S

A FISTFUL OF STRONTIUM

Johnny clicked off the time drogue and Slug's head exploded again. Johnny then clicked the drogue back on and watched with the others as Slug's head reformed once again. Slug groaned at this second resurrection, holding his head as if to stop it from bursting apart again.

"Let me rest in peace," he complained.

"Just as soon as you tell me what I need to know," said Johnny. "We're looking for your old leader."

"Kit?" said Slug in surprise.

Johnny made to click off the time drogue again. "Wait, wait," said Slug quickly. "I hear things, you know. I listen out for news. Things have been sweet since I took over the gang. I don't um, didn't want Kit coming back to muscle in on my rackets. Anyway, word is, since he broke out he's headed for Miltonia, and gonna get him some revenge on old Moosehead."

"Much obliged," said Johnny, and clicked off the drogue for the last time. Slug's head exploded almost gratefully.

Strontium Dog from Black Flame

BAD TIMING
Rebecca Levene

PROPHET MARGIN
Simon Spurrier

RUTHLESS
Jonathan Clements

DAY OF THE DOGS
Andrew Cartmel

More 2000 AD action from Black Flame

Judge Dredd

DREDD VS DEATH
Gordon Rennie

BAD MOON RISING
David Bishop

BLACK ATLANTIC
Simon Jowett & Peter J Evans

ECLIPSE
James Swallow

KINGDOM OF THE BLIND
David Bishop

THE FINAL CUT
Matthew Smith

SWINE FEVER
Andrew Cartmel

WHITEOUT
James Swallow

ABC Warriors

THE MEDUSA WAR
Pat Mills & Alan Mitchell

RAGE AGAINST THE
MACHINES
Mike Wild

Durham Red

THE UNQUIET GRAVE
Peter J Evans

THE OMEGA SOLUTION
Peter J Evans

Rogue Trooper

CRUCIBLE
Gordon Rennie

BLOOD RELATIVE
James Swallow

Nikolai Dante

THE STRANGELOVE GAMBIT
David Bishop

IMPERIAL BLACK
David Bishop

Strontium Dog and Middenface McNulty created by
Alan Grant, John Wagner and **Carlos Ezquerra**.

STRONTIUM DOG

A FISTFUL OF STRONTIUM

Jaspre Bark & Steve Lyons

BLACK FLAME

For Peter O'Donnell, master storyteller.

A Black Flame Publication
www.blackflame.com

First published in 2005 by BL Publishing, Games Workshop Ltd.,
Willow Road, Nottingham NG7 2WS, UK.

Distributed in the US by Simon & Schuster, 1230 Avenue of the
Americas, New York, NY 10020, USA.

10 9 8 7 6 5 4 3 2 1

Cover illustration by Philip Sibbering.

ISBN 13: 978 1 84416 270 3
ISBN 10: 1 84416 270 2

A CIP record for this book is available from the British Library.

Printed in the UK by Bookmarque, Surrey, UK.

CHAPTER ONE
KILLING TIME

"Whit did ye just say?"

A gloved hand shot across the hotel's reception desk and closed around the throat of the fat, sweaty man who stood behind it.

"Oof, sir, if you'll please just…" the hotelier choked. "Ow, please try to understand that it's the policy of this establishment to…" He was cut short as thick fingers tightened about his windpipe.

The mutant, who was obviously Middenface McNulty, leaned over the desk. He was shaking with rage, and the knobbly lumps that sprouted from the top of his hairless head glowed red to match his mood. "We paid good money fer yer best luxury suite, an' ye expect us tae sleep in yon stables with the animals," he snarled.

"Let it go, Middenface." His companion had to be Johnny Alpha. He spoke in a quiet growl, but his voice had a chilling authority. He was tall, lean and well-muscled, with curly, light brown hair. He lacked Middenface's bulk, but still he was able to calm the angry mutant with a firm hand on his shoulder. "We'll just get a refund and take our business elsewhere."

"I'm afraid that won't be possible," croaked the hotelier, released from the mutant's choking grip. "Cancellations have to be registered forty-eight hours in advance, and we, err, we don't give refunds to, um, muties." Nervously, he rubbed the tender flesh around his ample neck.

Middenface's nodules flashed angrily, but it was Johnny who stepped in with a firm but reasonable smile. "Listen," he said. "My friend here is not in a good mood. A two hundred light-year journey in a cheap transport ship will do that to a mutant. Add to that twelve hours in customs and third-class transportation from the space-port, and I'm sure you can see why you don't want to be upsetting him right now."

"I don't make the rules," insisted the hotelier in a ter-rified bleat. "It's company policy."

Johnny, at first glance, appeared to be a norm. Only upon closer inspection was he betrayed by his eyes, which emitted a fierce glow. Those eyes flared as he caught the hotelier's gaze and his hapless victim seemed unable to tear his own eyes away as his whole bulk trem-bled.

"You know what we are," said Johnny, his voice still calm and reasonable, "and you know what we're capable of. Do you mean to tell me you really want to try ripping us off?"

Tears streaked from the hotelier's eyes, and a dark patch spread across his crotch. "Oh God," he whimpered through chattering teeth. "Oh God. I... I'll get your money right away, and... and a couple of complimentary robes, and, uh, uh, please don't look at me again!"

And from a quiet corner of the reception area, unno-ticed as he always was, Cain Hine watched with resentment burning in his chest.

The fierce sun of Thulium 9 made the visitors shield their eyes as they stepped out onto the ramshackle boardwalk in front of the hotel. It was obvious from Middenface's curses that what he had seen of this world so far had not impressed him. Thulium 9 was a frontier planet out in the farthest reaches of inhabited space. Its climate was arid and inhospitable; its few small settlements based around scarce sources of fresh water. But it was Cain Hine's home.

Middenface surveyed the unpaved streets of the town of Bogweed with a scowl. "Who'd've thought anyone worth seven hundred thousand credits could've come frae a backwater like this?"

"It's not where you come from that matters," muttered his companion with the air of one who knew. "It's the prison you break out of, and the creep we're after broke out of the best. Maximum security, it was especially built to house the most dangerous criminals in the cosmos, and until a few weeks ago, thought inescapable."

"Aye, that's seven hundred thousand credits worth of egg on the authorities' faces, a'right, Johnny," agreed Middenface cheerfully.

Cain Hine passed almost close enough to touch the bulky mutant's tartan shoulder pads as he retrieved his broom from where he had left it, propped up against the hotel's front wall. Still, neither Middenface nor Johnny appeared to have seen him. He kept his head down, his ears flopping in front of his face. But he couldn't resist another stolen glance at the fiery-eyed Johnny, and at the circular red shield he wore over his heart.

Inscribed upon that shield, in black, were the letters: SD; the emblem of the Search and Destroy Agency, although to most people, mutants and norms alike, the letters stood for Strontium Dog. Warped like all mutants by the Strontium-90 isotope, they were the bloodhounds of intergalactic law enforcement.

Slug had been right. It had paid to bribe staff at the Doghouse, the orbiting HQ of the Search/Destroy Agency. His contacts had told him there were Stronties on the way to Thulium 9, and that they were after a big bounty, too. It had to be big if Johnny Alpha and Middenface McNulty had accepted the job. Slug had instructed Cain to watch out for the pair, punctuating his instructions with insults and the occasional slap as always, and now here they were.

"D'ye think there'll be *anywhere* fer us tae stay in this shitehole?" sighed Middenface.

"Who knows?" shrugged Johnny. "If we can get our job done before dark, maybe we won't have to stay the night."

He slipped a hard helmet over his head, hiding his brown locks. Despite his youth, he looked every bit as much a soldier as his partner: a stone-cold killer, whose very bearing spoke of the dangers that he had faced and survived. Cain could almost have admired him – admired both of them – but he shook himself and suppressed any similar thoughts. He reminded himself what Johnny Alpha and Middenface McNulty were: Strontium Dogs. Dirty, stinking traitors. Mutants who preyed on their own kind. Could there be any lower form of life?

They strode along the boardwalk, ignoring the hostile stares of passers-by as if they didn't care, as if they took a perverse pride in their badges of disgrace. In contrast, few people paid much heed to the wretched figure of Cain Hine, shuffling in their wake. Cain, who had dragged himself up from nothing to the gutter, and landed one of the most coveted jobs open to a mutant. Cain Hine, who had every reason to be proud of himself; who was worth a dozen of their filthy kind.

"D'ye really think this Identi Kit scunner'd come back here, Johnny?" asked Middenface. "Ye ask me, he's well shot o' the place!"

"Maybe," said Johnny. "But the best lead we have is the Chameleons, his old gang. Even if Kit's not hiding out with them, we might turn up a few leads."

They stopped to get their bearings on a street corner, apparently oblivious to a sizeable group of norms who glared at them from a table outside of one of Bogweed's saloons.

"The question is," Johnny sighed, "how do we go about finding the Chameleon gang?"

Cain Hine shuffled closer, eager to hear more. He thought about how pleased Slug would be when he heard that his snitch had not only found the Stronties, but had also learned of their plans. He basked in the imaginary warmth of the gang leader's praise.

And he cried out in alarm as, suddenly, Johnny and Middenface rounded on him and a pair of meaty, gloved hands fastened around the scruff of his orange overalls and yanked out a handful of the fur beneath them.

Before he could react, before he even knew what was happening, Cain Hine was bundled into a narrow side street and thrown to the dusty ground. He lost his grip on his broom and it skittered away from him. A booted foot came down on his chest and he flailed helplessly under Middenface's weight. He felt his fur curling and his tail shrivelling under the fierce stares of the two Stronties. He wasn't used to this kind of attention; wasn't used to being noticed at all. And his gaze was drawn irresistibly again to the mutant called Johnny, to those fiery eyes.

"Any particular reason why ye've been following us?" asked Middenface, his polite words belied by the curl of his top lip, baring his teeth.

Cain Hine couldn't speak at first. It had been so long since somebody had spoken to him and expected an answer. "I... I..." he stammered. "I'm sorry, I didn't mean to intrude, but I couldn't help... You... you gentlemen are Search/Destroy agents, aren't you? Oh geez, of course you are. I knew it as soon as I saw you outside the hotel. I could tell you were Stront... um, if you'll pardon the expression..."

"So, whit dae ye want? An autograph?" growled Middenface.

"Oh, geez, no."

Johnny's eyes searched Cain's face, and suddenly, they were inside him, filling his head with red pain.

"It's just… I was thinking that, you know, I might help you guys. People don't always pay me much heed, and they don't watch their mouths around me, so I pick things up, you know. Hey, I've thought about signing up to the agency myself, but gosh, those weapons you carry, they don't come cheap, and you need at least a couple of bounties to set yourself up, and…"

He stopped himself. The words had just streamed out of him as if they had been vomited up, and now his tongue lolled out of his mouth and he couldn't think through the pain. He had been searching for a lie to deflect attention, but somehow the lie had been turned back upon him to reveal a secret truth.

Those eyes filled Cain Hine's world, and he felt as if they were slicing into his brain, peeling away his memories sliver by sliver. Random flashes of smell, taste, sight and sound exploded against his senses, and suddenly, he was overwhelmed with bitterness, with every resentful thought he harboured against the norms. He was invisible to them. He relived every fantasy he had had of taking a gun to them, of watching their sneers freeze on their faces, of showing them that he was strong, and that he counted.

Yes, he had envied the Strontium Dogs. He had fantasised, in his darkest hours, about being one of them and betraying his people. And he was deeply ashamed of it.

"If you want tae help us," growled Middenface with an evil smile, "ye can tell us where tae find the Chameleons."

"It's true, then? About Kit? That *is* who you're looking for, right? Kit, who used to be their leader? They say he became some big-time crook. After he left Thulium, I mean. Only, we ain't heard nothing of him in years. They say he can disguise himself, look like any other mutant. Is that right? Huh?"

"The Chameleons," said Johnny, impatiently. "Where do they hang out?" And his eyes were inside Cain's mind again.

"Well, uh, I don't rightly know that, sir," stammered Cain through the pain, sweat matting the fur on his brow. "But... but..." And then the memories erupted again, and he was no longer lying in the road but in the sawdust of a seedy mutant bar, and the men standing over him were no longer Middenface and Johnny, but Slug and Beanstalk, and Cain could hear the snickering laughter of Weasel, and he was remembering all the times he'd been beaten and humiliated at their hands, the images of their fists and feet merging into an endless collage of abuse, but it was okay, it was all his own fault, he deserved it, because he was a traitor, a disgrace to his own kind, and they were only trying to teach him a lesson, to make him strong, to make him one of them.

And he would be one of them, one day. He would have the status, the respect that came from being a full member of the Chameleons. He knew this to be true because, although Slug may have despised him, he seemed to trust him. He had given him this mission, hadn't he?

Slug had entrusted Cain to this mission, and Cain wouldn't fail him. What could these Stronties do to him that he hadn't endured before? Whatever they said, however hard they beat him, he wouldn't break. He wouldn't tell them a thing.

It was with a creeping sense of horror that he realised he had been talking all this time; that the memories he'd been seeing inside his head had spilled out of him, involuntarily, in the form of words; that the Strontium Dogs knew everything about him, all the details of his miserable life that he had always been able to keep to himself simply because nobody else had ever been interested.

And still the words came, falling off his tongue before he could stop them. "See, you guys should be heading over to the west of town, that's where the mutant township is. Thing is, the Chameleons don't tell me where. That is, they always come find me when they want me. They got eyes everywhere. I reckon you should be looking for the Blades. They're, like, another gang around here. They've been muscling in on the Chameleons' rackets, and word is the Chameleons have decided it's time to settle the score and it's all going down tonight."

There was more. To his dismay, Cain heard himself telling the agents where the Blades' favourite hangouts were and giving directions to boot. A little more prompting and he gave up all he knew about the Chameleons' current membership. And, when there was nothing else to say, Johnny's burning eyes withdrew from his mind at last, and Cain lay panting with exhaustion in the dirt.

He felt Johnny's hand closing around his own and didn't resist as he was hauled to his feet. The fiery-eyed mutant's voice was surprisingly gentle, almost friendly. "We're obliged to you for the information, Mr Hine. Now, I suggest you go back to your work and say nothing about this meeting to anybody. And if I were you, I'd stay out of the Chameleons' way for a few days."

Cain felt sick. All he could do was watch through welling tears, trembling with helpless loathing, as Middenface and Johnny strutted away. He could well imagine how Slug would react when he heard about this, and he winced at the thought. Perhaps Johnny was right; maybe it was best to keep his head down, to say nothing, not even to warn Slug that the Stronties were on their way. But that would make him no better than them. It would make him a traitor.

The sound of a man clearing his throat jerked Cain out of his haze of self-pity. He looked up with a start to see that he was no longer alone.

It was the norms from the saloon around the corner; the ones he had seen watching the Stronties. A dozen or more of them. They had closed in, without a word, to surround him. He had been peripherally aware of their approach, but he had thought nothing of it, expecting them to pass him by as they normally would. Cain squirmed for the second time in as many minutes from the unfamiliar and unwanted sensation of eyes upon him.

"Thought it was your job to clean up the trash, kid, not kiss up to it."

"We don't like muties that don't know their place, y'hear?"

"Fixing to join up with those Strontium scum, kid? Cuz you's already a dog!"

The gang gave a hard and brutal laugh, and they were tightening their circle around Cain, raising their fists. He cowered from them, covering his head with his hands and letting out a plaintive whimper.

Then he heard footsteps, the crackle of electricity and an angry demand in a familiar gruff voice. "Whit did ye just say tae ma friend?"

Middenface and Johnny had returned. They tore into the lynch mob like twin hurricanes, scattering them this way and that. Their electro-nux – the charged brass knuckles that each of the S/D agents wore – flared and shot off blue sparks whenever they impacted with flesh and bone.

The fight was fast-paced and brutal and, caught in the middle, Cain didn't know which side to root for. Before he could make up his mind, Middenface had the gang's apparent leader – the one who had spoken first – pinned to the ground with a gun pointed at his face. It was a Westinghouse blaster. Cain recognised it from the tattered catalogue he had once kept hidden under his old blanket. The weapon was a powerful and adaptable handgun that fired small, variable-function cartridges. Middenface was jamming its barrel into the tender flesh underneath his victim's chin, and the loudmouth was sweating copiously.

"Hey, mister," he stammered. "We was just having a little fun with the kid, that's all. We didn't mean nothing by it."

"Well, the next time ye speak tae him, ye call him 'Mr Hine, sir', ye ken?"

A nervous tic pulled at the corner of the man's eye. "Sure, sure. 'Mr Hine, sir.' Anything you say."

Middenface stood, holstered his weapon and sauntered back over to Cain and Johnny, turning his back on his foe with the sort of easy confidence that came from knowing there was no threat from him. The mob exchanged panicked glances before picking themselves off the ground and scattered.

Cain would have run, too, had his legs not been frozen. His mind was whirling; his throat dry. He couldn't believe the Stronties had come to his aid like that, putting themselves out for him even after he'd admitted trying to snitch on them. Nobody had ever shown him such kindness. There had to be a catch, something else they wanted from him. Something that would hurt, again.

"Hey," said Middenface, throwing him a quick wink as if he had read his thoughts. "Nae problem. Us dogs gotta stick taegether, right? Maybe we'll see you roun' the Doghouse sometime. Ye can get us a roun' in, then."

Then Middenface and Johnny were gone again, leaving Cain's life as suddenly as they had entered it, with just a final snatch of conversation finding its way back to him on the hot, dry air.

"Looks like we mightn't have to spend the night here after all," said Johnny. "Saves us the price of a luxury suite, anyway."

It was only later that Cain realised what his brief encounter with the S/D agents had cost him. Only later, when he had found his broom and resumed his street sweeping duties, did he realise that wherever he went and whatever he did, it was against a background of pointing fingers and whispered suspicions. He began to think that it would have been better if Middenface and Johnny had left him alone with the mob, because at least the bruises they would have left would have faded. Not like this. This would change Cain Hine's life forever.

Everybody was looking at him.

CHAPTER TWO
GANG BANG

"Now this is more ma kindae place," said Middenface.

The mutant township was a vast, sprawling shanty-town. Its buildings, hastily erected from whatever materials could be scavenged and recycled, were clustered together to form an almost impenetrable maze of streets and alleyways. The whole place smelled of cheap liquor and exotic spices, but there was a vibrancy to it that the rest of Bogweed lacked.

Johnny and Middenface hadn't been searching long when the doors of a tumble-down bar flew open and a mutant hit the ground in front of them. He was writhing in agony, clutching at his third hand that grew from the top of his head. Another broad-shouldered mutant with a huge swollen head stood in the doorway behind him, and tossed a handful of bloody fingers in his direction.

"Next time you try and short-change the Blades, you won't get off so lightly," he growled. His victim gathered up his fingers and scampered off, whimpering to himself.

"Now there's a spot of luck," said Johnny, as they followed the swell-headed mutant back into the building.

The dim interior of the bar was a stark contrast to the bright sunshine outside. Even Johnny needed a moment to adjust to the oppressive gloom. There were about twenty mutants in the place: half of them gathered around the makeshift bar, and the rest sitting around packing crates. The swell-headed mutant marched past them and disappeared into another room at the back. The doorway was hidden by a curtain of animal hide, but it was no barrier to Johnny's Alpha eyes.

Unlike many mutants – Middenface included – Johnny's mutation was more than just cosmetic. His fierce red eyes emitted alpha rays that could see through solid objects and even pierce a man's soul. He had even named himself for their unique properties, after he had renounced his father and his birth name.

"Six muties in the back room," he reported to Middenface under his breath. "All of them packing." Middenface nodded.

None of the mutants around them dared to catch their eyes as they strode up to the curtain and pushed it aside. The room beyond was a lot more luxurious than the bar. There was proper furniture for a start, and carpet on the floor. Its six occupants were lounging around a table playing cards.

Swellhead spoke without looking up from his hand. "This is a private room, buddy. If you know what's good for you, you'll step back outside."

"And if you know what's good for *you*," said Johnny, "you'll listen to what we have to say." That got the attention of the whole gang. Six heads turned to give Johnny and Middenface the once-over.

"You Stronties ain't welcome back here," said another mutant with a giant rhinoceros horn growing out of his forehead.

"We're not here to collect any bounties," said Johnny. "We wouldn't waste our time with the chicken feed prices you've got on your heads. We're here to give you a warning that might just save your lives."

"Give us your weapons, then maybe we'll listen," said Swellhead.

"Ye'll have tae take them from us first," said Middenface, "and ah dinnae fancy yer chances." He placed his hand on the butt of his Westinghouse before any of the Blades could reach for their weapons.

"We're after the Chameleons and we hear they're not good friends of yours," said Johnny. "We also hear they're planning a surprise attack on you boys. We aim to save your hides as long as you stay out of our way and allow us to interrogate the surviving Chameleons when we're done."

"We don't need your help to take on the Chameleons," said Hornhead. "If they want to start something, we can finish it all by ourselves. You and your friend there would do best to stay out of our way."

The hide curtain over the door swished to one side, breaking the tension and drawing everyone's gaze. A barmaid stepped into the room carrying a bottle of Mac Mac and six shot glasses on a tray. She had giant front teeth like a bunny and an hourglass figure that kept everyone's attention. "Compliments of the house, boys," the barmaid said, laying the bottle down on the card table.

"Now this is what I call service," said Swellhead, patting the barmaid's behind as she bent over to pour each of the Blades a drink.

"You must be new here," said Hornhead. "Don't think I've seen you before."

"I don't imagine you'll see me again, either," said the barmaid over her shoulder. She reached inside her blouse and pulled out a small, metallic device. She pushed a button on its side, tossed it into the centre of the card table and bolted from the room.

Johnny recognised the device instantly. "Time snare!" he shouted. "Middenface, get back." He launched himself at his partner.

The snare was already emanating visible waves of energy. They rippled outwards to create a field of around three metres in diameter. As Johnny hit Middenface, the field overtook them both and they felt time slowing to a fraction of its normal pace. They were still moving, carried by the momentum of Johnny's leap, but each centimetre gained seemed to take an eternity.

By some quirk of the snare's operation, Johnny's mind was free to race at its normal speed, which only increased the torment of his situation. He was turning his head, trying to see what was going on behind him, but it was as if his muscles weren't responding, the movement was so slow, and he knew that in the meantime he and Middenface were sitting ducks.

Then they popped out of the energy field like corks, hit the back wall of the room and fell in a heap in one corner.

Simultaneously, the wall that separated the back room from the main bar was vaporised. One second it was there, the next, there was just a smoking hole through which five and a half members of the Chameleons made their entrance.

Johnny rolled to his feet and drew his blaster, but he and Middenface were trapped in their corner. If they shifted forward even a centimetre, they'd be caught in the time snare's field again.

They recognised Slug, the leader of the Chameleons, from Cain Hine's description. Slime ran in thick rivulets from every part of his leathery, grey hide. His clothes soaked up much of it, but the rest just pooled around his feet. His semi-automatic blaster was wrapped in industrial-strength plastic film to protect it from corrosion.

Slug fired off an opening salvo and the rest of the gang whooped and followed his lead. Their bullets and energy beams slowed as they hit the time field, as if they had been plunged into treacle, but the Blades, too, were moving in slow motion, still reaching for their own weapons and wearing expressions of dumb shock. Moving at twenty times the speed of their targets, the Chameleons were able to let off burst after burst of fire, filling the air with a slow-moving minefield, which the Blades could see coming but couldn't avoid.

"Eight ball inna corner pocket," said Weasel, a short mutant with beady eyes and a long thin face that stretched outwards like a rodent's. He fired off a cartridge from a short hand cannon and watched as it spun lazily towards the horn-headed mutant.

"Twenty credits says I can get four beams right in the heart," said Willian One-and-a-Half, a towering two-headed mutant with three legs. All four of his eyes squinted as he took leisurely aim with the blasters in his right and left hands.

"Fish in a barrel. Just like you said, Slug, fish in a barrel," cackled Beanstalk, a tall, impossibly slender mutant whose arms, legs and body were only slightly thicker than broomsticks. He began whistling a cheerful tune and the others joined in, providing a soundtrack for the Blades' slow motion dances of death as the first bullets and beams finally tore into them.

Weasel's cartridge burrowed into Hornhead's face and then exploded. Only the mutant's horn remained intact, floating slowly up above the bloody mess that used to be his face. The four beams from Willian One-and-a-Half's blasters inched their way, one after the other, into the same hole in Swellhead's chest.

Johnny had lived with death as a close companion for many years, but even he was appalled by the callous glee with which the Chameleons dispatched their helpless victims. There was no time to fret about that now, though. Weasel had spotted the two S/D agents in their corner and he motioned to the other gang members. Instinctively, the Chameleons turned and fired, but the intervening field worked to Johnny and Middenface's advantage, slowing the oncoming projectiles.

"We have to get out of here, fast," said Johnny, "before they can pin us down."

Middenface was ahead of him, already drawing back his foot. He booted a hole in the wall behind them, large enough for them to crawl out. The Chameleons saw what they were doing and four of them turned and raced towards the front of the bar. Beanstalk, however, headed towards them, impossibly squeezing himself through the tiny space between the time field and the wall.

Johnny and Middenface emerged into a dark alleyway and flattened themselves against the wall to each side of their exit hole. A moment later, the pursuing bullets reached the edge of the time field and regained their normal velocity, shooting out between them like a brief but furious fireworks display.

The next thing to emerge from the hole was Beanstalk's head, which was greeted by Middenface's Electro-Nux. A few good punches were enough to stun the spindly Chameleon. Then, Johnny and Middenface combined their strength to haul him out into the open and hurl him into the edge of the time field, which extended through the back wall beside them.

"Now ye're the fish," said Middenface, firing a single shot into the field after Beanstalk, "and this is ma barrel."

Hanging spread-eagled in midair, Beanstalk could do nothing to avoid the bullet that was slowly, inexorably, zeroing in on him. When it did eventually burrow a tiny hole between his eyes and blow a much larger one out of the back of his head, he would feel every slowed-down moment of its progress.

The Chameleons had split up at the front of the bar, hoping to catch their foes in a pincer movement. Slug had taken Weasel and Freddy Flat Face around the right-hand side of the building with him, leaving Willian One-and-a-Half to take the left.

Willian reached the back of the building and swallowed with both throats at the sight of Beanstalk, still trapped in the time field, facing death. There was nothing he could do about that. He looked around but couldn't see anyone.

Then, out of the corner of one eye, he saw movement. The glowing-eyed Strontie had just ducked out of sight between two buildings.

Willian grinned, twice over. "We're in luck," said his right head. "That's a dead end."

"Too narrow for us, though," said his left head. "Time to split, Will."

"Sure thing, Ian."

The two faces grimaced in pain as Willian One-and-a-Half began to tear himself down the middle. A split formed down his chest, then through his midriff and finally right down the centre of his sturdy middle leg. The leg became two separate spindly legs, each with three toes inside special padded boots that were held together with Velcro. Two one-armed mutants now faced each other, each slim enough to pursue their quarry. They exchanged malevolent grins and gave chase.

The Strontie was standing helplessly at the end of the blind alley when they reached him. He appeared to be unarmed, but was clutching something to his chest. Will and Ian flanked him, their blasters drawn.

"End of the line, Strontie," said Will.

"Four shots right through the heart, eh, Will?" said Ian.

"I was hoping you'd say that," said the Strontium Dog. He didn't seem to be afraid.

Will and Ian fired simultaneously. In the same split-second, their target revealed what he was holding: a small, circular device, which they recognised with horror as a beam polariser. He threw it down the alleyway between them, and the beams from their blasters bent impossibly back on themselves to follow it. In so doing, they sliced right through the mutants who had fired them.

Will and Ian looked down at the charred lines running across their abdomens. Instinctively, they reached out for each other, trying to join up again, but the top halves of their bodies toppled off their legs. Then their legs gave way and crumpled.

The last thing they heard, before their mutant bodies realised they weren't suppose to divide this way, was their killer's muttered growl saying, "Three to go!"

Weasel edged forward, cursing under his breath, knowing that there were a hundred places around him where an enemy could be hiding and trying not to look too hard in any one of them. He knew his part in the routine they were playing – the one Slug always played – but he didn't like it. He said a silent prayer to whatever gods looked out for mutant criminals.

Then Weasel felt a sharp blow to the back of his neck that almost drove him to his knees. Before he could draw breath, an arm locked around his throat, squeezing so hard it almost broke his neck. Weasel jerked and kicked as his bulky, tartan-clad captor lifted him off the ground.

That was when Slug and Freddy finally chose to reveal themselves, shrugging off the flimsy chameleon cloaks they were wearing. The cloaks were fashioned from a rare material that gave off variable light, allowing whoever wore them to blend into any background and become virtually invisible. The decoy ploy had worked.

Slug trained his blaster at the back of the S/D agent's head. "All right, big man, drop the little runt," he commanded.

The Strontie flexed the muscles in one arm almost casually, and Weasel gasped as he felt his neck break in one clean snap.

"Oops," said the Strontie.

"You'll pay for that, Stront!" snarled Freddy Flat Face.

Weasel believed him. But the Chameleons' revenge would come too late to help him. The arm around his neck loosened its grip, but the light inside him was

fading and he couldn't control his muscles any more...
Couldn't keep himself upright.

By the time Weasel's body hit the ground, he had
already come to terms with the terrible truth: that there
were no gods looking out for people like him.

"Okay, I know your partner isn't far away," said Slug,
raising his voice so that it carried to the shadows around
him. "He has ten seconds to throw down his weapons
and come out with his hands in the air."

"Dinnae listen, Johnny," shouted Middenface. "Take
the scunner oot."

"I wouldn't do that if I were you," said Slug. "This
blaster's got a hair trigger. Even if your partner's got a
bead on me, I can blow your brains out the front of your
face before I drop. Two seconds."

Slug was telling the truth and Middenface knew it all
too well. But the way he saw it, he was dead anyway,
which was fine with him. He had always known it would
end this way and, in fact, he'd been given a lot more time
than he could have asked for. The one thing he couldn't
face was if Slug got his own way, and if Middenface's
mistake brought his partner down with him. He prayed
that Johnny would do as he said and save his own skin
at least, but at the same time, he knew it was not going
to happen.

"All right," came a voice from nearby, causing Middenface's stomach to sink. "You win!"

A gun belt was lobbed out from behind an overflowing
dumpster, the blaster still in its holster. A moment later
Johnny appeared, his hands above his head, palms outward to show that he carried no weapons. Middenface
sighed and shook his head, both disappointed and overwhelmed with affection for his brash young friend.

"That's far enough," said Slug. "Remember, Freddy
here has you in his sights. Now, kick the blaster behind

you. I ain't touching it in case you booby-trapped it."
Johnny obediently kicked his weapon down a nearby
side street.

"Johnny, ahm sorry," said Middenface.

Johnny just shrugged and then nodded at Slug. "The
cloaks were a nice touch."

"We ain't called Chameleons for nothing. So, you must
be the infamous Johnny Alpha. You after the bounties on
our heads, or something bigger?" asked Slug.

"We're just after some information," said Johnny. "If
you put that blaster down and promise to tell us what we
need to know, you can still get out of this alive."

Slug laughed incredulously. "You got some balls,
Alpha, I'll give you that. You kill my men and then expect
me to spill my guts to you. The only thing you're going
to get from me is a long and painful death. Tie him up,
Freddy."

Freddy circled Johnny, wary of any sign of movement.
"On your knees!" he snapped, as he untangled a length
of rope from around his waist.

And then, without warning, Freddy Fat Face's head was
blown clean off his shoulders.

Slug was still staring in shock when Middenface
whirled around and knocked the blaster from his
hands. Slug leapt for the weapon but Middenface was
faster, drawing his own gun and pumping three bullets
into the gang leader's head before he knew what was
going on.

"It's okay," Middenface heard Johnny saying. "Everything's okay. Just put down the blaster nice and slow.
You don't want it going off again, do you?"

He was talking to someone Middenface couldn't see;
somebody in the street where he had kicked his weapon;
somebody who had evidently just saved their lives. Middenface gaped as he moved to Johnny's side and laid his
eyes on the wretched figure of Cain Hine.

The street sweeper was clutching Johnny's still-smoking Westinghouse, his whole body shaking from shock. "Aw geez. He's dead, ain't he? He's really dead and I shot him!"

"Whit the sneck are ye doin' here?" cried Middenface.

"I'm sorry. I didn't know where else to go. I lost my job. My supervisor, he said I'd been causing trouble, and... Oh heck, I didn't mean to... I just saw the gun, and Freddy was... And you'd been so good to me, better than anyone ever... I just killed someone, didn't I?" Cain dropped the blaster, put his hand to his mouth and threw up violently.

"Looks tae me like ye just decided whose side ye're really on," said Middenface, kindly.

Cain emptied his stomach, wiped his mouth and apologised.

"Divn't worry yourself. The first kill's always the worst. After that, it's doonhill aw the way."

Johnny, in the meantime, had retrieved his blaster, walked up to Slug's body and turned it over with his foot. Then he crouched down next to it and pulled out a time drogue: a round, handheld device that looked a little like a grenade. He clicked it on and reversed time in a small area of the street around Slug. The gang leader's brains rushed back into his freshly reformed head and he sat up with a start.

"Hello Slug," said Johnny. "Time for a little chat."

"I ain't telling you nothing," said Slug. "What you going to do, kill me again?"

"As a matter of fact..." Johnny clicked off the time drogue and Slug's head exploded again. Johnny then clicked the drogue back on and watched with the others as Slug's head reformed once again. Slug groaned at this second resurrection, holding his head as if to stop it from bursting apart again.

"Let me rest in peace," he complained.

"Just as soon as you tell me what I need to know," said Johnny.

Slug shook his head stubbornly. Johnny clicked off the drogue, let him die once more, then brought him back. "I can keep this up all afternoon if need be. No man ought to face his death more than once. Answer my questions and you can put an end to this."

"Okay, okay," Slug agreed, his shoulders slumping in defeat.

"We're looking for your old leader."

"Kit?" said Slug in surprise. "Sneck, I haven't seen him in over seven years. Not since that Strontie... What's his name? Moosehead, that's it. Not since Moosehead McGuffin brought him in."

Johnny made to click off the time drogue again. "Wait, wait," said Slug quickly. "I hear things, you know. I listen out for news. Things have been sweet since I took over the gang. I don't... um, didn't want Kit coming back to muscle in on my rackets. Anyway, word is, since he broke out he's headed for Miltonia, and gonna get him some revenge on old Moosehead."

"Much obliged," said Johnny, and clicked off the drogue for the last time. Slug's head exploded almost gratefully.

"Looks like we're headed for Miltonia," said Johnny, turning to his partner.

"Braw," said Middenface. "Ah've always wanted tae visit the place. Can't think why I havnae done so already."

"Because they detest S/D agents?"

"Aye, there is that."

"It'll be good to see old Moosehead, though, after all these years." Johnny and Middenface knew Moosehead McGuffin of old. Like them, he had joined the Search/Destroy Agency after the Mutant War, but he had retired some five years ago.

"What... what about me?" came the wretched voice of Cain Hine, stopping the agents in their tracks. "I've nowhere to go. I got nothing."

Johnny regarded him through narrowed eyes for a moment and then turned to Middenface. "What do you reckon's the combined bounty on six Blades and five-and-a-half Chameleons?" he asked.

Middenface shrugged. "Has tae come tae at least eight thousand."

"Reckon that's about enough to buy some useful weapons and set yourself up as an S/D agent, wouldn't you say?"

"Aye, Ah reckon it is," said Middenface.

"You guys don't mean..." Cain stammered. "You... You're going to give me the bounty on all these kills?"

"You saved our lives, Cain," said Johnny. "It's the least we can do."

"Aw geez, aw heck, I don't know what to... You don't know what this means... I mean, me, a Strontie, I... um..." Cain swallowed and stared at the ground, his expression betraying his conflicting emotions.

Johnny knew how he felt. He thought back over the events of the day, the lives that had been lost, and it wearied him. He placed a tired hand on Cain's shoulder and looked him in the eyes.

"You're wrong, Cain," he said gently. "I know just what it means. I know it all too well."

CHAPTER THREE
DETAINED

"Name."

"I've told you my name a dozen times already. It's Johnny Alpha."

"Real name."

"That *is* my real name."

"Occupation."

"You've seen my papers. I do freelance work for the Search and Destroy Agency."

"And your business on Miltonia, Mr 'Alpha'?"

The customs official had a face like granite – literally. His dour expression looked as if it had been chiselled into his tough, grey skin, and his hairless head was an uneven block, roughly square in shape and a little too big for his body. His eyes were tiny, sunken, black and piercing, but Johnny also knew how to give a hard stare.

"Again," he answered patiently, "you've seen my papers."

"And now, I want to hear it from you."

"My partner and I are in pursuit of a dangerous fugitive."

"Your partner. Yes. A Mr, ah..." Granite Face ran his tiny eyes over his clipboard in search of a prompt. "Archibald McNulty."

"He prefers to be known as Middenface."

"And this, ah, fugitive?"

"Kit Jones. I have a warrant for his arrest. You'll find it's in order."

"That remains to be seen. This Kit Jones, I assume he is a mutant?"

"That's right. He calls himself Identi Kit."

"And what makes you think, Mr Alpha," asked the granite-faced official with icy disdain, "that Miltonia is in the business of harbouring criminals?"

Johnny had been apprehensive about coming to this world right from the beginning. He hadn't known what to expect.

He had heard of Miltonia, of course. It was a relatively new colony, built by mutants fleeing oppression on Earth. It was one of many worlds settled in the uncertain aftermath of the Mutant War by the few surviving generals of that conflict, and where most of the others had floundered through lack of resources or fallen into norm hands, this planet had thrived.

The unlikely success of Miltonia could probably be attributed to its rich deposits of radioactive minerals that the settlers had discovered soon after their arrival. It was these minerals that had, in all likelihood, kept the norms away, at least in any great numbers. The minerals had also made those first settlers very, very rich indeed.

As a result, Miltonia had become a mutant paradise. It had grown quickly since both mutants and norms were drawn to it by its newfound prosperity, but still it remained the only known planet where mutants formed the majority of the population. At last count they had outnumbered the norms five to one and, inevitably, the mutants still controlled all the mining operations on Miltonia and thereby most of its wealth.

So far, so good. Certainly, Johnny had experienced his fair share of anti-mutant prejudice throughout his life. In his darkest hours, when the very fact of his birth had seemed like an intolerable burden to him, it had comforted him to know that Miltonia existed, and that in one tiny corner of this rotten universe at least, a mutant could aspire to be free.

And yet, paradoxically, another part of him had been afraid, too. Afraid that the legend or the dream of Miltonia might be better than the reality. Afraid that, were he ever to see this reputed mutopia with his own eyes, it would only disappoint him.

And then there was the other thing. The usual thing. His job.

If there was one thing that united mutants and norms alike, it was the mutual hatred of the Galactic Crime Commission's Search and Destroy Agency and the lowlife who chose to work for it: the Strontium Dogs. Johnny had seen a stark enough reminder of that shared hatred on Thulium 9. And he had heard from the other agents at the Doghouse that Miltonians were no different. Consequently, he wasn't exactly expecting a warm welcome.

And so here he was now, sitting in a simple plastic chair behind a simple, white plastic table in a simple, white-walled, stuffy side room into which he had been bustled as soon as the first official from Customs and Immigration had laid three of her eyes upon him. He had presented his papers, answered his interrogator's questions many times over, and now they were just holding him for the sake of making his life more difficult.

The fact that he was being questioned by a mutant, and not a norm, was the only small variation on an otherwise familiar scenario. Just like how, out in the main spaceport, there had been the usual two channels for incoming passengers – mutants and norms – only here, it was the mutants who were waved through while the norm line moved at a snail's pace.

No, Johnny hadn't known quite what to expect from Miltonia, but he needn't have worried. So far, this world seemed little different to any other he had seen.

"You can see my problem, Mr McNulty."

Middenface thought he could, but he was too polite to mention it. No, that wasn't strictly true. In fact, he was just too drunk to care.

"Miltonia is a wealthy planet," continued the granite-faced customs official. "A lot of people would like a share of that wealth."

"Ye think we wannae come live here?" asked Middenface, raising an amused eyebrow. "Ye're off yer head, pal. Once we've run down this Kit scunner, we'll be out o' yer hair faster'n ye can say 'seven hundred thousand credits'."

Granite Face leaned forward, placing his misshapen hands on the table in between them, and Middenface thought his tiny black eyes narrowed, if that was even possible. "Your partner made the same claim," said Granite Face, "but the pair of you were discovered sneaking onto this planet in the hold of a supply ship."

Middenface laced his hands behind his head and leaned back in his chair. It creaked beneath his weight. "Aye, well, dae ye have any idea how hard it is tae get a ticket tae Miltonia on short notice? The transports are booked up weeks ahead o' time. So we cadged ourselves a lift on a merchant ship, and a fair whack it cost us. But we wouldae gone through customs, if you'd given us a chance instead o' marching us awae like criminals."

Talk of the long journey here and of the hostile reception he and Johnny had received was almost enough to sober up Middenface there and then. His thoughts flashed back to the interminable hours in the supply ship's hold. He remembered the sawdust in his nose and the ceaseless pounding of the ship's ancient engines, their shielding shot, in his ears. He had had to wedge himself between two of the many stacks of wooden crates, their corners poking into his ribs, to keep himself from being knocked black and blue by the rickety vessel's unpredictable lurches.

But then Middenface closed his eyes and brought to mind one particular crate; the one that had broken free of its ropes and slid into him, hitting his knees, and came to him as if it had sensed his need. The one with the label that had spelled out the cure to his woes in six letters. And a smile returned to his lips.

Middenface had never been a good traveller. He hated the feeling of confinement, of putting his life in a stranger's hands. It was like being in prison. And when there was work to be done, like now, he chafed with impatience to get to it. The best way to drown those feelings, he had found, was with expensive whisky. And the booze had the additional benefit of helping him through the inevitable grilling at his destination.

Through many years of experimentation, Middenface had gauged the exact amount of whisky necessary to keep himself placid at least for the first few hours of this regular ordeal. This was important because petty officials like old Granite Face would invariably put S/D agents through as much inconvenience as the rules allowed and, as Johnny had had cause to point out on more than one occasion, if Middenface rose to their bait, he only gave them more excuses to hold him.

When Granite Face observed that Middenface and Johnny had arrived on Miltonia without return tickets, and suggested that this in itself was suspicious, Middenface presented him with his politest smile and explained that the supply ship had already left and that they intended to make alternative arrangements for their flight home as soon as they were allowed.

"Seven hundred thousand credits," said the official, chewing over the words thoughtfully.

"Aye," said Middenface cautiously, "that's right."

"Quite a bounty. There must have been some competition for that warrant."

"We had tae call in a few favours, right enough."

"And the fact that this Kit Jones was said to be on Miltonia, isn't that really why you fought so hard for this mission, Mr McNulty? So that the Search and Destroy Agency," he spat out the words with distaste, "would provide you with the papers you needed to gain access to this world?"

Middenface explained, again, how Kit's trail had first led them to Thulium 9, and about the information he and Johnny had received there.

"But we have only your word for that, don't we?" said Granite Face with a caustic smile. "Tell me, Mr McNulty, what makes you so sure this Kit Jones is on Miltonia at all? Our own records show that nobody of that name has presented himself at customs over the past month."

Middenface sighed. This was going to be a long day. And the whisky was already starting to wear off. He was getting a hangover.

"Kit Jones has total control over his own body," explained Johnny. "He can absorb the DNA patterns of any mutant he touches and reshape himself to resemble them, right down to the voice. He'd even fool the gene scanners you have out there. Believe me, if he is here on Miltonia, you almost certainly wouldn't know about it."

"Wouldn't we indeed?" sniffed Granite Face. "That all sounds very convenient, don't you think, Mr Alpha? Sounds like an excuse for you to harass any mutant whose face or other physical characteristics you don't like."

"I have an official warrant from the S/D Agency. That entitles me to pursue my target wherever–"

"It entitles you to nothing!" Granite Face interrupted with a snarl. It was the first time he had displayed any real emotion. "Not here! Miltonia was established as a mutant haven, Mr Alpha, a place where our kind can live free from persecution. We maintain the absolute right to refuse entry to anyone who, in our opinion, threatens that freedom, whatever papers you might have."

"You're accusing me of prejudice?" asked Johnny. "Against mutants?"

"That's what you Stronties do, isn't it? You hunt mutants!"

"I hunt criminals. I *am* a mutant!"

"You don't look like a mutant."

"What are you trying to say?"

"You'd be surprised how many people try this trick, Mr Alpha. They come through here, wearing prostheses or contact lenses, and they think we'll just wave them in. There are tests we can run, you know."

"I'm a mutant," said Johnny darkly. "Do you want me to prove it?" He felt the almost involuntary surge of alpha energy to his eyes and knew they must have flared.

The customs official's grey skin blanched a little, and he took a step back but continued unabashed. "Your paperwork is being examined. If it is found to be in order, it will be presented to the relevant authorities and your case will be evaluated. The process shouldn't take more than a day or two."

"A day or two!" exclaimed Johnny.

"Of course, the fact that you and your partner came so heavily armed could complicate matters. We have something of a backlog at the moment and it may take some time for the necessary permits to be issued for each of your weapons."

"Listen, pal," said Johnny. "I don't *have* time. My information is that Identi Kit came here to kill an old friend of mine; a member of your government."

Granite Face frowned. At least, that was how Johnny chose to interpret the crazed pattern that textured his stony brow. As the man had no eyebrows, it was difficult to be sure. "Who are we talking about here?" he asked guardedly.

"McGuffin. Moosehead McGuffin. You heard of him?"

"I'd be a pretty poor customs official if I hadn't heard of the Minister for Immigration," Granite Face said stiffly.

"The Minister for...?" Johnny grinned, seeing a way out of this. "I want to see him. Now."

Granite Face hesitated a long time before replying. Johnny longed to know what he was thinking but his tiny eyes betrayed nothing. He was tempted to use his alpha rays to rip the thoughts from the officious mutant's brain, but he thought better of it.

"That isn't possible," said Granite Face, at last.

"I told you, we're old friends. Get a message to Moosehead. He'll see me."

"And I told you that is not possible."

"Why not?"

It took Granite Face a moment to come up with an excuse. "I can't go calling the presidential palace every time some kook turns up claiming to know a minister. Why, next thing you'll be telling me is that you're a personal friend of the president himself."

"I fought alongside Moosehead in the Mutant War," said Johnny. "He was a scout then, serving under General Armz. He and I–"

"Please, Mr Alpha," said Granite Face curtly, holding up a hand to silence him. "Restrict yourself to answering the questions I put to you."

"I've answered your questions, over and over again."

"Not to my satisfaction. Name."

Johnny sighed and buried his face in his hands. "Johnny Alpha," he mumbled.

"Real name."

"That *is* my real name."

Middenface was getting restless.

He had taken to pacing; trying to walk off the pain that had begun to throb behind his eyes and the rage that was building inside his chest. It wasn't doing him much good. It took only a couple of his sure strides to cross the white-walled room. He was starting to feel cramped and dizzy from having to turn around so often.

He felt like busting down the flimsy door; one good kick would do it. He had caught glimpses of the guards on the other side as Granite Face had come and gone, and he knew he could take them, even with their guns. There would be others, though. Many, many others...

"So, let me get this straight," said Granite Face, seeming to enjoy his prisoner's discomfort. "You say Moosehead McGuffin is a friend of yours, and yet you didn't know he was our Minister for Immigration?"

"Aye, well," said Middenface, "it's been a few years. Ah'd heard he wa' some kindae political bigwig out here, but it's not exactly easy tae keep up with Miltonian current affairs, if y'knae what Ah'm sayin'."

"Oh, I know the norm media likes to pretend we don't exist," said Granite Face with a hint of bitterness. "After all, it wouldn't do to show mutants everywhere a better life, would it? They'd only get above themselves, and then who'd lick out the gutters and see to the trash?"

"Ye think I don't know that?" snapped Middenface. "I grew up on Earth, pal, in New Britain during the Kreelman era. I was sent tae a mutant jail when I wa' ten years old. Ye think I don't know whit it's like tae be treated like shite?"

"And now you're a Strontium Dog," said Granite Face.

Middenface clenched his fists and took a deep breath.

The worst thing was the disappointment. Sure, he had expected some trouble here – there was always trouble – but still, he had been optimistic about this trip, waving aside his partner's doubts. This was Miltonia, after all: the mutant paradise, a world built for people just like them. How bad could it be?

"I think I've heard all I need to hear."

Middenface ceased his pacing and glared at the customs official suspiciously. "What? Nae more questions?"

"No more questions."

"Then ye're letting me outtae here?"

"Not just yet, Mr McNulty. This interview was only the first stage of our investigation. Next, my colleagues will take you to our medical facility, where you will undergo a full examination and body cavity search."

Middenface felt the nodules on his head glowing red. "Ye what?" he growled.

Granite Face smiled and turned to a new form on his clipboard. "Now, to begin with, how many body cavities do you wish to declare?"

Johnny was sitting, slumped over the white plastic table, when he heard the howl of rage. It was followed a moment later by a series of dull thumps. Then, an ear-splitting crash as a shape was suddenly punched out of the white plaster of the wall in front of him. It was an uneven, roughly square shape... with a nose.

Johnny heard more shouting and running footsteps outside. He looked up at the clock above the door, nodded to himself and sighed.

Evidently, Middenface had just sobered up.

Johnny Alpha got his first look at Miltonia's sky – the first time he had seen a sky at all since Thulium 9, three days earlier – in a dingy back alleyway that smelt of rotting garbage. He was guided out of the spaceport building by two customs officials, each with a hand on one of his shoulders. His ankles were chained together with not quite enough slack between them for him to walk comfortably. Another length of chain connected his ankles to his wrists, which were also manacled.

Middenface was beside him, similarly bound and escorted, and looking very sorry for himself. A hovering police transport vehicle awaited them, its engine stirring up clouds of dust from the tarmac.

The alleyway, like the doorway behind them, was packed with more officials who wore black and white uniforms. Given the plethora of mutations on display and the imaginative ways in which their shirts and trousers had been altered to accommodate extra arms, legs, heads and tails, they may as well not have bothered. Each of them held a blaster trained nervously upon the S/D agents who, they had no doubt been warned, were highly dangerous. Some of them had the bruises to prove it, so they were taking no chances.

Granite Face stood a discreet distance away, his arms folded, with an ostentatiously large white bandage wrapped around one corner of his head. He had the same smug expression that he'd worn when he had informed Johnny that he and his partner had been designated a security risk, and would therefore be shipped to an internment camp for illegal immigrants pending the result of their visa applications.

Middenface bristled at the sight of his tormentor and Johnny spoke quickly to calm him. "Don't sweat it," he said. "As soon as Moosehead finds out we're here and what they're doing to us, he'll sort it out. He won't let us rot."

"D'ye think so, Johnny?" asked Middenface, miserably. "According to yon stony-faced chappie, our auld frien's in charge o' these here scunners. Ye think the Moosehead we knew'd let any mutant be treated like this?"

Johnny couldn't answer that. He had been thinking the same thing himself. It had been a long time since he had last seen Moosehead McGuffin. He hadn't even had the customary retirement party at the Doghouse and just announced that he was packing it all in and had gone. Could he really have changed so much?

He maintained a worried silence as his escorts pushed him into the back of the transport. He sprawled awkwardly on a narrow wooden bench where he was soon joined by Middenface. A thick grille separated them from the officers in front of the vehicle.

The last thing Johnny saw, as the door closed behind him with a soft *hiss* of hydraulics, was Granite Face talking to a mousey-looking young woman in a neat business suit. She kept pawing at her saucer-shaped ears and twitching her whiskers. Granite Face's smile had disappeared. He obviously didn't like what he was hearing.

A moment later the door opened again, and Granite Face was standing there, his face dark with fury.

"You're free to go," he growled in a voice that suggested it was a supreme effort to speak each word. He motioned curtly to two uniformed officers who scurried past him into the transport and began to unlock Johnny and Middenface's restraints. "My colleagues here will arrange for the return of your possessions. A car has been sent for you and will collect you from Gate Four."

He turned and made to stride away but Johnny called after him. "Hey, what's going on here? Why the sudden change of heart?"

"Looks like ye were right, Johnny. Moosehead came through fer us, and no' before time!"

Granite Face halted and took a few deep breaths before he turned back to face them. "Orders from the president," he said through clenched teeth. Glaring at Johnny, he continued: "It seems he *is* a personal friend of yours, after all."

CHAPTER FOUR
PRESIDENT OOZE

If his detention by Customs and Immigration had given
Johnny a bad first impression of Miltonia, his second
impression was most alarming. He had been wondering
why the guards, who a second ago had been about to
ship him and Middenface off to an internment camp, all
looked so tense as they accompanied the bounty hunters
across the spaceport's opulent plaza. Surely this must be
an easy and routine mission for them. The second he and
Middenface stepped through Gate Four's grand entrance,
he found out the reason for their tension.

The guards formed a tight-knit wall of bodies around
Johnny and Middenface. "Hey! Hang on a minute,"
yelled Middenface as he was crushed up against Johnny.
Then Johnny saw the banks of cameras all trained on
them and the sea of bodies waiting to engulf them.

The guards shuffled slowly towards the hover limousine that was waiting for them, taking Johnny and
Middenface with them. They were beset on all sides by
reporters from Miltonia's leading news agencies. The
reporters were the advance guard of a whole crowd of
mutants who had turned out to see the S/D agents. Many
of the crowd also pushed forward, desperate to get a look
at Johnny and Middenface, craning their necks and pointing. This made it slow going for the guards as they
pushed their way through.

"Hey, Alpha," a reporter with a giant mouth and no
nose called out. "Do you think becoming an S/D agent is

a good example for a former war hero to set young mutants?"

"Mr Alpha, Mr McNulty," said another long, thin reporter with three eyes and a prehensile fin growing from the top of his head. "Finnegan Trio from the *Clacton Fuzzville Courier*. Do either of you plan on applying for full Miltonian citizenship?" Finnegan's float-a-cam hovered in close, its lens whirring as it focused on Johnny and Middenface. It drew a spate of other float-a-cams with it, every orb-like camera shooting footage and snapping stills of the bounty hunters, who were astonished at their sudden celebrity.

A thin, snake-like mutant actually managed to slither between two of the guards and press herself up against the pair. "Johnny, Middenface, you don't mind if I use your first names, do you?" she purred. "I'm Sarah Saurus from the Modern Mutant web channel. I want to talk to you about cosmetic surgery. Do you think the modern Miltonian girl is complete with anything less than four breasts?"

Before Johnny could even begin to ask the woman what she was talking about, the guards stopped and parted just enough to reveal the open door of the limousine. Sarah Saurus was dragged to one side and the guards used their pistols to swat away the float-a-cams that tried to follow the S/D agents as they stepped into the vehicle's spacious interior.

"Gentlemen, welcome to Miltonia," said the smartly dressed mutant with four arms who sat opposite them. His head consisted mainly of an unnaturally huge smile. "My name is Grinling Gibson. I'm a special envoy attached to President Leadbetter's administration." He reached out and shook Johnny and Middenface's hands simultaneously, as his two left hands patted them on their shoulders. Grinling exuded so much charm and confidence that it seemed he must have been genetically bred for the sole purpose of meeting and greeting dignitaries.

"I'm here to make your audience with the president run as smoothly as possible. Are there any questions you'd like to ask me before we go any further?"

"Whit the hell was aw that aboot?" snarled Middenface, jerking his thumb back at the crowd they had just left behind at the spaceport entrance.

"Ah yes, the impromptu conference," Grinling said with a wry chuckle. "News travels extremely fast in the capital, and I'm afraid you've created rather a lot of interest. It isn't every day we get a visit from two genuine heroes of the Mutant War."

Grinling pressed a button and the thin stem of a holo-projector appeared from a hidden compartment in the upholstery. It began to play a holo-programme showing Miltonia from space as the first settlers' ships landed. Then it zoomed in to show the fugitive mutants building the first prefabricated shelters on the planet's surface.

Grinling's manner suggested that he had run through this patter with visiting delegations countless times before. "As I'm sure you're aware, Miltonia was settled soon after the Mutant War by British mutants from the ghetto of Milton Keynes: soldiers and civilians who wanted to build a new life free from persecution. The Mutant War is a defining moment in the foundation of our planet and people; a glorious and heroic struggle that began the long march towards the freedom and prosperity every Miltonian enjoys today."

"It didnae feel too glorious or heroic tae me," said Middenface. "Most of it was spent hidin' frae the Kreelers or cooling our heels in a holding cell."

"We fought because we had to," said Johnny. "It was our only way of staying alive. Kreelman and his government lackeys stirred up so much hatred among the norms, the only way we could survive was by fighting back."

"And you won," said Grinling with genuine admiration in his voice. "Nelson Bunker Kreelman was deposed as a minister, and his anti-mutant bills quashed. It was a decisive victory for mutantkind."

"We fought them to a standstill and they agreed to let us live as long as we left the planet," Johnny said in a bitter voice. "That doesn't sound like much of a victory to me."

"Nevertheless, it still led to the founding of Miltonia and the promise of freedom and equality that it offers to all mutants. The fact that you both played key roles in the victory of that conflict means you are held in extremely high regard here, even allowing for your, erm... unfortunate career choices."

The holographic image of early Miltonian settlement dissolved to be replaced by a dramatic reconstruction of the Siege of Upminster. It was the title sequence in a holo-show about the Mutant War. "This is still the most popular show in the history of Miltonian entertainment," explained Grinling. "As you can see, you're both lead characters."

Johnny *hadn't* seen, because the actors playing him and Middenface bore only the slightest of resemblances to them. "Johnny" was portrayed by a mutant with huge bulbous eyes that protruded from his head and glowed a dull red, while "Middenface" had enormous spots covering every inch of his bald scalp and face, and spoke in an incomprehensible drawl which was subtitled.

"Yon scunners look nothin' like us!" protested Middenface.

"Yes, well the programme makers took certain liberties in order to portray you according to Miltonian ideas about what's physically attractive," Grinling said. "You see, on Miltonia, the more mutated a person is, the more they are admired. It is a badge of status, and all mutations are displayed with pride."

"That sure makes a difference from everywhere else we've seen," said Johnny.

"Miltonia is quite different from everywhere else in the universe," said Grinling.

The holographic display changed once again to show the workings of a Miltonian mine.

"Due to the highly radioactive nature of the minerals we mine, only mutants can run the mining operations," Grinling continued, "which is why we control all the wealth on Miltonia. It's also why we admire mutation. The longer someone has worked in a mine, the more mutated they are likely to become and the richer they are likely to be. To be highly mutated is a sign of great prosperity and social standing."

"Incredible," Middenface muttered to himself.

"If we're so well-known, then how come the officials who held us didn't recognise us?" Johnny wanted to know.

"It's unlikely they believed you were who you claimed to be. You don't look a great deal like your popular images, and you did arrive in a–" Grinling paused to choose his words carefully, "somewhat unorthodox manner."

Johnny nodded, accepting the explanation.

"May I ask you gentleman a question?" said Grinling, leaning forward with an expression of polite deference.

"Okay," said Johnny in a guarded manner. His years hunting down the worst criminals in the universe had taught him to give away as little as possible about either himself or his mission.

"Were you close to your former comrade, President Leadbetter? I only ask because his mutation has increased considerably since the days when you would have known him and you may not recognise him."

"To be honest, we don't know him very well at all," Johnny admitted. "He was mainly a tactician. He rallied the troops when our generals were imprisoned after the Siege of Upminster failed, but he didn't see much activity on the front line due to his condition. He took control of what was left of the Mutant Army after Middenface and I left."

"That would have been just before he led our people to Miltonia," said Grinling with great reverence. "He named it after the ghetto we had left, so we should never forget our humble origins. We owe him so much. He is the founder of our people. But his condition, as you called it, has rather incapacitated him of late. He speaks through an advocate at all times now."

The limousine slowed down as it turned off the spaceport freeway and pulled into the centre of Clacton Fuzzville. Johnny looked out of the window at the grand buildings with their ornate architecture. It was a far cry from the ruined streets of the Milton Keynes he had known as a seventeen year-old lieutenant in the Mutant Army. Another crowd had gathered along the main boulevard that ran straight up to the presidential palace.

His stoic expression didn't betray it, but Johnny felt very uneasy about all the attention he and Middenface were attracting. For one thing, they had lost the element of surprise. Kit would have been tipped off about their arrival the minute it hit the news, and would already be in hiding. He would have had plenty of time to cover his tracks, too.

Worse still, he could be planning a pre-emptive strike on Johnny and Middenface; to take them both out before they even got a chance to come after him. Thanks to all the unwelcome publicity, he would now know exactly where both the S/D agents were.

"I hope you gentlemen won't mind if I put the roof down. The crowds at the palace gates are eager to catch a glimpse of our celebrated war heroes." Grinling leaned in confidentially to his two guests, his smile becoming apologetic but no less charming. "I'm afraid I have one request, though. Could you both remove your badges before the crowd sees you? President Leadbetter is very pleased to honour his old comrades, but it wouldn't look good for the image of his administration if he is seen to entertain Search and Destroy agents."

"Aye, that's right," grumbled Middenface. "Things aren't aw that different on this planet after aw. We're still considered scum for takin' on the jobs naebody else has the guts tae dae."

"I'm sorry to agree with you," said Grinling. "But most Miltonians believe that your profession projects a negative image of the mutant community. The president is offering you full hospitality and cooperation as long as you are sensitive to this little matter."

Johnny put a placatory hand on Middenface's shoulder, the way he often did when it looked like his partner's anger would get the better of him. "Take the badge off, Middenface," he said. "The less anyone knows about our reasons for being here, the easier our job's going to be."

Middenface snorted his objection, but he took his badge off all the same.

Grinling pressed another button, and the seemingly seamless plexiglass dome that covered the top of the limousine suddenly developed a split down the middle. The two halves of the dome receded slowly into the vehicle's sides, leaving Johnny and Middenface open to the full scrutiny of the crowd. The moment everyone caught sight of the pair, they let up a huge cheer and began to surge forward. A chain of soldiers, arms linked, strained to hold them back.

Johnny scanned the crowd for suspicious activity, chillingly aware that Kit could be any one of them. There was no way to guess what form an identity thief might take; that was what made their adversary so dangerous. Johnny and Middenface would have to be constantly on their guard. They could meet him at any time, in any place. They could even meet him at the palace. They could shake his hand, meet his eyes, and never know that he was sizing them up for a bullet in the back. All Johnny could trust were his instincts, and his undeniable talent for hunting down and capturing fugitive lawbreakers.

As the limousine finally reached the gates of the presidential palace, Johnny spotted a small group of old war veterans from the Fennsman Division of the Mutant Army. Above their heads was a holo-banner. The computer-generated, holographic image of a canvas banner fluttered in an imaginary breeze, and displayed the words: "REMEMBER GEORGE INCE!" For a moment, Johnny did just that. He cast his mind back to the escape he, Middenface and the other captured generals had made from Upminster Prison following the failed capture of Upminster Palace. The captured shuttle they were fleeing in had been hit by one of the spooker attack ships pursuing them, and they had been forced to crash land. That was when George, better known as General Clacton Fuzz, had become the last great martyr to the mutant cause.

Johnny recalled how the general had been hit by incendiary fire from one of the spookers as they were running for the cover of a disused blast shelter. The thick black hairs that covered every inch of Clacton Fuzz's face and body were quickly engulfed in flames. He went down fighting. His last act was to take out the spooker with a single shot, screaming, "Muties forever!" as he did. Johnny wondered what his old comrade would have made of Clacton Fuzzville, the city named after him. Would he have been plagued with the same unease that Johnny was? Would he, like Johnny, have found it all a little too good to be true?

* * *

"I'm afraid this is where I say goodbye, gentlemen." Grinling smiled graciously and shook Johnny and Middenface's hands again, clasping each of their hands between two of his.

They were standing in the middle of a huge antechamber on the ground floor of the palace. Johnny had been too lost in thought to register his surroundings as Grinling had led them down several long corridors, giving them a potted history of the palace's construction and pointing out architectural details that were of particular note.

As well as remembering his fallen comrade, Johnny had also been casing the palace for anything suspicious; checking for concealed corners from which an assassin might spring, and scanning each of the guards they passed for any sign that they were not who they pretended to be. As Grinling said his farewells, however, he snapped back to attention.

Grinling motioned to the large transparent tube behind them. "This is the special lift to the presidential quarters. I'm afraid I don't have the security clearance to ride it with you, but these gentlemen," Grinling motioned to the two guards stationed beside the lift, "will take you up."

"No, they won't," said Johnny, placing his hand on his holster.

"It's official policy," Grinling said reassuringly. "A simple matter of decorum."

"I don't care," said Johnny. "We're not getting in a confined space with two armed men we don't know. If the president wants to see us, we ride up alone. Otherwise, we can walk outside and explain to the press why we snubbed him."

"Well, we wouldn't want that. Maybe we can come to an arrangement."

Grinling looked to the guards for guidance. The guards gave Johnny and Middenface the once-over.

"Whit d'ye think ye're looking at?" growled Midden-face.

The head guard looked back at Grinling and gave a curt nod. Grinling gave his most winning smile, and took his leave.

The guards demanded that Johnny and Middenface relinquish their weapons, and they reluctantly complied. After that, there were no more objections. They were given the clearance codes to reach the presidential floor, and stepped into the lift.

When the doors opened again, they found their way blocked by two more guards.

They were about to start arguing when an officious voice barked, "It's all right, they're expected!" The guards stood to one side, and Johnny and Middenface could see the voice's owner as he marched up to them. He was a short, uniformed mutant with a forehead twice the size of the rest of his head. Four sets of eyes, each of them a different colour, looked down a small, pinched nose at the new arrivals as he came to attention in front of them.

"I am General Rising," said the mutant. "Head of Miltonia's armed forces. I understand you refused an escort." Obviously, the guards below had radioed ahead.

Johnny had seen General Rising's type before. He could tell from his supercilious manner and the way he held himself that he was no man of combat. He was a deskbound career soldier, the type who was happy to sign orders that saw men go to their deaths, but not to accompany them.

"The presidential guard are under instructions to let nobody past this point without a military escort," said Rising. "However ill-advised I consider it to be for the president to consort with bounty hunters, that task, it would seem, now falls to me."

Johnny could feel Middenface bristling palpably beside him. Before either of them could reply, though, the general turned on his heel and marched down a marble-lined corridor.

They followed him into the president's inner sanctum.

It was the president's eyes that Johnny noticed first. There was a sense of sadness about them, like he was pleading. They were the only things about President Leadbetter that he recognised.

Like most members of the Mutant Army, Leonard Leadbetter had a nickname. A mutie moniker, given to him by his own kind, that set him apart from the norms. Leonard had been known as the Ooze, on account of the liquefaction of parts of his body. It seemed as though this liquefaction had reached its apotheosis.

There, in the centre of the inner sanctum, in a large, round nutrient tank like an upturned dome mounted on a gold pedestal, two eyes floated in a giant puddle of sentient protoplasm.

This was the most powerful being on Miltonia: Leonard Leadbetter, the beloved President Ooze.

CHAPTER FIVE
ASSASSINATION

"Ooze, me auld mucker," said Middenface, a broad grin spreading across his face. "Nice tae see ye. Ye're looking well. Yer colour's good!" He strode up to the tank, his hand outstretched, before realising what he was doing and turned the proffered handshake into an embarrassed little wave. Johnny just nodded and smiled.

A small jet of bubbles streamed to the top of Leonard Leadbetter's mass, but Middenface didn't know if this was a greeting or just a random fluctuation in the fluid. The Ooze's eyes didn't give anything away either. They just stared up at the visitors and drifted serenely.

"The president returns the compliment. He says it has been too long."

The reedy voice drew Middenface's attention to the room's other occupant: a short, slight mutant who wore an immaculate black suit and stood with his hands clasped tightly behind his back. His skin was pale in contrast to the suit and jet-black hair, which was scraped back from his forehead. The only outward sign of his mutancy was a deformed nose, but this was prominent enough. It was huge; wider by far than the face from which it grew. It had at least three nostrils – there may have been more concealed beneath its irregular bulges – and, wherever it came to a point, it glowed a sickly red. Middenface had seen many, many examples of the random chaos that strontium exposure could wreak upon the human form, but still he couldn't seem to tear his eyes away from that misshapen nose. It drew attention like a magnet.

"Johnson," the mutant introduced himself, stepping forward and shaking hands. "Official advocate for President Leadbetter. You may call me Nose Job."

"Yeah," said Middenface. "I thought we might."

"Before we proceed, may I ask you to be careful with your eyes," Nose Job said.

Middenface realised that he was staring again and he jolted his head up. However, the remark had been aimed at Johnny.

Nose Job Johnson indicated to a cluster of machines at the head of the nutrient tank. "If you were to unleash your alpha radiation in the vicinity of the presidential vat, I'm afraid it would interfere with its rather delicate life-support equipment."

"Of course," said Johnny graciously.

"It is a great privilege to be invited into this chamber. The president thinks very highly of you both. I believe you fought together in the Mutant War." There was no trace of warmth in Nose Job's voice, but no hostility either. His tones were clipped and efficient.

"So yer the Ooze's new mouthpiece?" said Middenface, in an attempt to shift the conversation onto a more friendly footing.

"Hardly new," said Nose Job. "I have represented the president for almost ten years now."

"Dae ye still have tae go through that whole business o' injecting a part o' him into yer brain so as he can talk tae ye?"

"Nothing so onerous," said Nose Job. "Our scientists have refined the process, and now I can simply ingest a portion of the president's essence at fortnightly intervals. The telepathic link thus established is far stronger and has a much greater range than that provided by the old method."

"I wish we had time to sit down and talk about the old days," Johnny intervened. "But Middenface and I are here on an urgent mission."

"Yes," said Nose Job, "the president is aware of that. You have a warrant for the arrest of Kit Jones, alias Identi Kit, and you believe he is here on Miltonia."

"Drokk," hissed Middenface under his breath. "Can we no gae anywhere these days wi'out the whole world knowin' oor business before we even get there?"

"It wasn't hard to guess," said Nose Job. "Even without the report we received from Customs and Immigration. We may keep ourselves to ourselves on Miltonia, but we *have* heard about Identi Kit's escape from custody."

Something about Nose Job's body language must have alerted Johnny to the truth behind his words. "And you know he's here, don't you? You've seen him!" he said sharply.

Nose Job sighed and his head sank, which only drew Middenface's attention to the fact that his prodigious nose was as long as it was wide. The presidential advocate did not, however, answer the question. Instead, he glanced up at General Rising who was standing to attention in the doorway, and a meaningful look passed between them.

"Ah knew it!" growled Middenface. "Ah knew ah shouldae decked that stony-faced git sooner. If he hadn't kept us... Whit's happened?" He didn't know whether to address the question to Nose Job or to the Ooze himself, so he ended up aiming it awkwardly into the air between them. "Whit's that scunner been up tae?"

Nose Job cleared his throat. "The president thinks it would be best if I were to let you see for yourself. Would you follow me, please?"

* * *

They rode the lift back down to the ground floor, and beyond. Johnny didn't complain this time about sharing the confined space. If the Ooze trusted Nose Job Johnson, that was good enough for him and, although Rising was a different matter, an alpha scan revealed that the most deadly weapon in his possession was a pen.

The two bodyguards were still at their posts and they glared searchingly at Johnny and Middenface through the transparent tube as they passed.

They alighted on the third and lowest sublevel, and Nose Job led them down another maze of corridors. Evidently, this part of the palace didn't see much use. There was nobody around and the wall-mounted lights only activated when their sensors detected individuals in their proximity, so the for of them were always at the centre of their own travelling light bubble. There was a chill in the air and a taste of dust, and their footsteps rang off the concrete floor and echoed back at them until it sounded like they were being followed by an army of ghosts.

The foursome came to a concrete door, and Nose Job produced a plastic key card that he ran through the electronic lock. Johnny had already scanned the room beyond; unlikely as this was to be a trap, experience had taught him to err on the side of caution. Therefore, he was prepared when Nose Job cracked the heavy door open and a cloud of cold air rolled out into the corridor. Middenface, caught unawares, shuddered, stamped his booted feet and clapped at his upper arms.

It was precisely because Johnny knew what to expect, however, that he was reluctant to step into the cold room. He felt as if a clawed hand had reached into his stomach, bundled up his intestines, and squeezed. No matter how much death he saw, he reflected glumly, he never quite became inured to it – especially not to the death of a friend.

The body lay on a bier in the centre of the mausoleum, its hands clasped over its chest. It was draped in the red and black Miltonian flag. Although its head was covered, Johnny had already made out the shape of antlers beneath the cloth.

They approached the bier in respectful silence, and Middenface winced as Nose Job gently folded back the flag.

From the neck downwards, Moosehead McGuffin could have been any normal human being, but as Middenface had once joked, the rest of him looked like something you'd find on the wall of a hunting lodge. The joke hadn't gone down particularly well because Middenface hadn't known at the time that Moosehead's norm parents, revolted by their offspring, had sold him to a hunting fanatic who'd had exactly that fate in mind for him.

Moosehead had never talked much about that time. He once said, though, that every important lesson he had learned about hunting and survival had begun in the extensive forested grounds of his new owner, a younger brother of King Clarkie the Second. Against all odds, and thanks to a groundsman's negligence, the half-starved mutant had escaped to be taken in by General Armz's Salisbury camp near the ruins of Stonehenge. As a scout in the Mutant War, he had excelled, and later, like so many other soldiers in the Mutant Army, Moosehead had joined the S/D Agency and put his hard-won skills to the task of hunting down criminals with prices on their heads.

It hardly seemed fair that Moosehead's life should end like this, when he must have thought his struggles were finally behind him. But then, the life of a Strontium Dog wasn't one you could just walk away from, and none of them knew from where or when that fateful bullet would come.

"How did it happen?" asked Johnny.

"A Westinghouse," said Nose Job. "Single shot to the heart."

Johnny already knew that; he had seen the telltale burn pattern on Moosehead's chest. "I mean, how did Kit get into the palace?"

"Dae ye really need tae ask?" put in Middenface. "He couldae looked like anyone: Nose Job, the general here, one o' the guards... He couldae slithered in under the door disguised as the president himself if he'd a mind tae."

"Actually," confessed Nose Job, shifting his weight in embarrassment, "he wasn't disguised at all. That's how we could identify him. Our surveillance units filmed Kit Jones as he approached Minister McGuffin's office, although it was only later that we matched his likeness to the one in the news reports."

"You're saying you just let him walk in here?" Johnny asked incredulously.

"I don't think you appreciate how rare this type of crime is on Miltonia," said Nose Job. "Our citizens are happy and our government prides itself on its openness and accessibility."

General Rising cleared his throat and his eight eyes darkened. "I've been warning for some time that the political climate is changing. We've been too soft, letting in too many undesirables. This assassin is only the latest."

"We are in the process of tightening security in the presidential palace and other high-risk areas," said Nose Job.

"Too late for poor old Moosehead," muttered Johnny.

"When did it happen?" asked Middenface, his eyes narrowing dangerously.

"Four days ago," said Rising, adding pointedly. "Long before you arrived here and were detained by customs. There was nothing you could have done."

"Kit Jones made an appointment with the minister – under an assumed name, of course – to discuss an issue with his entrance visa," explained Nose Job. He swallowed and a tear came to his eye, but he struggled to remain stoical. "I walked in on them just as the gun fired. If I'd been a second earlier... I... I'll never forget the look on the minister's face. And his killer... Identi Kit was standing over him, the gun still smoking, and he turned and he just stared at me. His eyes were so cold and he was grinning. He was proud of what he'd done, and... And I think he wanted me to know it was him. I think he wanted everyone to know!"

"That's why he didn't disguise himself," surmised Johnny. "This wasn't just an act of revenge on the man who imprisoned him, it was a public statement."

"Dinnae mess wi' Identi Kit," Middenface muttered.

"You were lucky, Nose Job. Kit could have killed you, too, but he wanted a witness."

"I thought he *would* kill me, at first," said Nose Job, suppressing a shiver. "He was coming at me with that look in his eyes, and... I'm afraid I didn't cope very well. I've never had a gun pointed at me before. As I said, this is a peaceful world. At least, it was... I'm afraid I passed out. Just for a second. When I came to, he was gone."

"McGuffin was able to sound the alarm before he was killed," said Rising gruffly. "We had the ministerial wing cordoned off within ninety seconds, but we saw no sign of the perp, not even on the cameras. He'd vanished into thin air."

"He might not have used his abilities to get into the palace," said Johnny. "But it's a sure bet he used them to get out."

Middenface groaned. "Then we came aw this way fer nothing. Yon scunner's already done his worst. He's got nae more reason tae be hanging aboot here."

Johnny nodded despondently. "You're right. He could be anywhere by now."

"Actually," said Nose Job, "Kit Jones is almost certainly still on Miltonia. You see, we think there's more to this than just a personal vendetta – far more."

After Johnny and Middenface had paid their final respects to Moosehead, Nose Job Johnson suggested they continue their business in more pleasant surroundings. They retraced their steps to the lift, rode back to the top floor, and were led into a comfortably appointed room a few doors down from the president's sanctum, which Johnny took to be Nose Job's own office.

Johnny and Middenface sank into the soft, deep cushions of a black leather sofa, while Nose Job perched on a rigid chair beside his desk. Rising seemed content to stand guard at the door again.

"For some time now," Nose Job began, "we've been having some, shall we say, difficulties, with a group who call themselves the Salvationists."

"Norm supremacists!" spat Rising from the doorway. "It's not enough that they control ninety-nine per cent of the known universe. They can't stand the idea that there's a place, just one world, where mutants can be free of their bigotry."

"Thank you, general," said Nose Job. "The Salvationists began life as a legitimate pressure group and we recognised them as such. They campaigned for equal rights for Miltonia's growing norm population."

"The 'equal right' to persecute our kind," Rising grumbled.

"Over time, though, the movement has been hijacked by extremists, and has gone underground."

"Last week," said Rising, "they exploded a bomb on a school bus as it passed through the centre of Clacton Fuzzville. They sent a message by electronic mail to the palace, claiming responsibility. It was carnage: severed arms and legs everywhere."

"Fortunately," Nose Job hastened to explain, "there was only one person aboard: the driver. It's just that he had a lot of arms and legs."

"And there'd already been one attempt on McGuffin's life," Rising continued. "A norm took a shot at him during a press conference at the spaceport. He tried to make a run for it but my men were too quick for him. Four bullets right in the back; a perfect grouping. After that, I told McGuffin that he should be guarded at all times."

"But the minister was convinced that it was a one-off incident. He was determined to go on as before and not to give in to fear." Nose Job sighed. "I don't know... Perhaps we should have seen it coming. Perhaps we've grown complacent with our comfortable lives here. Perhaps we should have done something."

"You can't legislate against fanatics!" snapped the general. "They don't play by the rules. They'll do anything, use anyone, even sacrifice themselves for the sake of their own twisted goals. And they're cowards. They won't come out and fight, they only strike from the shadows. If the norms feel so oppressed here, if their life is so intolerable, why do they keep on coming? Why don't they go to one of the thousands of norm worlds, where they can live as happy as you please and lord it over the mutant scum they seem to hate so much?"

"I don't understand," said Johnny. "What does this have to do with Kit?"

"Did I not say?" asked Nose Job. "In Minister McGuffin's office, before I... Well... What I mean to say is, before Identi Kit left, he told me something. He said he was striking a blow for the Salvationists, and this was just the start."

Johnny frowned. "Why would a mutant be working with norm supremacists?"

"Who knows?" shrugged Middenface. "Who cares? Let's just go find the scunner. Ye got any questions, ye can ask 'em once ah've broken his face."

"We think the Salvationists engineered Kit's escape from prison," said Nose Job. "It's likely that they also planned the assassination of Minister McGuffin, and equipped Kit for the purpose. He owes them."

Johnny could see where this was going. "So, if we're to capture Identi Kit," he sighed, "we'll have to take on these terrorists, too."

Nose Job smiled. "Our intelligence reports suggest that the Salvationists have a base in the mountains to the south of Clacton Fuzzville. Unfortunately, we have been unable to pinpoint its exact location."

Johnny nodded grimly. "When do we leave?"

"There's one more thing," said Nose Job. "The Salvationists have a hostage: a Miltonian citizen named George Smith, better known as the Consoler. He was snatched from his home over six months ago. Since then, he's only been seen in video messages sent to the media by his captors."

Rising's thin lips twisted into a scowl. "At first, we thought they were forcing him to spout their racist propaganda, but now, we think it's worse."

"We think they've brainwashed him," concluded Nose Job.

"Why?" asked Johnny. "What's so special about Smith?"

"The Consoler has a unique ability," said Nose Job. "He can absorb the mutations of others into his own body. That means he can–"

"Turn mutants intae norms!" exclaimed Middenface, his eyes widening.

"Or, as the Salvationists would have it, 'cure' them," said Rising.

"They claim to have 'cured' over a hundred mutants already," said Nose Job. "We can't verify that figure, but you know as well as I do that many of our kind have been taught to loathe what they are; to see themselves as inferior. The Salvationists play on that self-hatred. They invite mutants to come to them, and they make them 'normal' in return for their support for the Salvationist cause."

"If we let this go on," said Rising, "they could shift the whole balance of power on Miltonia. We could find ourselves outnumbered by norms. There could be another Mutant War here."

"That's why the president has empowered me to make you an offer," said Nose Job Johnson. "The Miltonian government will give you all the assistance you require to find the Salvationists and arrest Kit Jones. We will also pay you an additional fifty thousand credits if you can rescue the Consoler and bring him back to us."

Johnny almost missed the muttered words of General Rising. "Whether he wants to be brought back or not."

CHAPTER SIX
CRIMINAL MAGNETISM

Middenface was longing for the whisky he had found in the hold of the supply ship that had taken them to Miltonia. The hold had been only marginally less comfortable than the military air cruiser in which he now found himself. The hunt for Kit had involved far too much travelling for his liking. He needed a drink to take the edge off his nerves.

The air cruiser lurched as it hit an air pocket, and then banked steeply. Middenface felt his guts turn over in complaint, but at least the mountain range to which they were headed had finally come into view. Hidden somewhere in this range was the Salvationist base camp where, according to their new allies in the Miltonian government, they would find Kit.

About time, too, he thought. He could take comfort in the fact that as soon as they had bagged their man, there was only one more journey to make, and that was back to the Doghouse to collect their seven hundred thousand credits. That was the only thing he *could* take comfort in, though. They were going after Kit practically unarmed.

The mountains were full of an extremely rare ore known as magnetinium. It only existed on a couple of known planets, and this particular mountain range had the biggest deposit ever found. Magnetinium gave off a huge field of... What was it Rising had called them at the briefing? Imps? No, it was EMPs: electromagnetic something-or-others.

Middenface had spent most of the briefing fighting the urge to blacken every one of the general's eight eyes. Stuck-up, self-important desk monkey! The general was happy enough for the S/D agents to fight his battles for him, but answering Johnny's questions, that was another matter. It was clear that he was holding back information, and telling them no more than he had to. Not that Middenface had listened to much of what the general had said. Listening and plotting was Johnny's field; laldy and handing it out, that was Middenface's forte.

Electromagnetic beans? No, wait, pulses. That was it. Yeah, pulses. Magnetinium radiated a field of electromagnetic pulses that disabled any electrical devices it touched. This made the mountain range the perfect place for a bunch of terrorist norms to hide out. No surveillance device could get close enough to find out where they were. What's more, any modern weaponry, or any type of technological doodad you cared to wave a stick at, was disabled the minute it got within the magnetinium's range, leaving General Rising's men unarmed against an enemy they couldn't find anyway.

The upshot of all this was that Middenface and Johnny were walking into this fight with nothing more than knives and clubs. They had had to leave all their weapons back with the palace guard for safekeeping. If they'd taken them along, they would have been knackered for good. Their weapons were the most expensive things they owned, and they couldn't afford to lose them.

Middenface did not like this one bit. Handing your weapons over to another man was worse than handing him your wife, naked and full of aphrodisiac. He was still chafing at the thought of it. He felt uncomfortable and undressed without the weight of them hanging off of him. He was so used to adapting his body to their presence that he didn't know how to stand or even sit without them. It was just one more thing that the whisky, if he'd had any, could have helped him forget.

Although Rising hadn't known the exact location of the Salvationist base, his covert operatives had been able to torture enough information out of the few Salvationists they'd captured to narrow it down to a rough area. The general had smiled proudly as he explained this. Johnny had gone quiet and grim, or rather even more quiet and grim than usual. Middenface could tell he didn't like the idea of acting on intelligence gained by torture. It probably brought back memories of the Kreelers back on Earth. He'd kept his mouth shut all the same.

So here they were, sitting in the bay of an air cruiser with two pilots and a lieutenant from the Miltonian covert forces. The lieutenant, who had ears growing all over his face (and probably much of his body), pulled out a military issue, handheld holo-projector, which emitted a three-dimensional map of the mountain range ahead.

"This is about as far as we can take you," he said. "Any closer and our instruments will start to malfunction, along with the engines." He pointed to a section of the holo-map which turned blue. "We're currently here and you want to be," he indicated another section, which turned red. "Here. We're convinced the base camp is within this two-mile radius. Any questions so far?"

"Aye," said Middenface. "Where do I tak' a leak?"

"Erm, you'll have to wait until you reach your destination," said the lieutenant. "You'll use jetpacks to get within walking distance of the target. We suggest you use this route." A dotted line appeared on the holo-map, which then zoomed in on the image of the mountain range to give an actual bird's eye view of the route in question. "Our readings show that the EMP field is weakest along this line, allowing you to get as close as possible before the jetpacks cease to function. They should take you to here," a section of the map turned green, "where you'll have to use parachutes to land. A bit low-tech, I'm afraid, but any standard anti-gravity device simply would not function in this environment."

The lieutenant handed Middenface and Johnny the jet-packs and two bulky backpacks to wear underneath them. "This button here jettisons the jetpacks," he explained. "Then you pull this ripcord here to activate the parachute."

Middenface was highly dubious about the parachute as he put it on. He had no faith in ancient technology, especially not when his life depended on it. Unfortunately for him, there was no turning back.

The bay doors opened and the lieutenant wished the two S/D agents luck. Middenface and Johnny jumped from the cruiser, their jetpacks roaring into life.

Johnny took a deep breath. The cool mountain air was mixed with the hot smell of the jetpack's burning fuel. The wind in his face revived him after the long journey in the air cruiser, and he felt good to be back in action. He and Middenface had spent far too long in stuffy rooms with politicians and officers that neither of them trusted.

He took a sharp left as he whistled through a gully and skirted a mountain pass. Middenface nearly overshot the turning, and Johnny had to yell loudly to bring the big lug back on course. Navigation had never been one of Middenface's strong points.

By Johnny's calculation, they were less than two kilometres away from the point at which the EMPs would cause their jetpacks to cut out. They didn't as yet have much of a plan of action upon landing. They would have to employ all their scouting skills to locate the camp and then study its defences carefully. They had no idea how well guarded Kit was or how they were going to apprehend him.

Like Middenface, Johnny sorely missed his weapons. They gave him an edge over most opponents and without them, all he had was cunning and guile backed up with a little muscle and determination. He was good with a knife and dangerous with a club, but his real area of expertise was as a marksman. His empty holster felt almost painful, like the hole of a freshly pulled tooth.

They shot over a ravine and approached a plateau where the EMP field was much stronger. Johnny signalled to Middenface to get ready to jettison his pack. They coasted over the plateau and felt themselves jerked sharply backwards as they hit the field and their jetpacks instantly cut out. Johnny pulled his ripcord and the parachute billowed out above him, slowing his fall. He looked up at the thin fabric that caught the air and slowed his descent with a sudden admiration. Maybe there was something to be said for the ingenuity of ancient technology, after all.

Middenface wasn't so impressed, however. Johnny was alarmed to see him plummeting past him, tugging violently at his ripcord and screaming out a tirade of profanities, some of which even Johnny hadn't heard before. He was relieved when the parachute finally opened out below him.

Johnny lost sight of Middenface then, as he was carried away by a light gust of wind. The ground raced up to meet him and he hit it and rolled as he had been taught. He clambered to his feet and unhooked the chute. It was only then that he realised he hadn't seen Middenface land.

He scanned the barren, rocky terrain of the plateau, and smiled broadly as he spotted his partner.

"Awright, very funny. Now git me doon frae here," cried Middenface, dangling from the branches of the only gnarled tree in sight. Trust him to find it!

Johnny took out his knife, clambered up and cut Middenface loose from the cords in which he had become entangled. He tumbled out of the tree, hitting several branches on his way down, cursing Miltonia, magne-tinium, and ancient technology as he went.

Johnny cut the parachute from the clinging branches and let it drop to the ground. They bundled both para-chutes up and looked around for a place to dispose of them. They didn't want to leave any trace that would alert the Salvationists to their presence. The plateau was too barren and rocky to dig much of a hole, and they didn't have a spade anyway, so they jammed the chutes into a crevice and covered it over with rocks.

"Where tae now, Johnny?" asked Middenface.

Johnny surveyed their surroundings. As he recalled from the holographic map, there was a gully with a large mountain stream some kilometres away. If there was water, it was probable that there was also some vegeta-tion and the opportunity to grow crops. A good place to begin the search, he decided.

"That way," he said, pointing to the top of a rise. Mid-denface nodded and fell into step beside him.

They hiked for about three hours. The sun sank lower in the sky, and Johnny reckoned they were approaching the middle of the Miltonian afternoon. As he recalled, there were approximately thirty-four and a half Earth hours in one Miltonian day.

The mountain terrain was heavy going at first. They had had two steep ridges to climb, the second of which was covered in loose shale. This caused them to lose their footing and slide quite often. When they finally got in sight of the gully, they were both out of breath and sweating quite heavily.

"By the time we've finished here, we'd have earned every penny o' that seven hundred thou," puffed Mid-denface.

Johnny still couldn't see any sign of habitation. He was beginning to accept, with some dismay, that they could be combing the two-mile radius for days before they stumbled upon anything. There was no guarantee that the intelligence they were acting upon was even true. He knew from experience that people would say just about anything under torture, and there was often no way to check their claims other than by inflicting more pain on them. This was just one of the reasons why he hated using information garnered by such means. The use of torture crossed a line into territory he wasn't prepared to explore. Even bounty hunters had ethics.

The gully contained the first real signs of life they had seen in the mountains. Bushes, shrubs and ferns lined its sides, and several clumps of trees sprouted down at the bottom. Johnny even spotted a few small furry creatures swinging from the branches. A clear, fast-running stream ran down a steep incline and through the middle of the flora.

From where they stood, Johnny could see two ways down. The first would be quite straightforward, but it would leave them exposed to the scrutiny of anyone hidden in the undergrowth below. The other way was far more precipitous, but it would afford them good cover throughout. There was no question of which route they should take. He outlined the latter course to Middenface, and they began their descent.

At the bottom by the side of the stream, they stopped and filled their water bottles. The water was cool and refreshing. After that, they decided their best bet was to cross to where the undergrowth was densest, and then follow the stream's course.

They were three-quarters of the way along the gully when suddenly an arrow shot out from nowhere, passing over their heads. They hit the ground and reached for their knives, trying to pinpoint the direction from which the attack had come. Behind them, they heard a chittering shriek as one of the furry creatures fell out of a tree, impaled and dying. The arrow had not been meant for them.

They crawled behind a clump of ferns and watched as two norms and a mutant broke out of the bushes and raced up to the fallen creature. They hadn't spotted Johnny and Middenface yet. As the three men drew closer, the S/D agents saw that two of them, not one, were mutants. The man they had mistaken for a norm only had the slightest of mutations: the fingers of his left hand were half as long again as normal fingers. He was carrying a bow.

"See, didn't I tell you?" the long-fingered mutant boasted as he picked up his quarry. "I never miss!"

"Fingers, that's the first thing you've shot all day," said the norm, good-naturedly. "Which is lucky because that's your last arrow."

"Get out of here," replied Fingers. "You're still sore because you missed that lizard."

"That wasn't my fault," the norm countered. "Tell him, Whispers, it wasn't my fault." A tall mutant who also looked near-normal except that he had the tiniest of mouths just shrugged and shook his head.

"What's the matter?" joked the norm. "Are you just going to stand there and let him talk to me like this?"

"He ain't gonna stand there," said Fingers. "He's going to walk back to the camp with me. You can stay here and argue about lizards for as long as you like."

"Okay, okay," said the norm, jogging along behind them as they set off at a brisk pace. "But you wait until our next hunting expedition. I'll bag the biggest lizard you ever did see. Just you wait and see if I don't."

Johnny and Middenface exchanged smiles. Luck was with them. When it came to the matter of hunting down their men, it seemed it always was.

* * *

They followed the three Salvationists at a safe distance. It was not difficult as their quarry was not on its guard. They tramped merrily through the gully making a huge racket: laughing, joking and arguing playfully, obviously convinced that nobody was watching them. While this made it easier for the bounty hunters to tail them, it also put them on their guard. There had to be a reason for the Salvationists' confidence and, whatever it was, it could prove highly dangerous to them.

The three men walked to the end of the gully where the sides were the least steep and took a hidden route upwards. Johnny and Middenface had to hang back a moment as the trio had the perfect vantage point from which to see any pursuers. As they disappeared from sight, the pair broke cover and raced across the open ground after them. It was a risky but necessary manoeuvre and it almost backfired. The path that the Salvationists were following must have doubled back on itself, because they suddenly came back into view above Johnny and Middenface's heads. Had they only been a little more vigilant, they would have spotted them.

The S/D agents ducked out of sight, emerging when the coast was clear and scrambling up the hazardous path in pursuit. They caught one more glimpse of Fingers, not far ahead of them, but by the time they reached the spot where he'd been, he had vanished into thin air. There was no sign of any of the three men. They stood for a moment, perplexed, looking for anywhere their quarry could be hiding.

"D'ye think we've bin steered blind, Johnny?" Middenface asked.

Johnny shook his head. "I know it looks strange, but I don't believe those three would have been up here by themselves. We're too far from civilisation. They have to be connected to the Salvationists somehow."

"Even if two o' 'em were mutants?"

Johnny stroked his chin thoughtfully. "I get the feeling there's more to all this than we realised," he considered.

Suddenly, he heard a scraping sound behind him.

Middenface heard it too, and they spun around in unison, their hands reaching for their knives. They were too late.

The shapes in front of them were wispy and grey, like ghosts. It took Johnny a moment to realise that he was looking at two human figures, their clothing blending perfectly into the shapes and colours of the mountainside behind them.

"Sneckin' chameleon cloaks!" groaned Middenface under his breath, and Johnny was just as chagrined as his partner at having being caught out in the same way twice.

"Hold it right there!" growled one of the cloaked guards.

"Out for an afternoon stroll in the hills, are we?" said the other with an unpleasant smile. "I think you two better talk fast!"

Sturdy bows, with arrows notched and ready, protruded from their cloaks. Johnny's mind raced, calculating the distance between himself and his enemies, and their likely reaction time to any attack. They were only a few steps away. If he could surprise them, he could disarm one of them before he had time to fire. Probably. He felt Middenface tensing beside him and knew he was thinking the same thing. But some ingrained warrior's instinct told Johnny that that would be a bad move and, a moment later, he saw why.

There was a third guard situated further away, maintaining his cover, but now that Johnny knew what to look for, he could see him by the way the light bent around him creating a ghostly ripple effect in the air. With a nod and a look that was almost imperceptible to anybody else, Johnny communicated the bad news to Middenface.

They were surrounded.

CHAPTER SEVEN
CAPTURED

"Don't shoot!" said Johnny. "We aren't your enemies."

"What are you doing here?" asked the first guard. He appeared to be a norm, but his chameleon cloak distorted his contours and made it impossible to know for sure. Johnny kept his eyes downcast and concentrated on keeping the alpha fire out of them. He had been mistaken for a norm at the spaceport, and with any luck, his captors might make the same error.

"I... I... Well, geez, I don't rightly know," he said, slipping into an impression of Cain Hine. "I just heard about youse fellows up here and... Well, it ain't easy being a norm on Miltonia and I think you got the right idea. I think they should treat us better. I mean..." Remembering the mutants in the hunting party, Johnny thought it best to hedge his bets. "Don't get me wrong, some of my best pals are muties." He nodded towards Middenface. "But it ain't nothing to be proud of it, is it? The muties here, they act as if they don't wanna be cured."

"And you do?" The guard had turned his gaze upon Middenface who shifted his weight from one foot to the other. Johnny sensed his partner's discomfort with the deception. Middenface preferred to speak plainly, preferably with fists and guns.

"Go on, um, Nodule Head," Johnny urged him. "You don't have to be shy around these good people. Tell them how you feel."

Middenface shot him a murderous glare before mumbling, "You dinnae ken whit it's been like. All ma life, Ah've been kicked around and spat upon, and ah know ah deserve it, but sometimes ah think, if ah coulda have a second chance, if ah could just be rid o' this filthy curse, ah could be a good person, ah know ah could."

"We thought things'd be different here," said Johnny. "We were told everyone was equal on Miltonia. We thought it'd be a good life for both of us. But I guess we know now what happens when you let the muties take over. It ain't their fault, they just ain't equipped to rule."

Middenface let out a plaintive howl, surprising even Johnny, and fell to his knees, beating his chest in anguish. "Oh, the pain, the pain!" he wailed. "Ah only wannae be normal, fer Drokk's sake, why did ye have tae make me this way?"

Johnny winced inwardly and aimed a surreptitious kick between his partner's ribs. But Middenface's hammy performance had had the desired effect. Johnny heard the skittering sound of sliding shale; the third guard had closed in, drawn by his own curiosity. His shape was as clear as the others, now. He was another norm (probably), watching the strangers mistrustfully along the length of a notched arrow.

"How did you find us?" he asked curtly.

Johnny feigned surprise at this new voice, and contrived to lose his balance on the uneven surface and stumble towards the source of it. The third guard froze him with a pointed glare and a movement of his bow. The arrowhead was now aimed at his heart.

"Oh, you know," said Johnny vaguely. "People talk, and you fellows are making something of a name for yourselves. We just... Um, people don't always pay us much heed, and they don't watch their mouths around us, and we pick things up, you know. We did hear right, didn't we... That you can help us?"

"The pain," howled Middenface. "The pain!"

"But, hey," said Johnny, beaming at the third guard and spreading his arms wide to show that he meant him no harm, "this was a lucky break for us and no mistake, finding you guys so soon." He took another crucial step towards the guard. "How long have we been out here, Nodule Head? Can't be more than, oh, about four days."

This time, Johnny ignored the guard's warning gesture. There were only a few feet between them; they were close enough to see the change in the bowman's posture and the shift in his face that betrayed his intention to fire. Johnny made eye contact and tore into his would-be attacker's brain. The guard gasped and tears came to his eyes.

With a perfect coordination that came from years of working together, Middenface made his own move at the same time. The other two guards had taken their eyes off him, seeing his partner as the greater threat. Their mistake. His fist closed around the first guard's arrow even as it left its bow, bound for Johnny's back. A flex of his fingers was enough to snap the shaft in two. By the time the second guard had found the presence of mind to use his own weapon, Middenface had the first by the throat and was using him as a shield. The first guard yelped as he took an arrow to the shoulder. Then, Middenface threw him at the second guard and brought them both down in a tangle of limbs.

The third guard struggled manfully but was no match for Johnny's alpha eyes. His legs buckled and his arrow twanged into the stone ground. Johnny moved in to finish the job even as Middenface leapt joyously upon the man's comrades.

The fight was over in seconds.

Middenface slung an unconscious guard over each shoulder, while Johnny took the third. They dropped them out of sight behind a rocky outcrop where Johnny bound and gagged them with their own clothing.

Now that his adrenaline rush had subsided, Midden-face felt empty and troubled. He sank to the ground with a heavy sigh. "Ah didnae mean it, ye know," he said in response to his partner's questioning look. "All that stuff ah said about being ashamed. ah'm proud o' what ah am. I always have been... Even when it hasnae felt like such a blessing."

Johnny smiled indulgently at him. "I know."

"It makes ye think, though. Whit'd make ye so unhappy, so short on self-respect, that ye'd come begging to these scunners fer this so-called 'cure'?"

"I guess you'd have to be pretty desperate," said Johnny. "Desperate to be somebody else."

Middenface mumbled a grudging acceptance of that point. After all, he knew what life was like for most mutants. But how was it going to get any better if they didn't all fight for their rights? If they just gave up? Many norms already viewed mutancy as a disgusting disease. If a "cure" now existed, what did that mean for those mutants who chose not to receive it, who remained true to themselves? They could only be stigmatised further.

Then, thought Middenface gloomily, there would doubtless be people who believed they shouldn't have that choice.

He shivered at the thought and tried to turn his mind to other matters. Johnny was scanning the area, his eyes blazing, seeking out clues to the disappearance of the hunting party. All of a sudden he beckoned his partner towards a black, dead-looking patch of scrub bush, and pointed to something behind it.

There was a fissure in the side of the mountain. It was narrow and rocks had been arranged in front of it to protect it from view. It was almost invisible until you were right on top of it. It didn't look as if it could lead anywhere, but Johnny's alpha eyes had clearly told him otherwise.

Communicating only with hand gestures, Middenface and Johnny returned to the unconscious guards and divested them of two of their chameleon cloaks. They wrapped the flimsy material about themselves; a tight fit around Middenface's broad shoulders. Then they drew their knives and Johnny slipped into the crack and was swallowed by darkness.

Middenface followed suit. At first, he had trouble squeezing through the narrow confines of the rocky passageway, but the fissure soon opened out into a larger tunnel, which appeared to be natural. The light from the entrance behind them died out and Middenface stumbled several times. He tried to keep Johnny in sight, but it wasn't easy since the chameleon cloak fooled his senses, merging the shape of his partner into the shadows around him.

They proceeded with caution, Johnny scanning constantly in case they ran into more concealed guards. The way remained clear, however, and soon they saw a dim, flickering light ahead of them. A moment later, they became aware of a faint humming sound and of the ground vibrating beneath their feet.

The sound became louder and the vibrations stronger as the tunnel broadened out and became lighter. Now, they could also hear a discordant rhythm of *hisses* and *clanks*, like the workings of some great machine. Middenface realised that the temperature had risen considerably. He was sweating.

They hugged the walls, letting the chameleon cloaks do their work, until they reached the end of the tunnel.

"This is getting stranger aw the time!" gasped Middenface.

The tunnel opened out into the wall of a huge crater at least a kilometre in diameter. Its floor, about twenty metres below them, was covered haphazardly with tents and ramshackle wooden huts. Halogen lamps were bolted to the wall of the crater at regular intervals; they fizzed and flickered, casting an eerie blue pallor over the whole scene.

They were standing inside a huge dormant volcano and could see the source of the mechanical noises. It was a mammoth steam turbine standing in the centre of the settlement, ingeniously constructed from all manner of recycled parts, and obviously powered by the heat and natural gases of the volcano itself. Rickety pipes ran from the turbine carrying steam to the various dwellings all over the camp. Somehow, Middenface reasoned, the steam had to be powering the lamps, too.

It was an amazing sight and he could have stared at it a while longer, but there were people moving between the huts and he was painfully aware that the chameleon cloak didn't make him invisible and it only camouflaged him. He and Johnny withdrew down the tunnel before they were noticed to discuss their next move.

They had to go down there, of course, and it had to be a stealth mission. They were too badly outnumbered to take the direct approach. The chameleon cloaks were their greatest asset, and the irony that the Salvationists themselves had unwittingly provided them was not lost on the pair.

"Strictly recon," suggested Johnny. "We split up, scout around for an hour or so, get the lay of the land and see if we can set eyes on Kit or the Consoler. With luck, Kit'll think he's safe in here and wouldn't have bothered to disguise himself."

"Ye really think we'll find him?" asked Middenface. "Ah've been thinking about that Rising character, and ah'm nae sure I trust him, Johnny. Whit if he lied tae us so as we'd tak' out his enemies fer him?"

"That has occurred to me," said Johnny. That didn't surprise Middenface; his partner had always been a quick thinker. "But the material in these cloaks isn't easy to find – impossible, in fact, in this part of space – and the cloaks are the Chameleon gang's trademark. I'd lay odds that Kit has been here."

Middenface accepted this point and they finalised their plans. As they crept back towards the crater end of the tunnel, another thought occurred to him and he clapped a hand on Johnny's shoulder to get his attention.

"Nodule Head?" he repeated, frowning.

The short descent from the entrance passageway was simple enough. Iron rungs had been hammered into the crater wall and a knotted rope trailed beside them.

Johnny took his time, carefully testing each rung beneath his feet. He knew there was more chance of being spotted this way, but with luck, the Salvationists inside the base would be as overconfident in their ability to remain hidden as the hunters outside. Even if they saw the telltale distortion of his chameleon cloak, he hoped they would mistake him for one of their own guards. So long as he kept his movements unhurried, confident, natural.

He knew the plan made sense. He knew it was the best they had. But still his nerves were fraught, screaming at him that he had made the worst mistake a warrior could make: he had turned his back to his enemies. He felt exposed and his neck hairs prickled with the sensation of imaginary eyes upon him. He felt he had been climbing down this ladder for an age, and that it extended a greater distance still below him.

He wouldn't even hear them coming over the din of the turbine. The first he would know about it would be when he was struck down with an arrow in the back.

Then, at last, his foot touched stone and he was on firm ground once again. He allowed himself a quiet breath of relief before casting a furtive glance around. Nobody was waiting for him. He couldn't see anybody at all. He turned to his left and slipped behind the nearest hut.

Middenface stepped onto the ladder a moment later. Johnny watched him until he, too, had reached the bottom without incident. He looked around, caught sight of Johnny, and pulled back his cloak to flash him an "OK" gesture, his thumb and forefinger touching to form a circle. Then he crept off to the right and out of sight.

That was the easy part over with.

Johnny skirted around the edge of the hut and scuttled across a narrow gangway to the next one. He could hear low voices now and he made his way towards them. Five norms were sitting around on packing crates, swigging beer from cans and swapping jokes. Johnny was just in time to hear the punch line of a particularly bad one about a mutant, a nun, and a hoverbus driver. It hardly bothered him that the mutant was the butt of the joke; he was used to that. But after the bomb attack that Nose Job Johnson and General Rising had described – the one that had claimed a bus driver's life – the joke seemed especially inappropriate.

The norms, however, laughed uproariously. Only belatedly did the slender, blonde-haired woman stifle her giggles and appeal for quiet. "We don't want the Consoler to hear us, do we?" she said with a conspiratorial grin.

"Don't care if he does," grumbled an overweight man with a square chin and heavy brow. Johnny recognised his baritone voice as that of the joke-teller. "He ought to know how we feel. Then maybe he'd do something about it."

The blonde woman sighed. "That's not fair, Jim. We're all impatient for change, but the Consoler can only do so much."

"Jim's not good with patience," said one of the other men. "If he had his way, we'd march on the palace tonight with torches and pitchforks."

"Damn right!" The overweight man slammed a fist into his crate. "I'm sick of these hit-and-run tactics. The longer we sit around here, the more time we give them to prepare."

"Security has got tighter since McGuffin was killed," someone else pointed out.

"And we're getting stronger," asserted the blonde woman. "Our numbers are growing all the time. We will make our move, but it has to be the right one at the right time, or all the good work we've done will be wasted."

"If you ask me," said the overweight man gruffly, "every day we let that scum Leadbetter stay in power is one day too long." He pushed himself up from the crate and marched away, his fists clenched and his head bowed.

For a brief moment, Johnny had a good view of his back, and he was startled to see a short, thin tail dangling over the waistband of the man's loose-fitting trousers. For the second time in as many hours, he had mistaken a mutant for a norm.

Deep in thought, he moved on.

A baby was crying.

The sound came from inside one of the huts, insistent and penetrating. Middenface had ignored it at first, thinking that whatever was happening in there, it was nothing to do with him, but now the sound was playing on his nerves. The child was obviously in distress. He found himself drawn to the hut's back wall, wishing he had Johnny's alpha vision to see through it. Fortunately, the building was not very well constructed, and he found a gap between two planks that afforded him a restricted view of its interior.

He saw the edge of a makeshift cot, and a flickering shadow that suggested movement inside it. There was no sign of anybody else.

The wailing continued so Middenface made up his mind. He marched around to the front of the hut and shouldered open the door.

It was dark inside the hut's single room. The only light came through a glassless window beside the door that carried in the halogen light from outside. A steam pipe ran along the back wall, and a pan of milk was warming on it. But Middenface hardly noticed any of this. His gaze was immediately drawn to the cot and to its occupant, which had to be the biggest baby he had ever seen.

It was six feet tall and as bulky as Middenface himself. There was no denying that it was a baby, though, with its scrunched-up features and its hairless head. It was wearing an enormous patchwork nappy which appeared to have been stitched together from scraps of curtain material. And it was still crying, as if it were in dreadful pain.

No wonder, thought Middenface. The cot was barely large enough to hold it. It was wedged up against both sides, the wooden slats straining to breaking point. The baby *had* to be uncomfortable.

And then the mutant baby saw him and burst into a renewed bout of bawling and shrieking, pedalling its feet with their stumpy, underdeveloped toes as if in a hopeless attempt to get away from him.

Realising that he looked like a ghost in his chameleon cloak, Middenface shrugged it off his shoulders. The sight of his mutated form, however, was evidently no less upsetting. Not knowing what else to do, he raised his hands and backed away.

"Um, there, there," he said awkwardly. "Dinnae cry. Ah dinnae wannae hurt ye."

He almost collided with a middle-aged woman in the hut's doorway. They both recoiled and stared at each

other in horror. The woman was a norm so far as Middenface could see. She was grey-haired and stooped, and
her face had been crinkled by lines that were probably
caused by worry rather than age. He expected her to
scream or to raise an alarm, and if she tried, he would
have to knock her out, discomfited as he was by the
idea.

But instead, she just asked in a quiet voice: "What are
you doing in here?"

"Ah, um..." Middenface's features twisted in concen-
tration. He was halfway through concocting an
explanation for his unlikely presence in the Salvationist
camp when he realised that the woman was only concerned with his presence in her hut. "Ah heard this, uh,
bonny wee bairn of yours crying out, and ah thought..."

She nodded, seeming to accept that. She moved past
him to see to the pan on the pipe. Middenface didn't
know what confused him more: the fact that, here in the
very lair of the norm supremacists, his mutation had
passed without comment, or that the woman had hardly
spared a glance for her crying child.

She caught his gaze with tired eyes as she filled a plastic bottle with warm milk. "I know it seems dreadful of
me," she sighed, "but it never stops. Night and day...
There's nothing... You become inured to it. That's why I
came here. The Consoler... He's my only hope. My Little
Billy's only chance for a real life."

Middenface's eyes widened. "Ye're getting him... Ah
mean, ye've brought him here tae... Shouldn't that be the
bairn's choice? When he grows up, ah mean?"

The woman fixed him with an odd look. "He's thirty-
four years old," she said. "Oh, I've heard all the
arguments about how he was born a mutant and how he
should stay that way. It's what he is, and I love him, I
really do. But we aren't talking about an extra arm or a
tail or whatever. The doctors say my boy is in constant

pain and there's nothing they can do about it. Doesn't he deserve a chance? If I can end his suffering..."

"And the Consoler's okay with that, is he?" asked Middenface, sceptically. "He's happy to help ye?"

"He can't absorb the whole of Little Billy's mutation at once," said the woman. "It would overwhelm him. But he says he'll do what he can. He'll take it one stage at a time. He's a wonderful man."

Middenface didn't know what to say. He was more confused than ever. He settled on a mumbled "I'm sorry," but it didn't seem adequate. He turned and left the hut as the woman took the plastic bottle to her gigantic baby, which gulped at it greedily, still snuffling and grizzling. He took one final, forlorn look back over his shoulder, and was therefore completely unprepared for what awaited him outside.

Six norms carrying crossbows and longbows formed a semicircle in front of the open door, and Middenface cursed himself for having let down his guard.

He had walked into an ambush.

Johnny paused for thought by the side of the steam carbine in the crater's centre. He had been here forty minutes now, and all he had seen were norms and mutants apparently mixing peacefully. Had Rising lied to him? Had he misjudged the Salvationists' motives? Even if he had, he thought, the threat they posed seemed real enough.

He was still standing, wondering which way to go, his bones rattling in sympathy with the carbine's deafening rhythm, when they came for him.

One second, there was nobody. The next, he was surrounded. He didn't even have time to draw a weapon, not that it would have done him any good. Johnny couldn't understand how they had done this, how they had got the drop on him so completely and so suddenly.

Somehow, he reasoned, they must have known his exact location despite his cloak. He wondered if they had been aware of his presence from the start.

Johnny weighed up his options. If he let them take him, he was as good as dead. If he fought, he was still dead, but at least he might take one or two of them down with him.

As if reading his thoughts, one of the bowmen said: "Don't try anything stupid. The Consoler only wants to talk. We're to take you to him."

"The Consoler?" repeated Johnny, nonplussed.

"You're looking for Identi Kit, aren't you?" said the bowman. "Well, the Consoler has some information that might interest you."

CHAPTER EIGHT
THE CONSOLER

Johnny winced. Middenface swore. The Consoler merely laughed. It was a warm laugh, full of understanding and humanity.

The laugh shamed Johnny, but it also put him at ease. He and Middenface had both grown up around deformity and mutation. They had not only come to accept it in others and in themselves, but they also felt more comfortable in its presence. It meant they were among their own kind, away from the prying eyes and accusatory stares of the norms. But neither of them had ever seen anyone quite so hideously mutated as the Consoler. Not even President Ooze came close.

It wasn't any one particular feature that made him so grotesque; it was the agglomeration of so many different ones. Johnny would have found himself hard-pressed to give a precise and accurate description of the Consoler. Even a genetic specialist would have had a hard time documenting all his manifest mutations. There were eyes, noses, legs, arms, and some unidentifiable limbs sprouting from the most unlikely parts of his body. His skin was a vast patchwork of colours and textures. Mutation was piled on mutation to create a whole new set of hybrid deformities. There were parts of his body that were so mutated that Johnny had a hard time even visually registering them. His brain could just not take in what his eyes were seeing.

The two guards who had accompanied them into the Consoler's living quarters knelt in front of him, and the grotesque mutant placed a ceremonial hand on each of their heads. The guards stood, bowed slightly, and withdrew to join the others gathered outside the hut. Johnny couldn't help thinking it was a strange way to behave around prisoners.

"Please, do have a seat," said the Consoler as he sat down on a faded cushion and motioned to Johnny and Middenface to do the same.

The Consoler's living quarters were sparsely furnished. The floor was covered with matted reeds. There was a bedroll and a few blankets in one corner, some cushions scattered on the floor, and a writing table against the far wall. Apart from the armed guards outside his door, there was nothing about the dwelling that suggested he was being held against his will.

"I am sorry for asking you here in such a forcible manner," said the Consoler. "I hope my men did not mistreat you."

"Yer men?" exclaimed Middenface in surprise. "Ah thought ye were a captive."

The Consoler chuckled. "There are many stories told about me by those who are opposed to our aims. However, I assure you gentlemen that I am most definitely here of my own free will, as is every other member of our camp."

"Whit aboot the guards?"

"They are there for my protection only, not to ensure that I don't escape."

"From the way you talk, it sounds like you're the leader here," said Johnny.

"I provide guidance and tactical advice to the Salvationist cause," said the Consoler. "So in that capacity I imagine many would see me as a leader, yes."

"The Consoler is more than a leader; he is an inspiration and a saint. He suffers for the redemption of the whole of Miltonia," said a voice – or rather, two voices – from the doorway. Johnny turned and saw that another mutant had entered the room. He was quite short and slight, and carried himself in a very officious manner. He had a second mouth in the centre of his forehead that was identical to his first. When he spoke, both mouths voiced the words. The mouth in his forehead had a slightly higher register, however, giving the impression of two people talking in unison.

"Permit me to introduce my adviser, Doubletalk Daley," said the Consoler.

"I hope I am not intruding, Consoler," said Doubletalk. "I heard that you were alone with the pris... Er, guests, and I wanted to see if I could lend my support."

"You're not intruding at all," said the Consoler, tossing him a cushion. "Come and join us." Doubletalk sat next to his boss with an affected air of nonchalance that Johnny could tell was meant to mask his deep suspicion of the bounty hunters.

"How did ye know we were here?" asked Middenface. "Did ye find the guards we took oot?"

The Consoler turned to Doubletalk. "Did we locate the missing perimeter guards yet?"

"We found them behind an outcrop near the entrance to the main antechamber," replied Doubletalk. "We're attending to their injuries now." He shot Johnny and Middenface a hostile look.

The Consoler nodded and returned to Middenface's question. "I have been aware of your presence since you entered the camp. I wanted you to have a look around before I summoned you. Your thoughts were so full of suspicion and violence that I wanted you to see our community and the way it operates. I trust you did not find the den of extremists and murderers that you were expecting?"

"So ye read oor thoughts then?" asked Middenface.

"Not exactly. One of the benefits of my condition is the ability to form a psychic picture of my surroundings, somewhat similar to a radar. I am able to pick up an impression of the feelings and mental activities of any mutant within that area. Over time, and given a bit of practice, I can monitor an area as large as this camp. This is more effective than any surveillance system and provides us with excellent security."

"So, if you admit that there are benefits to being a mutant, and you're not a prisoner, why are you forcing innocent mutants to change against their will?" Johnny wanted to know.

"Everyone who comes to me," said the Consoler, "does so of their own free will. They ask me to take their mutations into myself, and I am pleased to oblige. Their reasons are many. Some, as you have seen, simply cannot live with the horrors that nature has inflicted upon them. Others have their appearances changed at my hands by way of a protest against the prejudice of their fellow mutants. You might be surprised to learn, by the way, that many norms also come to me because they wish to develop a mutation. Doubletalk here was one of them."

"And I was honoured that you agreed to minister to me," said Doubletalk.

"Our aim is to remove every boundary between the norms and mutants in our midst. To remove the barriers that set us apart and pit us against each other, in order that we can become consoled to each other's differences."

"That is why we named him the Consoler," Doubletalk interjected.

"It aw sounds like anti-mutant pish tae me," said Middenface.

"That's because you know little of what life is really like here on Miltonia," said the Consoler. "The regime we are resisting is little different from the one you fought against back on Earth."

"These men fought in the Mutant War?" said Doubletalk, both his mouths hanging open in surprise. "I thought they were Strontium... I mean, S/D agents."

"Forgive me, Doubletalk," said the Consoler. "I'm afraid I've been a little circumspect about the identities of our two intruders. This is the renowned Johnny Alpha and Middenface McNulty."

Doubletalk didn't quite know how to react to this revelation. He eyed Johnny with a newfound respect, seeming almost apologetic for his former suspicions. "But they look nothing like they do in the holoprogs!"

Middenface bristled at this and Doubletalk quickly changed the subject. "Are you here to collect a bounty, or do you intend to join our cause?"

Before Johnny could voice his contempt for the question, the Consoler tactfully cut in. "Mr Alpha and Mr Middenface are here under the auspices of the Search/Destroy Agency. However, you have rather indelicately expressed one of my own hopes. Perhaps if our guests see that our efforts here are for a good cause, the same cause, indeed, that prompted their struggle against Nelson Bunker Kreelman, they might throw in their lot with us."

"We didnae plant any bombs on school buses in the Mutant Army," said Middenface with a contemptuous sneer. "Or murder innocent muties."

"If you are referring to the assassination of Minister McGuffin," said the Consoler, "then I assure you he was no innocent. Nevertheless, our organisation was not responsible for his killing, nor for the recent spate of violent protests for which we have been blamed."

"Doesn't exactly sound like you're condemning them, though," growled Johnny.

"Hold on," protested Middenface. "If ye did nae do those things, then why did ye admit tae it? We heard ye sent an electronic mail to the palace."

"I'm afraid you are mistaken. We don't have the means. As you can see, what little technology we have here is very basic, and all powered by steam."

"It's a smear campaign; an attempt to blacken our name and discredit our cause," said Doubletalk.

"I can't imagine your cause is particularly popular on Miltonia as it is," said Johnny. "Why would anyone go to such trouble to discredit it?"

"Leadbetter would," said the Consoler. "It's the perfect way to prop up his brutal regime. The more afraid the general populace is of the terrorist threat that we are supposed to pose, the more they want to see something done about it. His administration has introduced increasingly draconian laws, attacking the civil liberties of every citizen of Miltonia. Discrediting our movement and driving us underground was the first step in establishing Leadbetter and McGuffin's reign of terror."

"Now just a minute," snarled Middenface, leaping to his feet. "Ah fought alongside both o' those mutants. At times, ma life depended upon them. Ah've just seen an auld comrade laid oot on a slab by one o' yer men. So don't ye start tryin' tae blacken their name in ma presence or ah'll tak' ye doon right here an' ah don't care how many guards come fer me."

Johnny was used to Middenface's outbursts. Usually he would make a move to curb the worst of their excesses. He'd pulled his partner out of many a bar brawl, and saved countless poor unfortunates from a beating at his hands. This time, however, he had no inclination to hold him back, whatever the consequences to both of them. He didn't like the Consoler's tone any more than Middenface did. His piety reeked of self-righteousness, and his claims about Moosehead and Leadbetter had to be lies. Johnny, too, had fought with both men and he knew them as intimately as only men who have seen combat together can know each other. They simply weren't capable of the crimes of which the Consoler had accused them.

Doubletalk quailed and practically hid behind his leader. The Consoler, however, raised his hands in a conciliatory gesture. "I am deeply sorry for the loss of your friend," he said. "But once again I assure you that our movement had no part in his assassination. I can understand your strong feelings towards your former comrades, but political power is a great corrupter, and the men you knew are not the men who held and still hold office here on Miltonia."

"An' whit would ye know aboot it?"

"I know that, like you, Leadbetter and McGuffin were heroes. They fought to free our kind. I confess I am at a loss to understand how such people could then go on to pass laws that oppress mutants. Nevertheless, that is the situation. Difficult as it may be for you to believe, I'm afraid you will have to accept that your former comrades have changed quite considerably since you knew them."

"Whit are ye talkin' aboot, 'laws that oppress mutants'?" Middenface demanded suspiciously.

"Things have not been easy for many of us since Moosehead McGuffin was made Minister for Immigration," said the Consoler. "As I'm sure you both must have discovered by now, a great many Miltonians fear and mistrust norms."

"Is it any wonder," said Johnny, "considering how they treat us on most worlds?"

"Maybe not, but here, the prejudice extends to those with only slightly noticeable mutations like your own. It is this attitude that brought Moosehead McGuffin to power five years ago on a raft of hard-line policies. One by one, the rights of anyone who is not heavily mutated have steadily disappeared."

"So why should ye be bothered?" asked Middenface. "Ye're hardly likely tae suffer any discrimination in yer condition."

For the first time there was anger in the Consoler's voice. "When innocent people are taken from their homes in the middle of the night; when families are split up and forced to suffer the most brutal conditions in internment camps; when anyone's rights and civil liberties can disappear overnight due to a simple accident of birth; then I think everyone should be concerned. And if we allow these things to happen on our world, then we are all responsible, if not through our direct support, then equally through our inaction."

"Internment camps?" repeated Johnny, sceptically.

"One of the first things McGuffin instigated was the widespread building of camps to contain so-called asylum seekers. Anyone who does not have a job when they arrive on Miltonia is classified as such. Even those lucky enough to get through customs are closely monitored, and if they don't find work within a period of three months, they are 'relocated' to a camp while their immigration status is 're-evaluated'. Even those who have lived here for years, if they find themselves unemployed for three months, they can have their visas and work permits revoked. The government can reclassify them as asylum seekers and intern them too."

"I thought your economy was booming," said Johnny. "Surely there's enough jobs for everyone?"

"Only if you're the right sort of mutant," said Doubletalk, emerging tentatively from cover.

"The elite mine owners who run most of the planet are making it almost impossible to gain any kind of employment unless you are quite noticeably mutated," said the Consoler. "This leaves a considerable minority of the population vulnerable and persecuted. It is these people who make up the ranks of our movement. Many escaped captivity or managed to slip through the net before they were taken. We have an underground network of cells operating all over the planet ferrying people to safety. This is why the Miltonian government perceives us as such a threat."

Johnny looked over at Middenface. He could see the big mutant was getting more and more aggravated. Middenface was a man of action who saw the world in simple opposites and broad definitions. Leadbetter and Moosehead were their friends, and therefore the Consoler had to be lying about them. To him, it was simple.

Johnny was not so sure. Brainwashed or not, the Consoler was certainly no captive to be rescued and dragged back to Clacton Fuzzville. Nose Job Johnson and General Rising had lied about that, at least. He didn't yet know why, but it didn't much matter. It didn't make him more sympathetic towards the Salvationist cause. Johnny made it a rule not to get involved with local politics, and he wasn't about to break that rule here, of all places. Apart from anything else, he needed to keep on good terms with the authorities. He and Middenface would need their compliance in transporting Kit offworld when they finally caught up with him. Not to mention the fact that they were still holding all the S/D agents' extremely expensive weaponry.

He eyed the Consoler, thinking about the fifty thousand cred reward for his capture and wondering if they should complete the job anyway. The Consoler was too well-guarded to kidnap, though, and Johnny certainly didn't want to jeopardise the far greater bounty on offer for Kit. He was inclined to leave this one alone.

"I'm sure you have your reasons for what you're doing," he said. "What I've seen of the Miltonian government hasn't impressed me all that much either. All the same, we came here to do a simple job. We need to capture an escaped felon. You brought us here with the understanding that you would give information that could lead to Identi Kit's apprehension. Are you prepared to give us that information?"

"I am," said the Consoler, "but with one proviso."

Johnny nodded and smiled a bitter half-smile. He had expected this. One thing you soon learned when you chased bounties for a living was that no one does anything for free.

"We're not mercenaries and we aren't hit men," he said, laying out his terms for negotiation. "We don't know anything of importance about the Miltonian government and we probably wouldn't trade you the information if we did. We're bounty hunters, but we are true to our word. Time is of the essence. With every hour, Identi Kit's trail is growing colder. We need to bag him as soon as possible. Once we have him in our custody, we'd be happy to return the favour you would be doing us."

"This won't take up more than a day or so of your time," countered the Consoler, "and I have reason to believe that Kit won't go anywhere. At least, not yet."

"He's nearby, then?" guessed Johnny. But not in the camp itself, he thought. If that were the case, he was sure he would have known about it by now.

The Consoler didn't answer. Several of his mouths twisted into what Johnny guessed was an attempt at a smile.

Johnny sighed. "Okay, I'm listening."

"We've been keeping the nearest internment camp under covert surveillance for a while now," said the Consoler. "I would like you to accompany a small scout party on a routine reconnaissance mission."

"That's all you want?"

"That's all. I realise there is an element of risk to this venture, but I don't expect you to do anything other than witness our reasons for opposing Leadbetter's government. You may even take the chameleon cloaks you, ah, borrowed from my guards. We don't have many, but we are happy to share them with our friends. They should help you remain undetected."

Johnny's eyes narrowed as the Consoler's words reminded him of an earlier suspicion. "I meant to ask you about the cloaks. Where did they come from?"

The Consoler waved a hand vaguely. "Oh, I picked them up on some world or other. I did a good deal of travelling when I was a more able man. And of course, being entirely natural rather than electronic, the cloaks have been of great use to us here in the magnetinium field. Now, I don't wish to rush you, but I am eager to hear your response to my offer. Unless you would like more time to consider, of course."

Johnny turned to his partner. "What do you say, Middenface?" he whispered.

"Ah dinnae like it Johnny, and ah dinnae trust these tinpot revolutionaries," Middenface replied in hushed tones. "But if it gets us one step closer tae gettin' oor man and gettin' off this planet, ah'm willin' tae gae along with it."

"There's been too many diversions," Johnny quietly agreed. "But this is our best lead so we may as well play along."

He turned back to the Consoler. "We're in," he said clearly.

CHAPTER NINE
IMMIGRATION CAMP

To Middenface's dismay, there was still more talking after that.

The Consoler sent for a young mutant who rejoiced in the name of Elephant Head. With her grey skin, flapping ears and long trunk, she was one of the most mutated people the S/D agents had seen in the base other than the Consoler himself. Elephant Head, it seemed, was bound for the immigration camp to collect reports from a surveillance team there. She would travel by night to arrive at dawn. It was agreed that she would take Middenface and Johnny with her.

She cautioned them that it would be a long journey; almost three and a half hours by foot. The Salvationists, said Elephant Head, had a small supply of pack animals for when speed was essential, but they were too conspicuous for everyday use. She showed Middenface and Johnny to an empty tent and advised them to get their heads down. Thanks to Miltonia's slow rotation, they could snatch at least six hours of sleep before they had to set off. Elephant Head found a couple of old sleeping bags for them but they weren't really necessary. A steam pipe ran right by the tent so it was already warm inside.

Middenface wasn't happy about sleeping in what he still thought of as the enemy camp, but Johnny pointed out that if the Salvationists wanted to kill them, they would have done so already. Johnny urged Middenface to take Elephant Head's advice and get some much-needed sleep. After all, it had been a long day – literally.

They were woken at what they assumed was the appointed time, although in the constant artificial light, they had no way of telling if it was night or day. They were offered a light breakfast of tinned goods foraged from Clacton Fuzzville and warmed up on the pipes. After they had eaten, Elephant Head showed them to the Salvationists' pitiful armoury and kitted them out with a crossbow and a case of six bolts each.

"Self-defence only," she said. "Remember, this is strictly a reconnaissance mission. We've been mapping the layout of this camp and observing its routine for over a month now. It's a prime target for us, and the last thing we want is for the fascists who run it to know that."

Outside, a bloated moon hung in the black sky, its surface scarred and pockmarked. If there was a man on this moon, thought Johnny, then it was an appropriately grotesque one.

There were four of them in all: Johnny, Middenface and Elephant Head had been joined by a middle-aged norm called Mason who was to relieve a member of the surveillance team. Mason said little else about himself. Indeed, none of them spoke much as Elephant Head set a relentless pace across the difficult terrain. They wore their chameleon cloaks but let them hang open, rippling in the cool night breeze. Only after they had walked for almost three hours did Elephant Head put up the hood of her cloak and slow down a little. Johnny guessed that they were entering hostile territory and he followed her lead.

The sun was returning at last, its first few tentative rays bathing them in shades of crimson. It looked to Johnny as if the rocks were awash with blood. He felt weary. Of course, as S/D agents, he and Middenface were used to physical hardship. If an enemy were to attack now, their training and experience would kick in and they would fight as hard and as skilfully as ever. In the absence of such a development, though, there was nothing to distract his mind from his aching muscles. He was tired, too. Despite his encouraging words to Middenface, he had slept with one eye open in the Salvationists' base. It hadn't quite made up for the night and a day they were stuck in a supply ship hold, another night of interrogations by customs, and another day of hiking through the mountains.

He was almost relieved, then, to hear a new sound in the never-changing landscape; a sound that had no right to be there. A sound that put his senses on the alert and drowned out his pains in an adrenaline rush.

It was a guttural rumbling, like the growling of an asthmatic beast, but with a regular quality that made it seem more mechanical than natural. It echoed off the rock faces around them until it filled the air and Johnny couldn't tell which direction it came from. Elephant Head knew, however, and she led the way to cover.

Crouching behind an oversized boulder and tightening their chameleon cloaks around themselves, Johnny and Middenface stared in awe at the misshapen contraption that spluttered into view below them. It was made up of two boxlike shapes, the smaller of which was jammed onto the front of the larger. Both boxes were olive green, but the front one was forged from metal with windows all around it and the back one appeared to comprise a heavy canvas sheet stretched over a framework. Smoke belched from the rear of this larger box, wreathing the contraption in a faint blue haze.

It was wending its way through the mountains, twisting and turning as if its course was set on no more than a random whim. Johnny realised, however, that it never turned back on itself; its route may have been circuitous but it had a destination in mind.

"Government transport," snarled Elephant Head. "They must be bringing in more prisoners to abuse."

"Whit the sneck is it?" whispered Middenface.

Johnny had just realised the answer to that question. The contraption had taken another turn and for a moment he had a clearer view of it. He could see the six large wheels that protruded from its underside, sheathed in protective rubber.

"It's an ancient land-crawling vehicle," he said. "Driven by combustion. We're still within the magnetinium field, aren't we? Normal transports won't work here so they must have to transfer incoming prisoners to that thing for the last leg of their journey."

"We thought it was a weapon when we first saw it," said Elephant Head. "We thought Leadbetter's thugs were trying to poison us out of the mountains."

Johnny shook his head. "If I remember right, that smoke is a by-product of the combustion process. That's why those things were outlawed on most worlds."

"Ah dinnae get it," said Middenface. "Why would Rising have built his camp oot here? Did he nae realise that none o' his gadgets'd work with aw these imps aboot? Nae alarms, nae electronic locks and nae guns fer his guards."

"He knew," said Elephant Head. "But Rising didn't build this camp. That honour goes to our late Minister for Immigration, Mr Moosehead McGuffin. He was the one who chose this site. He said the magnetinium emissions would make the camp easier to secure and that there'd be no need for expensive precautions against so-called terrorists with hi-tech weapons, or jetpacks or teleport devices."

"Makes sense, I guess," said Johnny, ignoring the implied slur on his late friend. Middenface, however, couldn't stop his lips from curling into a snarl and his nodules turning red.

"All lies!" Elephant Head spat. "The truth is, no one wants norm immigrants on their doorstep. Pack them off into the mountains, lock them up without even the most basic amenities, and no one has to worry about them. This is the dark secret at the heart of our paradise: buried out of sight, out of mind, so that Miltonia's mutants can live their privileged lives without feeling the pricking of their consciences."

"You obviously feel strongly about it," said Johnny, "for a 'privileged' mutant yourself." Elephant Head didn't answer that.

The ancient truck had crawled out of sight by now, so Elephant Head led the way down a steep incline to a relatively flat area. The truck had passed this way and its exhaust smoke still hung in the air, scratching at Johnny's throat. Its wheels left faint tracks in the dust and Johnny realised that the vehicle's erratic path had been calculated to avoid obstacles on the ground.

"Just a little further now," said Elephant Head darkly, "and you'll see the truth for yourselves."

Another two chameleon-cloaked norms greeted them at the top of a ridge. They eyed Johnny and Middenface suspiciously until Elephant Head explained that they were "potential new recruits". Middenface opened his mouth to dispute this but Johnny silenced him with a quick shake of the head. Again, it wasn't worth it.

They lay on their stomachs, peered over the edge of the ridge, and got their first look at the immigration camp. Although it was encircled by two mesh fences topped with coils of barbed wire, their vantage point afforded them a good view over these obstructions to the compound where the prisoners were kept.

The space between the fences appeared to be the guards' domain. There was a large barracks, a mess hall, and a smaller building that was obviously an officers' mess. Also within this space were too large wooden towers, one to each side, atop which guards manned large, ancient weapons. Elephant Head explained that these weapons were called machine guns. Like the prison transport, they were mechanical in nature and so were unaffected by the magnetinium, but they were still lethal.

"There's also a small artillery in the barracks," she said. "Five or six antiquated rifles, maybe a few more, brought from offworld. Luckily for us, they're hard to come by these days, and ammunition is even harder. If all the guards had them we'd be dead before we reached the gates."

Johnny accepted an old-fashioned telescope from one of the Salvationists. He couldn't work out how to operate it at first until he realised that it had no zoom function and its focus had to be set manually. No electronics, of course. Looking down the metal tube, he confirmed that the majority of the prisoners within the inner fence were norms, though he saw some mutants too.

The sun had risen and most of the camp's inmates were already up. They shuffled around aimlessly, pale and miserable. There were hundreds of them wearing dull beige coveralls and packed into a space barely large enough to contain them. Some huddled together beneath canvas lean-tos; the only shelter available to them.

A row of troughs stood in the middle of the camp beneath a corrugated iron roof supported by wooden beams. From these troughs, four inmates were dispensing bowls of a filthy-looking grey broth, watched over by mutant guards in uniform. More guards were moving beneath the lean-tos and chivvying inmates who were trying to sleep. If they responded too slowly, the guards made them stand and hit them with batons.

Setting his telescope to rove further, Johnny found four cages in the far corner of the camp, each of them just large enough for one person. Three of them were occupied. The cages were too low for their prisoners to stand upright, and too narrow to let them sit down. As a result, they were forced into uncomfortable hunched positions, the pain of their confinement evident in their expressions.

Middenface cursed under his breath. "We ought tae git doon there and bust the whole place open," he seethed. He knew as well as Johnny did, though, that the suggestion was impractical. The guards were armed as well as the magnetinium field allowed, and they had whips as well as their batons, and crossbows slung across their backs. And, of course, there were the rifles, of which Johnny could see three… No, four.

"Do you see now?" said Elephant Head, bitterly. "Do you see what we're fighting against? I heard what happened to you two at customs. Make no mistake, if Leadbetter hadn't spoken up for you, this is where they would have brought you. This, or one of the many other camps just like it."

Johnny didn't know what to say. He prayed it wasn't true and that the Salvationists were trying to mislead him, and that this facility housed only the most dangerous terrorists. But even if it did, that hardly excused what he was seeing. A mutant guard had taken out his whip and was laying into a norm for some misdemeanour that Johnny hadn't even seen. Another guard was looking on, laughing cruelly.

Two more guards had gathered four inmates together and chained them, just as Johnny and Middenface had been chained at the spaceport. They were leading them to the gate beyond which stood the truck they had seen earlier. Its engine was still running, pumping out fumes. It appeared to have been left unattended.

The inmates parted to let the procession through, those that moved too slowly earning swift baton blows. One of the chained prisoners stumbled and fell, and he too was repeatedly beaten until he struggled to his feet.

"Probably being taken into town for visa application hearings," muttered Elephant Head, following the direction of Johnny's gaze. "Chances are, they'll be back by sunset."

Johnny knew that trouble was brewing before it broke out. It had something to do with the body language of the prisoners – nothing he could put his finger on, just something that experience had taught him to sense. It happened outside the gate. The guards were prodding their charges into the back of the truck, the vehicle blocking them from prying eyes within the camp. Some subtle signal must have passed between the prisoners, because they spun around and launched coordinated attacks upon their tormentors. Although their chains restricted their movement, one guard was winded by an elbow to his stomach while the other was sent sprawling by a head butt to the chin. This latter guard reached for his whip, but found himself pinned down by the weight of a burly norm who quickly divested him of his key card.

The second guard, however, was already recovering and yelled for assistance. Johnny wasn't sure he had been heard over the general hubbub of camp life, but it could only be a matter of time. It had been a spirited attempt, but the prisoners, chained as they were, had no chance.

And, in the moment that Johnny saw this, he also realised that Middenface had left his side. He was racing, slipping and sliding down a treacherous slope towards the fight. The four Salvationists were horrified. Elephant Head took two steps after the S/D agent but pulled up short when she saw she could follow him no further without breaking her own cover.

"Don't move," said Johnny grimly. "They can't know you're here. With luck, when Rising hears about this, he'll think we were acting alone."

"We?" queried Elephant Head, raising an eyebrow.
"I have to go after him. I'm sorry."

The guards hadn't seen him coming.

They had gained the upper hand over the would-be mutineers and were angrily whipping them into submission. Middenface felt his chest burning with fury. The fact that he was rushing to the rescue of norms against mutants was only just beginning to dawn on him, but it made no difference. He knew what it was like to be a prisoner, to be brutalised. He knew whose side he was on.

Something whistled by his ear and one of the guards jerked rigid and fell. It took Middenface a moment to realise that he had been struck in the back by a crossbow bolt. Johnny, he thought with a grin. Middenface had quite forgotten about the range weapon he'd been given, though in any case he preferred to do his fighting up close. A second later, he cannoned into the remaining guard and bore him to the ground. The prisoners, defeated a moment ago, were only just beginning to see that the tide had turned again. The norm with the stolen key card began fumbling with the padlocked chains of one of his comrades.

The guard fought back valiantly but helplessly. One good punch to his head knocked him cold. Then Johnny was there, urging the prisoners into the back of the truck and warning them that the sounds of combat had reached the camp and that more guards were on their way. Half-chained and confused, they were made to obey, and Middenface gave them a hand by lifting two of them and hurling them bodily through the canvas flaps. As if to underline Johnny's warning, a bell was ringing somewhere, and he could hear voices raised in excitement. Bullets thudded into the ground behind them, coming in a steady stream from one of the machine gun towers. Fortunately, the guards seemed to be bad shots.

"Reckon we can pilot this thing?" asked Johnny, indicating the truck.

"Auld technology," Middenface reminded him. "And the engine's already running, so how hard can it be?"

There was a door on each side of the truck's front section, but they ran to the one that faced away from the camp. Johnny entered first, found two seats within, and clambered over to the far one so that Middenface could get in behind him. Even as he reached it, the far door was yanked open by a guard from the barracks. Johnny drove a booted foot into his face and he disappeared from sight as suddenly as he appeared.

Middenface, meanwhile, had taken the near seat and was dismayed to find himself faced by an array of strange controls. An old-fashioned key protruded from a slot, so reasoning that this turned the engine on and off, he left it alone. And the huge wheel in front of him could only be for steering. But the switch by its side appeared to do nothing at all. He was beginning to panic. He needed propulsion.

He found it by accident when his clumsy feet alighted upon a row of pedals in front of him. He stamped on them at random, hearing the pitch of the engine rise and fall but still gaining no ground. Johnny joined in the desperate search and was wrestling with a lever that rose between the two seats. It didn't seem to want to give at first, but suddenly it clunked into a new position and, to Middenface's elation, the truck surged forwards. The engine was screaming as if it were about to explode, but they were moving.

Towards a rock wall.

Middenface wrenched the steering control around and winced at the high-pitched squealing that came from the truck's wheels. They were facing the camp and he could see more mutant guards emerging from it, trying to work out what was going on. He pressed down hard on the pedal that he now knew controlled the vehicle's acceleration. Nothing happened.

"The engine!" cried Johnny. "The engine's cut out!"

Middenface swore. What sort of a clapped-out old wreck couldn't cope with a simple U-turn? He seized hold of the key he'd noticed before and twisted it back and forth to no avail. "Electric ignition," Johnny realised. "The EMPs will have fried it. That's why they left the engine running. It won't start again now."

The guards had seen their weakness and were already advancing, crossbows raised. Middenface pounded on the partition between the driver's cab and the back of the truck and yelled to the would-be escapees: "We're dead in the water! Run fer it!"

He and Johnny leapt out of the truck simultaneously through opposite doors, splitting their enemies' fire and trusting their chameleon cloaks to make them difficult targets. Middenface ducked and rolled as crossbow bolts flew around him. From the other side of the truck, Johnny was firing back, forcing their pursuers to scatter and find cover. Middenface tried to do the same, but his chunky fingers fumbled with the fiddly firing mechanism of his crossbow, and his first bolt described a feeble arc and clattered to earth about one metre in front of him.

He discarded the bow and ran instead. The last prisoner was just climbing out of the back of the truck – thankfully, they were all unchained now – and Middenface took charge of them, urging them to follow him as Johnny laid down more covering fire.

He didn't know where he was leading them. All he could do was keep them moving, find cover where possible, try not to lead the guards toward the Salvationist scout party, and pray that their pursuers gave up before they did.

He was beginning to think that maybe, just maybe, this hadn't been such a great idea after all.

Two hours later, they were reunited with an angry Elephant Head on the ridge above the camp. She lectured them about the irresponsibility of their actions, how they had made the Salvationists' work here all the harder. Johnny was able to calm her down, though. They had freed three prisoners, after all. Two of them were eager converts to the Salvationist cause, while the third just wanted to find his way to the nearest city and disappear. The fourth member of their escape party had, regrettably, fallen behind and been recaptured.

One of the rescued norms turned out not to be a norm at all. Youngblood had a perfectly human appearance, but his blood was green and acidic. He had told Johnny and Middenface his story as they hid from their pursuers and waited for the right moment to circle back around them. His eyes filled with tears as he described how an accident at work had revealed his secret. He had lived as a norm for almost thirty years, and to find himself suddenly cast out from everyone and everything he had known had been unbearable. That was why he had taken his life savings and headed for Miltonia, believing that here he would be accepted as he was. Instead, found himself being stigmatised for not being mutated enough.

"Moosehead cannae have done this," Middenface insisted loyally. "He mightae built these camps, but it wouldae been fer good reasons. He was just tryin' tae be fair tae everyone. It'll be scunners like Rising who've twisted things around."

"You're probably right," said Johnny with a sigh. "But that doesn't do us much good. We have to face facts, Middenface. Miltonia was supposed to be a paradise, a place where everybody is equal. Instead, we've just swapped one form of prejudice for another. I'm afraid everything the Consoler told us is true."

CHAPTER TEN
REVELATIONS

They arrived back at the Salvationist base as the Miltonian sun was setting. Johnny was reluctant to admit it, but he was glad to see the place. The journey back from the internment camp had been longer and more arduous than the outward leg. They were slowed down by the three detainees they had rescued, weakened and exhausted by their ordeal. Elephant Head had also insisted on taking a different, more perilous route back up into the mountains and performing a lot of evasive manoeuvres in case they were being followed.

Then there had been the small detour they had had to take to put the former detainee who did not wish to join the Salvationists back on the path to a populated area. Elephant Head had given him the best directions she could, and as much water and provisions as she had about her. Middenface had wanted to know why they couldn't just take him with them for the present, but Elephant Head thought it was better for him that he knew as little as possible about their group. She could not risk having him picked up and tortured for information.

"Are we nearly there?" asked Youngblood. "You said we'd reach the camp before nightfall. The sun's setting and I still can't see any sign of it." The green-blooded mutant had fallen in with Johnny and Middenface during the journey.

"We're there awready," said Middenface with a smile. "It's just well hidden, that's aw."

Youngblood looked a little nervous. "Is the place full of hardened terrorists?" he asked.

Johnny shook his head. "It's mostly full of everyday norms and mutants, much like yourself."

Elephant Head led them up a slope and stopped at the opening of a side entrance. Once again, it had been impossible to spot until they were right on top of it. She turned to Youngblood and the other norm, her manner relaxing for the first time and her stern elephantine features softening into an expression of sympathy.

"You're safe now," she said. "There's nothing to fear here and no one will judge you for what you are. Your days of hiding are over."

Johnny exchanged a wry look with Middenface as they followed her through the entrance.

"We didnae mak' speeches like that in the Mutant Army, that's fer sure," said Middenface.

Another fissure wound through the mountain, but this one was a lot narrower than the last. They had to walk in single file, and at times the passageway was so narrow they had to squeeze through it sideways. Johnny knew they were nearly at the centre of the extinct volcano when he felt the familiar vibrations at his feet and heard the *clanks* and *hisses* of the carbine.

They arrived at the Salvationist camp to receive a very different reception from the one they originally had when they were first discovered. Word had obviously gotten round that the Salvationists had two mutant war heroes in their midst. Tent flaps were pushed open and makeshift curtains twitched as the bounty hunters walked by. Mutants and norms began to gather around them, pointing and smiling. Some even plucked up enough courage to greet them, shake their hands and pat them on the back.

Elephant Head motioned to two norms: a man and a woman outside a building that Johnny recognised as the supply hall. They came over and she introduced them to Youngblood and the norm.

"These two will take you for some food," she told them, "then show you where to get materials to build a shelter and how to hook yourself up to the steam turbine for energy." She turned to Johnny and Middenface. "I've got to report to the Consoler and the military council now," she said. "I know he'll want to speak with you again in a little while."

"That'll be fun," Middenface muttered.

"I suggest you return to the quarters we allocated for you and get some rest," said Elephant Head, ignoring Middenface's remark. "You look as though you could use some."

"She's right, big guy," said Johnny before starting back for the tent where they had spent the previous night.

"Aye, ah s'pose she is at that," agreed Middenface, following him.

Middenface awoke with a start. He had fallen asleep sitting up and was roused by a hand on his shoulder. His reflexes kicked into gear before his eyes had even properly opened. He grabbed the wrist of the hand that had shaken him and had his knife at the throat of its owner before his eyesight came into proper focus. When it did, he found he was staring into Johnny's bright alpha eyes.

"You'll have someone's eye out with that," said Johnny with a smile. "Get your things together. The Consoler wants to see us."

Middenface stood and stretched, chasing the sleep out of his stiff limbs. "Mustae nodded off fer a second there," he said sheepishly. He still felt cautious in the camp since there were people he couldn't account for and didn't trust, so Johnny had suggested they sleep in shifts and Middenface had volunteered to take the first watch.

"Thought you might be keeping an eye out for killer nightmares," said Johnny sardonically.

Middenface huffed at this. Johnny was like a brother to him – the man had saved his life more times than any other mutant he could think of – but at times he could be a real son of a bitch. It wasn't so much what he said, or even what he did, but there *was* just an air of moral superiority about him. It was like he wasn't just hunting bounties, but that he was on a mission of some sort. When he thought about it, which wasn't often, this made him feel rather isolated from Johnny. He was mainly in it for the crack, plus the pay could be pretty good at times.

"Ah hope we dinnae have tae go through aw that talkin' again," he said. "Ah hope he just tells us where the scunner is and has done wi' it."

He didn't.

Even though he had previously spent several tedious hours in the Consoler's company, Middenface still wasn't prepared for the sight of him. Before he could catch himself, he exhaled sharply and held his hand up over his face as though he was shielding his eyes from a bright light. "Sorry," he said, remembering his manners.

"I've been hearing reports of your reckless exploits," said the Consoler with a smile. Also in the room were Elephant Head, Doubletalk, the captain of the camp guards, and a norm called Walrus on account of his huge blond moustache. "Come and join me for some purple tea," he offered, pouring himself a bowl of exotic-smelling liquid.

"If ye dinnae mind, ah think ah'll pass," said Middenface.

"Suit yourself." The Consoler squeezed ink from what looked like a tiny squid into his bowl. "It's very good for the liver." He manoeuvred his misshapen bulk onto a cushion and bid everyone else to sit, too. Middenface groaned inwardly as he remembered how numb his backside had gotten the last time he had been in this room.

"I have to say, I did hope that if you saw what we were up against you'd at least show some sympathy for our cause," the Consoler continued. "I didn't imagine you'd respond quite so actively, though."

"It was grossly irresponsible," barked Walrus. "It put months of intelligence-gathering at risk and the security of the camp in danger, leaving us wide open to detection by the enemy."

Middenface clenched his fists, grinding his teeth as he bit back the urge to feed Walrus his own facial hair. "Now just a minute," he growled. "We rescued three innocent people. Two o' them norms, mind, from the men ye're supposed tae be fightin'…"

The Consoler stepped in just as Middenface was thinking of the best four-letter word to describe Walrus. "Please forgive my associate," he said. "He has worked very hard to guarantee the security of our camp. He's not as used to taking the offensive as you both are."

"I'll be ready when the time comes," said Walrus, pushing his chest out.

"I'm sure you will," the Consoler placated him.

"That's why we need men like you on our side," said Doubletalk. "To help us take our campaign to the next level. We need to liberate this camp and others like it."

"I might not have approved of your methods," said Elephant Head. "But you certainly proved yourselves under combat conditions. If anyone could lead a successful raid… Consoler, don't you see? We can take action, at last. With Johnny and Middenface on our side, we can liberate *all* the camps and build an army large enough to destroy this corrupt police state!"

Middenface didn't like the way the conversation was going. Neither did Johnny.

"Listen," he said. "I admit you've got a reason to fight for what's happening here on Miltonia, but it's not our struggle. We're not here to get involved in local politics. We came here to capture an escaped felon. We just want to collect him and then go pick up our bounty."

"Best o' luck to ye and aw, but we're bounty hunters ye ken," added Middenface.

The mood in the room completely changed. Elephant Head, so enthusiastic a moment ago, retreated into sullen silence. Walrus sneered and gave the others a look that said, "I told you so." Doubletalk was crestfallen and, not knowing how to respond, he looked to the Consoler to save the situation.

"You did promise to tell us the whereabouts of Kit," continued Johnny. "We made good on our side of the bargain. Now we need you to uphold your end."

The Consoler nodded, then went very quiet and stared at the floor. Middenface couldn't believe it. The flaming mutie did nothing but talk for hours, and then, just as he was about to say something interesting, he suddenly shut up. Finally the Consoler looked up.

"Would you leave us alone?" he said to Elephant Head, Doubletalk and Walrus.

"You're not going to start collaborating with these Strontium Dogs, are you?" snarled Walrus.

"I gave my word," said the Consoler firmly, "and I mean to honour it."

"But Consoler, I th-thought w-we..." Doubletalk stammered.

The Consoler silenced him and sent them all outside. The three high-ranking Salvationists seemed angry and confused at being dismissed in such an offhand manner.

The Consoler didn't speak for what seemed like an age after they had left. Middenface didn't know what to say himself, so he left it to Johnny.

"I know you might be reluctant to betray a former comrade," said Johnny. "But if you knew the things that Kit has done and what he's capable of, you wouldn't feel anywhere near as loyal to him."

"I know all too well what Kit has done," said the Consoler quietly. "And I don't think anyone is as aware as I am of what he is capable of doing. You see, Kit is my brother."

"Yer brother!" Middenface blurted.

"My twin, to be exact."

Middenface's brain whirred slowly into action. "But... Now hold on a minute! Ye said yer boys here had nothin' tae do wi' killin' Moosehead. Now ye're tellin' us ye sent yer ain brother in tae dae the job!"

"Kit has nothing to do with the Salvationists and never has," said the Consoler. "He and I parted company a long time ago, and we haven't remained in touch. I even changed my name. I arrived on Miltonia as George Smith. News of Kit's criminal exploits was rife at the time. I feared that, even back then, if my connection to him were known, I would have been turned away."

"He's your twin, you say," said Johnny.

"We're identical, or at least we used to be. I've absorbed and passed on so many mutations that I've changed quite considerably. We even share the same mutation. We've chosen to develop it in different ways, but we have essentially the same abilities: to adapt our own DNA using that of others as a template."

"Then that's why he came here," guessed Johnny. "He was looking for a place to hide out after he killed Moosehead and turned to his long-lost twin brother for help. Did he want you to smuggle him off the planet?"

"I don't know," said the Consoler.

"Whit dae ye mean, ye don't know?"

"I never got a chance to talk to him. Kit turned up much as you did. He slipped past the guards at a side entrance and infiltrated the camp. I kept expecting him to come and see me but he never did. I wanted him to come to me of his own free will, so I didn't alert the guards to his presence. After spending a day and a half among us, he began to arouse suspicion. A few people were talking about him, realising that they hadn't seen him before and didn't know where he had come from. As soon as he heard this, he fled."

"Why didn't he use his shape-changing abilities to disguise himself?" asked Johnny.

"I don't know that either," said the Consoler. "I tried to read his thoughts, but sadly–"

"Hey!" Middenface interjected again. "Ah thought ye said ye couldnae read minds!"

"As a rule, I can't. However, Kit and I had a strong psychic bond from the moment we were born. Our thoughts have always been an open book to each other... Until now. I could feel Kit's physical presence in the camp but I couldn't make mental contact with him no matter how hard I tried. Somehow, he has found a way to shield his thoughts from me."

"Then you don't know where he is now?" asked Johnny with a worried expression.

"I didn't say that," said the Consoler. "Sometimes, when I concentrate and block out the rest of the camp, I can extend my radar just far enough to find him."

Middenface leaned forward eagerly. "Where?"

"I can't tell you exactly where he's hiding out because he slips in and out of my range. I suspect he has unfinished business with us. In any case, the signal comes from the same direction. But it's a bit of a strange signal, I must confess." The Consoler sighed, evidently reluctant to impart the information but bound by his honour. "I believe that, if you proceed on a bearing of approximately one hundred and twelve degrees from this base for a little over two miles, you will reach the optimal area in which to concentrate your search."

"Thank you for this information," said Johnny solemnly. "You're the first person we've met since we came to Miltonia who's remained true to his word."

"Without his word, a man is nothing," said the Consoler. "I know my brother has done terrible things and I know he hasn't finished paying for them, but I would dearly like to see him just once before you take him back. I promise he'll remain in your custody. In return, I'll arrange for your safe and quick passage out of these mountains."

"You've treated us okay so far," said Johnny. "It's a deal."

"Thank you," said the Consoler, sadly.

Even Middenface could see how hard it was for him to turn in his own brother. He almost felt sorry for him. The Salvationists' leader may have liked the sound of his own voice a bit much, but he had kept his word. He was beginning to earn Middenface's respect, and that wasn't an easy thing to do.

Middenface eyed the cooling bowl of congealed tea as they shook hands and said their farewells, and commended himself for having had the good sense not to try any.

Word of the daring rescue that Johnny and Middenface had pulled off had spread right through the camp by the time they were ready to leave. Unfortunately, the news that they weren't planning to stay had not. Johnny noted guiltily that their ill-advised stunt had brought a whole new mood to the encampment. The residents seemed filled with hope and determination, as if they sensed a change coming in their fortunes.

Everyone wanted to shake his and Middenface's hands, share a meal or a cup of tea with them. Several Salvationists offered them prized delicacies they had managed to scavenge and save for a special occasion. Johnny watched as, for the first time in his life, Middenface turned down hard liquor. It was good stuff, too; ten year-old single malt scotch from another world. Middenface sorely needed a drink – they both did – but neither of them had the heart to accept the precious liquid under what they knew were false pretences.

Youngblood bounded up to them as they stood at the iron rungs in the crater wall that would take them back to the surface. "Are you guys off on another mission already?" he asked.

"Not exactly," said Johnny.

"I've been made a scout," said Youngblood proudly. "I'm going out on the next reconnaissance trip. There's even talk of liberating more prisoners. You've inspired the whole camp. I don't know how to thank you for rescuing me. I only hope I can prove myself worthy of fighting by your side when the time comes."

"Look, Youngblood," Johnny looked into the eager mutant's eyes, finding it painful to say what he had to. "We're not going on a mission for the Salvationists. We're not a part of this cause, we never have been. We're S/D agents. Everything we've done while we've been here has been in the cause of tracking down a felon."

Youngblood's face fell. He didn't know whether to believe Johnny at first; it was obvious he didn't want to. "You're not going to fight to save all those people you saw locked up in that place?" he said. "Then why did you help me? You rescued me for nothing if you turn your back on everything you saw and just walk away."

"I'm sorry that we're not the men you thought we were," said Johnny. Then he turned and began to climb up the crater wall.

Middenface punched the disillusioned mutant affectionately on the shoulder. "Ye tak' care of yerself," he said, and followed Johnny up the rungs and out of the camp.

Neither Johnny nor Middenface could bear to look back at the brave mutant whose illusions they had just shattered.

CHAPTER ELEVEN
THE FACE OF THE ENEMY

The arrows flew out of nowhere; six from the right and six from the left. Caught in the crossfire, Johnny had a fraction of a second to react before he was skewered. His combat reflexes kicked in, twisting him around and bearing him to the ground almost without the need for conscious thought on his part. An arrowhead grazed his temple but didn't break the skin. Middenface, who had been a short way ahead of him, wasn't so lucky.

Johnny's heart sank as he heard the grunt of pain and realised that his partner had been hit. Middenface's ample frame spun around, seemingly in slow motion, and fell like a brick.

Johnny scrambled over to him, keeping low, painfully aware that a second volley could come at any moment. To his relief, just one arrow had pierced Middenface's shoulder, sinking into the muscle tissue. It was painful but they had both seen worse. He would survive... that was, if they could find a way out of their current predicament.

Johnny was glad of one thing. He had begun to fear that their cause was a lost one, even armed with the Consoler's information. It had been another long day of plodding through the grey, dead mountains, and watching the sun sink inexorably beyond the farthest peak, until the task of finding a single fugitive out here without technology had begun to seem impossible.

Evidently, their target had found them. And he had friends.

Or had he? There should have been more arrows by now. The bowmen certainly had time to reload. Johnny dared to raise his head and take a look around him and as expected, he saw a broken tripwire which had been strung between two rocks. Middenface followed his gaze and looked suitably chagrined. He had walked into a trap.

The bounty hunters rolled to their feet and ran together as one. The first arrows may have been unleashed automatically, but chances were the wire had also been linked to some sort of alarm system. There was no way of knowing how long they had to find cover before somebody responded to that alarm.

The question was soon answered. Even as Johnny and Middenface dropped behind a convenient outcrop, another arrow whistled over their heads. Then, there was silence. Their unseen attacker was waiting for them to show themselves.

Johnny longed for the weight of his Westinghouse blaster in his hands. Even a Salvationist crossbow would have been useful, or one of their chameleon cloaks, but when they had turned their backs on the Consoler's guerrilla band, they had been obliged to hand their equipment back to them.

Middenface braced himself against the mountainside, and he clenched his teeth to bite back a scream as he pulled the arrow from his shoulder. As always, Johnny admired his fortitude. The arrowhead came free, at last, in a spray of blood, and Middenface flung it aside in disgust. He sat back, breathing heavily, his face shining with sweat and his eyes moist with relief. Johnny didn't ask how he was because the question would have been useless. Whatever his state of health, Middenface would have maintained that he could keep fighting. Johnny knew he would have to keep an eye on him, though.

He removed his helmet and raised it cautiously over the top of the outcrop. An arrow flew past it, missing it by a hair. It was followed a couple of seconds later by one that struck the helmet squarely and glanced off it. This told Johnny three things: their opponent hadn't moved, he was an excellent shot, and he was probably alone.

"Kit Jones," he called out on a hunch. "We know you're there. You're surrounded. There's nowhere to run. Lay down your weapons and step out into the open with your hands in the air." There was no reply.

"We know where he is," said Middenface. "Ah say we split up an' come at him frae both sides."

"Whichever way we go, it means crossing open ground," Johnny pointed out. "He'll have a clear shot at us."

"He can't tak' us both doon at once."

"I don't know, Middenface. The Consoler said Kit's powers are essentially the same as his. What if he shares his brother's psychic radar? We can't get the drop on someone who can sense us coming."

"We don't chance it now," said Middenface, "we'll be pinned doon here till we die of exposure. If we gottae gae out at all, ah say we do it in a blaze o' glory."

Johnny had to admit he had a point and nodded curtly. He scanned his surroundings and looked for the least hazardous route out of their hiding place. When his gaze returned to Middenface, he was alarmed to see that he hadn't moved. He was breathing heavily and his eyes had glazed over.

"It's ma blood, Johnny! It feels like it's on fire!"

Johnny quickly retrieved the arrow that had wounded his partner. One sniff at its tip was enough to confirm his worst fears. "Poison," he said grimly.

"All the more reason we... should rush the scunner now, before ah'm too weak tae... haul ma carcass over there and hand out some... some well-deserved..."

Middenface made a determined effort to rise but it was
no use. He collapsed into a panting heap, sweating ever
more profusely. He clenched his fists, and his eyes
betrayed his pain and his anger at himself for his weakness.

Johnny had rarely felt more helpless. He never felt the
need for technology more than at that moment, when
there was none to be found. Civilisation, with its hospi-
tals and medical equipment, seemed an impossible
distance away with no hope of a hovercar or jetpacks to
speed up their journey. There was an outside chance that
the Salvationists could help Middenface, but given the
evident speed with which the poison was working its
way through his system, Johnny knew he couldn't carry
his heavy partner back to their encampment in time to
save his life. What he wouldn't give for his short-range
teleporter right now! Trapped out here, he didn't even
have water to bathe his friend's wound. All that he had
was the small, precious amount left in their bottles.

He only had one hope and it was a desperately slim
one. Controlling his voice, he called out to Kit again and
forced himself to speak calmly and slowly despite the
urgency of the situation.

"Don't be an idiot, Kit. You can't keep this up forever.
You're outnumbered and we can wait as long as it takes –
for days if necessary. You have to sleep some time."

For an unbearably long time, there was silence again.
Then, even as Johnny was beginning to despair, a voice
rang out across the mountainside as calm and confident
as his own had been.

"That's twice you've lied to me," said Kit Jones. "I
don't think I *am* surrounded and I don't think you *can*
wait. There are only two of you, aren't there? And thanks
to the magnetinium field, you can't call for backup. You
don't even have ranged weapons or you would have used
them by now. I think you're the ones who are in trouble.

I only caught a glimpse of you as you ran, but it was enough to see that the big guy was stuck by one of my special arrows, and there's blood on the ground. By now, I expect he's lost all muscle control. Has his tongue turned black yet?"

Johnny couldn't stand to hear any more. "Listen," he interrupted. "We don't want to hurt you. The Consoler sent us to find you."

"I've nothing to say to him."

"He's worried about you, Kit. He's your brother for drokk's sake!"

"He's no brother of mine!"

"He only wants to talk. He told us he wants to," Johnny thought furiously, "to console your differences."

"I've told you people before, I only want to be left alone!" For the first time, Kit's composure was slipping. "I don't want to meet the Consoler, I don't want to join the Salvationists. I... I've been lied to too many times already and I need time to think."

Johnny smiled grimly. His gamble was paying off, so far, at least. By his own admission, Kit had caught no more than a glimpse of his enemies. He obviously hadn't seen their S/D insignia. He had no real reason to want them dead.

Then he looked at Middenface again and the smile faded. His partner's eyes were closed, his skin pale and his face puffy. His breath was coming in painful wheezes. Johnny gasped his name in alarm and Middenface's eyelids fluttered, but the effort of raising them defeated him. He tried to talk but his tongue was swollen and black, as Identi Kit had said, and it trapped the words in his throat.

"Okay, you win," called Johnny hurriedly. "We'll back off. You let us go and we'll go back to the Consoler and tell him everything you said. He won't bother you again. Only you were right about my friend. He was hit. He's been poisoned. He won't last all the way back to base. If you can help him…"

"How do I know I can trust you?" Kit asked suspiciously.

"You're the one with the weapon."

"You said I was surrounded. You demanded my surrender. Doesn't sound like the words of someone who just wants to talk. How do I know that you're Salvationists at all? How do I know you're not with the government?"

"Kit, listen to me. My friend is dying. Can you save him?"

"There's a cure, yes. But if I give it to you, if I let you go, you might tell your friends where to find me. I can't risk that. No, the only way for me to stay safe is to kill you both."

Kit didn't sound like a killer. That surprised Johnny. It made him feel, not for the first time, that he had been misinformed, and that things weren't as they appeared to be. A real killer wouldn't have been as hesitant as Kit was now, nor would he have tried so hard to justify his actions. His words had sent a chill down the bounty hunter's spine, but they hadn't been a threat. It was more like a plea, thought Johnny. It was as if Kit wanted a way out of this, and wanted to be given an alternative to murder.

The only problem was, he couldn't think of one.

He only had one gambit left and it was the most dangerous one of all. He could tell the truth.

"What if I told you," he called, "that we aren't from the Miltonian government, and we aren't Salvationists either?" He took a deep breath. "We're S/D agents!"

There was no response from Kit. Johnny waited a moment before calling his name again. Still nothing.

"You know why we're here," he continued, knowing his cause was probably lost already. "We have a warrant to bring you in, alive if possible. I figure that makes us your best friends right now, Kit. I don't know what's going on here, but it seems to me there's a war about to erupt on Miltonia and you've made enemies on both sides. At least in prison you were safe and you had three square meals a day. What are you doing now? Cowering in some cave, scavenging for lizards, just waiting for the day when they find you? We're the best chance you've got of getting off this world with your skull intact, Kit, but you've got to help us first."

Silence.

Middenface was trying to say something, but he was too incoherent. Still, Johnny knew him well enough to guess that he was urging his partner to forget him, to take down the enemy, and to save himself, in that order.

"If my partner dies," he called, "you'll have to kill me too, and you know what'll happen then. They'll send more agents after you. It took us a few days to pick up your trail; how long do you think you can stay ahead of the entire Search and Destroy Agency? Because that's who you'll be running from, then: every bounty hunter in the cosmos. And you know what they'll do to you when they find you. We don't like it when one of our own gets taken down. We don't like it at all."

Silence.

"I'll make you a deal. Keep my partner alive and we'll let you go. We can fake your death and send a report back to the Doghouse. We'll get you to any world you choose and help you build a new identity. You'll be free, Kit. There'll be nobody after you."

The echoes of his voice died away to nothing. That was it, thought Johnny. He was out of cards. He had blown it.

Then, Kit's voice came again, quieter than before. "Who are you?" he asked.

"I told you, we're S/D agents. It's the truth, Kit. I can prove it to you. I can throw you my badge."

"I mean, what's your name?"

"Johnny Alpha. And my partner is–"

"Middenface! Middenface McNulty! I should have recognised the big lug!"

"Um…" Johnny hadn't expected that response.

"Listen to me," called Kit. "You don't have much time. I poisoned the arrowhead with sap from a plant that grows around here. The antidote is the plant's own leaves. They're purple and shaped like seven-pointed stars. Can you see any?"

Johnny looked around and finally called back: "Yes. Yes, I can see them."

He spotted a jagged streak of purple amid the grey. They looked more like weeds clinging tenaciously to life in an area where life had no right to exist. But in order to reach them, Johnny would have to show himself.

He agonised over his decision. He knew he couldn't trust Kit, but what he had said made sense. Nature often saw to it that poisons grew in tandem with their own antidotes. He knew what Middenface would have said if he could talk, but this was his partner's only chance and Johnny had long since understood that he would give his life for him.

He didn't give himself time to think about it. He leapt and rolled towards the vital leaves, making himself as small and hard a target as he could. Feverishly, he tore the four biggest ones from their stems. It took him only a second, but during this time he was a sitting duck. Still, no attack came.

He hurried back to Middenface, leaping the last few feet to land beside him. The big man wasn't moving at all now, and his breathing was shallow. Kit called to Johnny again, instructing him to tear the leaves up into small squares and mix them with water. Johnny did so, stuffing them into the narrow neck of his bottle. He was still suspicious, but the medicine could hardly make his partner's condition any worse. He forced it past Midden-face's swollen lips and urged him to swallow.

For the next few long, tense minutes, he sat over his partner and watched intently for a sign of recovery. Compared to the onset of the poison, it came slowly, but finally, thankfully, Johnny was sure that the swelling was easing, and that Middenface's breathing was becoming more regular and less laboured.

"I think we should talk."

Johnny jumped. Kit's voice sounded much nearer. His attention had been focused on Middenface, but even so, it had taken some skill to creep up on him like this.

He peered out over the outcrop and saw his enemy at last.

Kit Jones, also known as Identi Kit, was standing there in the open. He had made no attempt to disguise himself; he was just as he had appeared in the video that Johnny had been shown at the Doghouse. He was slight of stature, and his skin was pale almost to the point of whiteness. The years in prison and the days on the run since had taken their toll on him, and his eyes were sunken and haunted. He looked weak and ill; hardly the wild, violent criminal after whom the bounty hunters had been sent. But then, Johnny reminded himself, Kit excelled at looking like something he wasn't.

Kit saw that he had Johnny's attention, brandished his bow and made a show of tossing it to one side. He shrugged a makeshift quiver of arrows from his shoulders and discarded this too. It was quite an impressive gesture of trust, but of course, Kit knew he had nothing to fear. Since Johnny was so ill-equipped, he couldn't take advantage of the situation. Not unless he could get closer.

His hand shifted reflexively to his knife, checking that it was still there. If it was a choice between a seven hundred thousand credit bounty and a deal made with an enemy under duress, he would just have to live with the stain on his conscience.

Johnny looked at Middenface to see that his eyes were still closed, but the pain had drained out of his expression. Johnny stood slowly, showing Kit his empty hands. He stepped out from behind the outcrop.

"I'm listening," he said.

And he took one, two, three steps forward.

"That's far enough!" warned Kit too soon. There were still several yards of uneven ground between them. The identity thief knew what he was doing. He was watching Johnny closely, alert for any threatening moves. If he was quick, he could still retrieve and use his weapons in the time it would take the bounty hunter to reach him.

"I'm sorry about Middenface," said Kit. "I'm sorry it has to be this way, but I have something to tell you, Johnny. It's something I've been trying to tell people for five years and no one will believe me. And I think you're close enough now to use your alpha eyes and see into my mind. I invite you to do that. See for yourself if I'm lying, or if five years in that hellhole of a prison have driven me mad."

Johnny would have suspected a ruse, but he didn't see what Kit had to gain by this request. If he'd wanted to kill his pursuers, he most certainly would have done so by now. Johnny nodded and fired up the alpha radiation in his system. A low dose to begin with... Kit wouldn't be compelled to tell him anything and he would feel no discomfort. But Johnny would see the electromagnetic patterns in Kit's brain and read them like the contour lines of a map. Even the smallest deception on his part would cause a spike in those patterns which Johnny would perceive.

"Go ahead," he said.

"I'm not the man you think I am," said Identi Kit. "I'm not the man who committed all those crimes. I'm not the man you're looking for. I'm not Kit Jones."

Then, he said something that Johnny *wouldn't* have believed, had it not been for the fact that his eyes told him it was the truth.

"It's me, Johnny. Your old friend. I'm Moosehead McGuffin."

CHAPTER TWELVE
BODY DOUBLE

Moosehead could not believe his good fortune.

He'd been down on his luck for so long that he had almost forgotten what it was like to catch a break. When he heard the perimeter alarm go off earlier, he thought his luck had gone from bad to worse. Now, he was beginning to think that things might finally be turning his way.

Aside from Moosehead himself, there were only two, maybe three S/D agents who could have picked up his trail so quickly, but Moosehead was the best of them all. He had a nose for these things. If he'd had to put money on which one would trace him to this remote hideaway, he'd have bet on Johnny Alpha. The minute he realised who'd found him he knew his luck had changed. Johnny was probably the only agent who would believe his story. With those alpha eyes of his he could easily read the truth within someone's mind and even pluck individual thoughts right out of their brain.

Moosehead had never forgotten his first encounter with Johnny. Back when he had been a scout for General Armz in the Mutant Army, he had helped catch a Kreeler spy who'd been watching their Salisbury camp. The man was tough and had stood up to interrogation until the general had brought in one of his lieutenants.

Even at seventeen, Johnny Alpha looked formidable. There was a determined set to his features that said nothing short of death would stop him from doing what he had to, and he didn't look as though he'd die easily.

Johnny had taken the spy's head in his hands and stared deep into his eyes, his own eyes lighting up like two glowing embers. The Kreeler began to writhe and tried to pull away, but Johnny had him fixed. At first, he told General Armz what he could read on the surface of the Kreeler's mind, and then he probed deeper until, sobbing and squirming with self-hatred, the spy had been forced to confess everything he knew.

Johnny had impressed every mutant at the camp with his abilities. He had also scared them. Moosehead was twenty years old at the time. He had never forgotten his first encounter with Johnny Alpha.

"I'm awright now, I'm okay," said Middenface. He pushed Johnny and Moosehead away, held up his hands to show that he could walk unaided, and took two steps before his legs gave out.

Moosehead leaped to catch him and ended up flat on his back underneath him. He still wasn't used to the body he was in. Kit was shorter and slighter than he was, or rather than he had once been. Since he had broken out of prison, he kept attempting to do things that he previously wouldn't have thought twice about, only to find that he physically wasn't up to it anymore.

Johnny lifted Middenface off Moosehead, and then they both helped the wounded mutant to his feet. Middenface was still feverish with the effects of the poison. Moosehead had never actually used it on anyone before, so although he was sure the antidote would work, he had no idea how long it would take or how painful the process of recovery would be.

"Only a few more steps," Moosehead said encouragingly. "Then you can lie down and get something to eat."

"Ye've been sayin' that fer the past half hour," Middenface grunted. "If I have tae listen tae it one more time, I'll cut yer snecknin' heart out. I dinnae care how weak I am."

Moosehead had set up several boltholes in the mountains, and had regularly moved between them. Johnny and Middenface had caught him just as he was clearing one camp in preparation for a move to another. This meant that they had to now trek across some inhospitable terrain to get to a place where there was food and water.

They were standing now on the rim of a steep crater, and Moosehead explained how to reach the bottom by sitting and sliding down the thick dust and loose shale of the crater walls.

"Och Johnny," groaned Middenface. "Can we no just kill him now and pretend he was the real Kit?"

Moosehead had forgotten just how many swear words Middenface knew. He counted fourteen different ones, from languages he was pretty sure weren't even human, as the big guy bounced down the side of the crater on his backside.

"Ye better have a sneckin' palace in there," said Middenface as his colleagues helped him to his feet.

Moosehead pulled aside a sheet of parachute material that had small leafy branches stuck to it as camouflage. Behind it was a small cave into which he invited the others to follow him. It wasn't five-star accommodation, but after five years in a solitary cell, anything was, as Middenface had put it, "a sneckin' palace".

He lit a torch from the embers of that morning's fire, and helped Middenface get comfortable on a pile of furs by the back wall. Then he rebuilt the fire, filled a canteen with water from a large clay pot, gave Middenface a drink, and put a pan of water on to boil.

"Hope you gents like tree skeeters," he said, reaching into a bag, "'cos that's all we've got."

"You said you were going to explain everything once we got under cover," said Johnny. "Now seems a pretty good time."

"You know how I caught Kit in the first place?" asked Moosehead as he gutted a tree skeeter and squeezed its innards into a jar to use as gravy. "I got a nose for these things." Johnny nodded and helped Middenface take a little more water from the canteen.

"You got them alpha eyes of yours that can see into a man's soul." Moosehead tapped his nose. "I got an acute sense of smell. Leastways, I *used* to have an acute sense of smell. You wouldn't believe what you can learn from the way a person smells. You can build a whole profile of them from the scents they leave behind in a single room, if you know what you're doing. And I knew what I was doing. I spent years training up my instinct, improving my knowledge, and honing my nose. Then I threw it all away in one stupid moment."

He paused, thinking about the best way to tell a story that was almost impossible to believe. It was all so complicated, so utterly incredible, that he didn't know where to begin.

Moosehead's norm parents were unable to have a child by conventional means so they'd opted for *in vitro* fertilization. Unfortunately for them, something had gone terribly wrong with the process. The clinic they went to provided them with sperm that had been somehow contaminated with Stontium 90. They later claimed that they had taken every precaution, but life following a nuclear strike had its difficulties, to say the least, and you couldn't account for every bit of fallout, even in a hi-tech medical clinic. Their insurers agreed to stand by them in court, and Mr and Mrs McGuffin didn't want to expose themselves to the social stigma of publicly admitting that they had a mutated child, so they kept quiet.

The McGuffins kept their offspring well hidden after that and strategically moved house so as not to arouse too much suspicion. When Moosehead was twelve they found an answer to their problems.

"This really is for the best, son," his father had told him. "Your mother and I couldn't give you anything like the life he'll be able to. He's the king's brother, son. He's royalty."

"He doesn't mind about your appearance, either," his mother had explained. "You won't have to hide anymore. The prince purposefully sought us out because you're a mutant."

"He's offered us an awful lot of money, son. We'll be set up for life. All he asks is that we never see you again, and he'll make certain you're properly looked after. It's an opportunity to die for."

Moosehead very nearly *did* die for it.

He didn't want to go when the footmen came for him. He kicked and bawled and clung to his mother, begging her not to send him away. He had never known another life, and he didn't like the way the footmen smelled. His parents shed a few tears as they waved him goodbye, but Moosehead suspected they would soon dry them on the cheque the prince's men left for them.

He saw nothing of his new owner's remote Wiltshire estate as he was driven through it in the back of a black, windowless van. He was taken from the vehicle and thrown in a pen with other mutant children like himself, all with animal characteristics. The pen's fences were electrified, they were fed from a trough, and they had to go to the toilet in the same straw they slept in.

Five days after he arrived, Moosehead was taken from the pen with four others. The keepers told them that they should feel honoured. The prince had important guests that day. They were set free in an open green and given a twenty minute start before the prince and his cronies let the dogs loose and rode after them.

That was when Moosehead's ability first kicked in properly. Faced with the prospect of death, all the body's natural senses sharpen as it looks for any means of escape. Moosehead had never felt his sense of smell open up quite so incredibly before. He caught every scent that hung on the breeze within a kilometre of him. There was so much scent information that it almost overloaded his brain's ability to process it.

The other children just screamed and ran, crying for their mothers. Moosehead, however, stood stock still and sniffed out the best route to take in order to avoid capture.

He found a row of dead rabbits hanging from a barbed wire fence, and used their carcasses to mask his scent and put the pack off his trail. By nightfall they still hadn't caught him. From the scent of freshly spilled blood that he caught on the downwind, he knew their other quarry had not been so lucky.

He was hungry, weak, and shaking with fatigue as he smelled the beaters closing in on him with the dogs. He was by the perimeter fence and he could smell the fierce heat of the static coming off the voltage that ran through it. Moosehead had concentrated hard on that smell and discovered a gap in the electrical field about two hundred metres away, where part of the fence was down.

Somehow, he found the strength to keep running.

"This is all a little difficult to take in," Johnny said. "You look like Kit and you sound just like him, too. I can tell you're not lying to me, but you have to help me understand how this happened."

"I'm not sure I understand it myself," Moosehead admitted. "I was one of the best manhunters that ever worked for the S/D Agency. That doesn't mean I didn't get tired of the work, though. Happens to us all, I know, but I wanted out of the life. All I needed was one big score: a bounty that could set me up with real prospects for the future. When they put Identi Kit's capture out to tender I knew it was my big chance. A lot of agents wouldn't touch the job; said it was impossible to catch a mutant who could change his shape and assume anyone's identity. Not me, though. I had a nose for these things. Took me a year and a half of chasing mock leads to find him, and another six months to bring him in."

"Aye, we know aw this, and ye're burning yon tree rats," said Middenface, who seemed to be recovering from the poison.

Moosehead turned the skewered tree skeeters over and continued his story.

Kit was knee-deep in some major-league corporate fraud when Moosehead caught up with him. His victims were mostly Miltonian mine owners who were looking to invest their substantial wealth offworld. Their business was necessarily covert since few norms would deal with them at all, but there were always those for whom greed was stronger than prejudice. The many layers of secrecy that surrounded these mutant businessmen were perfect for Kit's purposes.

Posing as various mutant millionaires, he'd been able to embezzle trillions of credits. He had become overconfident, though, and Moosehead had been able to quite literally sniff out the paper trail he had left.

He cornered Kit in the executive washroom of Microhard's central HQ. The identity thief was standing over an unconscious mutant executive who had been able to hide his nature until now. Kit was halfway through the transformation from one form to another when Moosehead zapped him with a paralysis ray.

Moosehead was all set to retire after that. He'd heard about the opportunities opening up on Miltonia and planned to use his half-a-million credit bounty to buy shares in a new mining development. He was just about to book his passage to the remote planet when

the Intergalactic Bureau of Investigation got in touch
with him.

Kit had offered to turn world's evidence and rat out his
accomplices. He was offering up big-time gang bosses
and senior figures from the sphere of high finance. He
had one condition, though. He wouldn't talk to anyone
but Moosehead.

Moosehead smelled a rat from the beginning. It was
nothing he could put his finger on, just an uneasy feeling
in the pit of his gut. But he was intrigued. A hunter can
build up a great deal of respect for his quarry, especially
one as clever and as formidable an opponent as Kit. In
his vanity, Moosehead assumed that the respect was
mutual. After tracking Kit for two years, he knew him
intimately but had never had a face-to-face conversation
with him. It was almost for this opportunity alone that he
agreed to a meeting. That, and the credits, of course.

The IBI was offering exclusive rewards for the capture
of any major criminal named by Kit. With so much
money on the table, Moosehead chose to ignore his
instincts. It was a big mistake.

The Shawshank Penal Colony was far worse than he
could have imagined.

Moosehead had sent more than a few inmates to the
colony himself, and that responsibility weighed heavily
on him as he walked through its gates. The authorities
demanded that he leave all weapons at reception. It was
the colony's regulation that all visitors should also don
the drab prison uniform before they were allowed into
the main compound.

Moosehead did not like the way the stiff fabric of the
uniform felt against his skin as the prison guards
escorted him to a secure room in the visitors' wing. Kit
was brought into the room in special shackles; his hands
and feet encased in large metal spheres from which

heavy chains hung, and his head was entirely covered by a helmet that obstructed his view. Kit could only change shape and steal someone's identity if he could lay his hands on them. The prison authorities were obviously taking no chances of that happening.

The guards bolted Kit's shackles to the floor. Moosehead told them to remove the helmet and leave them alone, but the guards were dubious. He showed them his IBI clearance credentials and they reluctantly did as they were told.

"Are you sure you're safe in here alone with me?" said Kit with a sneer. Moosehead could smell his adrenaline levels rising and, beneath the stench of the stale sweat that clung to his prison uniform, he could pick up the salty tang of fresh perspiration. Kit was gearing himself up for something.

"I don't think I have too much to fear," said Moosehead.

"Don't let these shackles fool you," said Kit. "You don't have any toilet stalls to hide behind here."

Moosehead felt his gorge rise. Kit was goading him and, despite his better judgement, it was working. He took a deep breath and got down to business. "You have something you want to tell me, I understand."

Kit laughed a short, derisory laugh and leaned forward. Moosehead could smell the bland prison food on his breath and the caustic prison soap on his skin. "I have lots of things to tell you. Let's start with a few home truths, shall we?"

"I'd prefer names and dates."

"You'd prefer me to give it to you all on a plate. You haven't got the wit or the balls to find out for yourself. But you know what your real problem is?"

"Tell me," said Moosehead.

"Your total lack of vision or imagination. You caught only the faintest glimpse of my entire operation and you didn't have the sense to see what it might have meant for you. I could have made proper use of your meagre talents. I could certainly have made you twenty times richer than you are now."

"I don't want any of your blood money," said Moosehead.

"No," Kit countered. "You prefer the blood money of the stinking norms who spit on you and wipe their backsides on every note they hand you. The money you make isn't cleaner than mine, it's just paltry in comparison. You're too stupid and cowardly to make it any other way than to prey on your own kind."

"I was clever enough to catch you."

"But not brave enough to take me face to face. You had to shoot me in the back, skulking in a toilet cubicle like some filthy microbe clinging to the seat."

Kit was pushing all the right buttons. Moosehead had expected him to be impressed by his ingenuity, not mocking and superior. Kit's words ate Moosehead up inside, and without thinking, he lunged for Kit's throat.

That was probably the biggest mistake of his whole life.

The moment he put his hands about Kit's throat, he knew something was up. He could smell the blood moving faster in Kit's veins as his heart beat more quickly, signifying a burst of hope. As his thumbs closed on Kit's windpipe, a jolt of energy surged though him. He was gripped by a sudden paralysis. He felt his muscles begin to writhe and distort beneath his skin. His bones felt as though they were being ground to powder, and he passed out with the unbearable pain.

He awoke to the sound of the security alarm.

A squad of guards burst into the room, armed with batons and electric prods. "He broke free," he heard a voice say. He recognised the words as his own, but he didn't sound like himself. "I don't know how he did it," his voice continued. "He overcame me and locked me in these shackles."

Moosehead got unsteadily to his feet. Something was very wrong. His prison uniform suddenly felt too big and hung loosely off him. Worse still, he could hardly smell his surroundings, and his mirror image was sitting in shackles at the very spot where Kit had been.

Two guards approached him, wielding their prods. "Wait," said Moosehead. "Something's not right. I..." He stopped short as he realised that Kit's thin, reedy voice was coming out of his own mouth. Then the guards hit him. Bright lights flashed behind his eyes as his whole body convulsed from the shock. He fell to the floor, foaming at the mouth.

"Thanks for acting so quickly," he heard the other Moosehead say as the two guards pounded him with their boots. "I'm sorry I didn't listen to you before. I didn't realise he was going to pull anything like this."

"He's a wily customer, make no mistake," said a guard. "Did you get any information out of him?"

"No, it was just an elaborate escape ploy," said Moosehead's lookalike. "He might have gotten away with it, too, if you hadn't have acted so swiftly."

"He'll pay for this, you can be sure of that," said another guard as he joined the two who were already beating on the real Moosehead.

Moosehead's double left the room and more guards came in. He curled into a ball to protect himself as their fists, boots and batons rained down on him. The guards didn't stop until they were physically exhausted. Moosehead was already unconscious by then.

He came to in a cell that was too small to stand up or lie down in. Every part of his body was bruised or bleeding.

After what seemed like days, a small grille opened up in one of the walls, and someone pushed a stale chunk of bread and a bowl of water through it. In the dim light of the cell, Moosehead stared into the bowl and caught sight of his reflection. Tears spilled from his eyes and his whole body shook with rage and hatred as he saw Kit's bruised and battered face staring back at him.

He knew now what had happened to him, although it still took him some time to accept the truth. Kit's powers had obviously developed to a degree that no one could have foreseen. Along with the ability to change his own shape, he could now also alter the DNA of other mutants. He had not only taken Moosehead's likeness, he had also changed Moosehead into a perfect replica of himself. He had effectively swapped bodies with him.

Kit had walked out of the prison a free man, leaving the S/D agent who had put him there to serve his sentence for him. It was the perfect revenge.

Not that any of the prison guards would believe that.

After an eternity of discomfort and near starvation, Moosehead was taken out of his cell and marched to the showers where five other prisoners were waiting. The guards had passed the word about how he had been cooperating with the authorities, grassing up his friends and allies. The inmates didn't take too kindly to this. Moosehead made the best attempt he could to defend himself, but he was weakened from starvation and his previous beating, and his new body just wasn't as strong as his old one.

The weeks dragged into months and Moosehead spent every day cursing himself for having fallen for Kit's stunt like a total sap. He also spent the time planning his escape. He might have lost his sense of smell, but he still had years of valuable experience and training. He didn't intend to stay locked up forever. He had a score to settle.

After four years, he eventually landed a job in the refuse section of the penal colony. It was the filthiest and most lowly form of employment the prison had to offer: packing loads of decayed garbage into a trash compactor and then loading it into containers to be shipped out of the prison.

After many months of carefully studying the schedules of the vehicles and ships that transported the trash out of the colony, then cross-referencing this information with the watch rotas of the guards, Moosehead took an opportunity to only partially fill a container, and then climbed in with the compacted trash. His bold but desperate gambit was timed to perfection and he made it out of the prison undetected.

Moosehead had always had a near-photographic memory. In the long months and years he had spent staring at the dull grey walls of his isolation cell, he'd gone over every single detail of the paper trail he had followed to Kit. This included hundreds of bank accounts set up with false or stolen details that were used to hide and launder money. Once he was out of prison, Moosehead checked out these accounts and found that a few of them were still active and contained funds. With this pilfered capital, he set about trying to find his adversary again, and picked up his trail with surprising ease.

Kit was on Miltonia.

"Okay," said Johnny. "I'm willing to buy your story so far. What I don't understand is why you killed Kit when you got here. He was the only person who could either prove who you were or turn you back to your old self."

"I didn't kill him," said Moosehead. "I hacked into his schedule to find out when he would be alone in his office, when his aides and secretaries would be away from their desks. I made myself an appointment and I walked into the presidential palace to confront him. I was pretty surprised that no one tried to stop me, actually."

"So were we when we found oot," said Middenface with a slight groan as he shifted his weight on the pile of furs.

"I walked into the office and the first thing I saw was my old body lying dead on the ground. I can't tell you how that felt. It seemed like everything was over. Then an alarm went off and steel shutters came down over the door. Before I even had time to panic, a side door opened and some guy ushered me through it. He told me the guards were coming and it was my only way out. He said they wouldn't believe my story and, after five years in prison."

"Who was the guy?" asked Johnny.

"He called himself Nose Job."

"Aye, we've met that scunner," said Middenface.

"He told me he was working for the president at an above top secret level, rooting out corruption in the cabinet. He said they'd been onto Kit for a while. According to Nose Job, Kit had been doing some arms deal with a bunch of terrorists called the Salvationists. He'd been in a secret meeting with the terrorist's leader just before I walked in. Seems the leader, a mutant by the name of the Consoler, had found out Nose Job was onto Kit and told him so. Nose Job claimed that the Consoler thought he had been set up and that Kit had lured him into a trap. Nose Job told me that they argued, Kit swapped bodies with him and then killed him, seconds before I arrived.

"Nose job explained to me that Kit thought this would give him the perfect alibi. No one would prosecute a dead man, after all. Then he headed out to the Salvationists' secret base in the guise of the Consoler. What Kit hadn't counted on, though, was that Nose Job knew all about his abilities. He even guessed my real identity. He said he'd square things for me with the authorities, but it would be easier if I was out of the way. He smuggled me out of the palace and even gave me an airlift into the mountains. I scoped out the Salvationist camp and infiltrated it. I was there about two days before they rumbled me. It was long enough to work out that I'd been lied to. So I left there pretty quick and holed up here to figure things out."

"Come to any conclusions?" asked Johnny.

"As a matter of fact, I have. I've had a lot of time to think things through since I got here. Haven't done much else."

"'Cept fer layin' traps and poisonin' arrows," muttered Middenface.

"Anyway," said Moosehead, "I soon realised the truth was staring me in the face. Kit didn't swap places with the Consoler and kill him. He swapped places with Nose Job and killed *him*. Then he sent me out here to get this Consoler chap for him."

"Hang aboot," said Middenface. "Ye mean ye're tellin' me that the body we saw on yon slab was Nose Job?"

"The *real* Nose Job Johnson. And the guy you spoke to who called himself Nose Job was the same guy we're both after: Kit Jones. Only thing I can't work out is why he didn't just bump me off or hand me over to the guards."

"I think I know," said Johnny. "Nose Job isn't a military intelligence officer, he's the president's mouthpiece and right-hand man. Kit was probably looking for the perfect moment to swap bodies with him. Posing as Nose Job, he could run the whole government, and in his current condition, President Ooze couldn't have done anything to stop him."

Moosehead nodded thoughtfully. "Kit must have known I'd escaped and was waiting for me. When he saw me coming on the security cameras, he finally had his opportunity to get rid of Nose Job and take his place, pinning the blame on me and charging me with my own murder. That's why he had to get me out of the palace so quickly without anyone seeing me."

"Och, he's a wily snecker and no mistake," said Middenface.

Johnny went quiet for a moment. Moosehead had seen that look on his face before, with his jaw clenched and his eyes burning with determination.

"You know what this means," he said at last. "If we're going to bring Kit in and collect seven hundred thousand credits, we're going to have to take down the whole Miltonian government."

"Aye," said Middenface. "And fight some of oor oldest comrades alongside a bunch o' norms and misfit mutants."

CHAPTER THIRTEEN
REVOLUTION NOW

"Pardon me for staring," said the Consoler. "You look so much like my brother, as he would look now. So much like the man I once was myself." He passed a tired flipper-like appendage over his eyes and sighed. "I know it was foolish of me, but when I thought you were Kit, when I thought he had come here to find me, I allowed myself to hope. I thought we could put the past behind us, at last. Now you tell me he was our enemy all along. Minister McGuffin, the man most responsible for all of Miltonia's troubles, is actually my own twin brother!"

"Kit *was* McGuffin," Johnny reminded him. "Now he's Nose Job."

"I should have seen it," the Consoler lamented.

Johnny had never seen the Consoler like this. During their previous encounters, he had been so composed, but now he was completely miserable.

"I should have realised when I couldn't feel our psychic bond. And this new ability of his, to alter the appearances of other mutants... It's so like my own."

"You weren't the only one fooled by Kit's tricks," muttered the man in Identi Kit's body. Johnny still found it hard to think of him as Moosehead. It wasn't just his appearance; he also seemed so subdued, like his old fire had been extinguished. "I knew what he could do, and I still let him play me. He easily manipulated me and sent me after you. I guess that's what five years in prison will do to you: it dulls the senses by teaching you not to think too hard if you want to get by."

"I cannot apologise enough for what my brother has done to you, Mr McGuffin," the Consoler said quietly.

"The important thing now," said Johnny, "is to see that Identi Kit pays for his crimes."

Doubletalk, the fourth and final occupant of the Consoler's hut, had kept his own counsel so far. It was likely, thought Johnny, that he felt embarrassed by his boss's discomfort. Now, however, his eyes widened in excitement and his two mouths blurted: "Are you saying you've reconsidered? You'll join us after all?"

Johnny chose his words carefully. "It seems we have the same goals."

He had thought long and hard about his next move as he and Middenface had led Moosehead back to the Salvationist camp. He could have kicked himself for being so close to the real Kit without realising it, but they had been unarmed and were watched over by the menacing presence of General Rising. Even if they could get that close to Nose Job again, it would be no simple matter to take him into custody. Too many people would give their lives for the man they thought he was.

It was dark when they reached the entrance to the volcano; it was the one they had first come across. The guards regarded them with a mixture of awe and resentment, but let them pass without any argument. Someone had evidently warned them that the S/D agents may return with a prisoner.

At the end of the entrance passageway – the last point at which they could talk without being overheard – Johnny had taken a deep breath and told his partner what he had concluded. Middenface wasn't happy, but he had bowed to Johnny's tactical expertise. He had drawn the line, however, at having another conference with the Consoler.

"Ah'm afeared he might talk ma ears off, Johnny. Ah'm gonna go see if there's any o' that booze left fer us. Ah reckon we deserve a drop now."

Johnny allowed Middenface his escape. It was the least he could do after all that he'd been through recently.

The Consoler had been asleep but Johnny had persuaded Doubletalk to wake him up. Refusing the offer of purple tea, Johnny had Moosehead repeat his sorry tale, and watched as the Salvationists' leader sunk ever deeper into a pall of gloom.

"We need to talk tactics," said Johnny brusquely. "I need to know how many people you've got, and what resources other than the ones we've seen."

"You have seen everything," said the Consoler. "It is a small army, but we are growing day by day. In a few short months–"

"We don't have months. You know the damage Kit did when he was posing as Moosehead. Now, he's the president's mouthpiece and quite possibly the most powerful person on this world. We have to act now."

"No!" The Consoler said sharply. "I understand your motives, Mr Alpha. You told me yourself that you have no interest in our politics. You come to us now because you need our help. Well, I tell you, I will not let you take my people into a war for which we are ill-prepared, simply because you are impatient for your bounty."

Johnny smarted at the harsh words. They stung all the more because they were true. Even so, he wasn't prepared to give up. "The longer you take to build up your forces, the longer you give Kit to do the same," he insisted. "Rising is slowly zeroing in on your location. He's already sent us after you. Do you think he'll stop at that?"

"The Consoler's right. Under his leadership, we've achieved so much in so short a time. If we act too hastily, it will all be for nothing."

No sooner did Johnny realise that only one of

Doubletalk's mouths had spoken than the other chimed in with a completely different point of view. "We've waited long enough. There may be few of us, but we're ready. Delay any longer and our people will lose the will to fight."

"This is not up for discussion, gentlemen," said the Consoler darkly. "It was agreed that I, and I alone, would decide when we are ready, and that moment has not yet come. Mr Alpha, you know how happy I would be for you and your partner to join our cause, but you must realise that you must also abide by our timetable. If you can see a faster way to achieve your aims, then do as you must without us. I will not lead my people to slaughter at your whim." He hung his misshapen head and added quietly, "I have done them enough harm."

"That's typical of the Consoler," said Elephant Head after Johnny had told her the news. "He's a good man, but an idealist. He formed the Salvationists to offer refuge to those who were mistreated by Leadbetter and his cronies."

"By Kit," Johnny reminded her, "not Leadbetter."

She nodded brusquely. "It took us months to make him see that this is war, and you don't win wars by hiding in caves and sending polite letters to the media. Even now he talks about fighting, but I always knew he'd bulk at the idea when it came to it." She clenched her fists in frustration and Johnny smiled to himself.

A little groan emerged from the space between the crates on which they sat. Middenface lay there, a wet towel draped over his face. He claimed to be just "resting his eyes" after the all-night party he had instigated – the party that had drained every drop of liquor from the camp.

"Is that how most of you feel?" asked Johnny.

"Many of us. You saw the excitement when you and

your friend turned up. We thought this was it; that it was finally time to get out of this cave and do something! We're beginning to fragment, to turn against each other. Our worst enemy isn't Leadbetter's government anymore; it's boredom. People are starting to say that if the Consoler won't act, they will."

"The terrorist attacks in Clacton Fuzzville? The hoverbus bomb?"

Elephant Head's eyes clouded. "The official word is that they were faked by Lead... umm, Kit himself. Unofficially... I don't know. It's not the sort of thing you can talk about openly."

"If you were in charge," said Johnny, "what would you do?"

She answered without hesitation. "You saw the immigration camp. We've been watching it for weeks. The Consoler says we need to learn more, but every day the reports are the same. We know the camp's routine to the second. We'll never be more ready to make our move than we are now."

"And when you've liberated the camp?"

"We'll have the numbers to make a real difference. We could storm the presidential palace!"

"With bows and arrows?"

Elephant Head scowled. "Liberating the camp would be the first step. After that, we'd take stock of the situation and see how many recruits we've got and what skills they have, and then we'd plan our next move. If nothing else, it'd give morale a boost."

But it'd get us no closer to Kit, thought Johnny. "Why do you think the Consoler won't give the order? I didn't have him pegged as a coward," Johnny said.

"Guilt!" said Elephant Head firmly. "I believe he'd give his life for Miltonia, but to sacrifice other people's lives and send them to their deaths? I just don't think he can. And you can't fight a war without casualties."

"Last night he said he'd 'done enough harm'."

"The Consoler sees himself as a martyr, a pariah. You told me his brother can reshape his own DNA. Well, ask yourself, why can't the Consoler do that, too? Why does he have to bear the mutations he takes from others?"

Johnny frowned. "You're saying he could look normal if he wanted to?"

"I don't think it's that simple. He told us his powers and his brother's were the same, but they developed in different ways. I don't think the Consoler consciously makes himself suffer."

"But subconsciously," muttered Johnny.

Elephant Head glanced around to make sure nobody was listening, then leaned in closer to him and spoke in a conspiratorial whisper. "He told me something once. The Consoler was a criminal, a gangster. It's true," she insisted as Johnny's eyes betrayed his disbelief. "Back on some dustball of a planet where he grew up. He ran the biggest, most vicious gang there. Went to prison for it. He said the experience changed him."

"I think I'm beginning to see," said Johnny.

"The Consoler's brother looked up to him. It was he who introduced Kit to a life of crime, and he's had to live with that ever since. He blames himself for all the crimes that Kit commits, and he's spent the whole of his adult life trying to atone for it."

"By fighting against injustice on Miltonia," concluded Johnny. "Only he's just learned that everything he's fighting against, that was all Kit's doing, too."

"I'm disappointed," said the Consoler. "I am very disappointed. I invited you into my home, I have treated you as allies and this is how you repay me."

It was late afternoon and Middenface and Johnny were back in the Consoler's hut. Middenface's hangover had cleared up, but he almost wished it hadn't because at least it had blotted out the tedium of being underground

for so long. It had been his fondest hope that the Consoler had summoned them to give the word, to say it was
time to prepare for battle. But, of course, he had only
wanted to talk. Again.

"I don't know what you mean," said Johnny.

"No? Then perhaps you can explain the rumours I have
been hearing all day, that you are poised to lead the Salvationists to victory. You have been fomenting dissent;
turning my people against me for your own purposes."

"We've been talking to them, that's all. And they've
been asking us to help them, not the other way round.
They're sick of waiting."

Amen to that, thought Middenface.

"And I share their impatience," the Consoler insisted.
"Of course I want to see an end to Miltonia's troubles,
but to act prematurely would be worse than not to act at
all. We are our world's last chance, Mr Alpha. We cannot
afford to fail."

"Who said anything about failing?" said Johnny. "I've
been talking to Elephant Head. We've been drawing up
plans to attack the immigration camp."

"We need more people, more training and more
resources."

"We can do it now. We can bust that camp wide open,
Consoler, with the minimum of casualties."

"But there *will* be casualties. People will die on both
sides."

"Of course they will!"

"Innocents will be caught in the crossfire. I don't know
if I can be responsible for that. I don't know if I can bear
the blood on my hands," the Consoler admitted.

"So, what's your plan?" challenged Johnny. "To talk
about change but not act on it? How many more camps
are there, Consoler? How many more are being built each
day? Word is that people are dying out there through
malnutrition, exposure and mistreatment. But that's okay

with you, is it? Their blood doesn't matter? You said yourself that if you let these things happen, you share responsibility for them. How many more deaths, Consoler?"

Middenface let out a cheer at Johnny's impassioned words and then wished he hadn't as all eyes turned towards him. He looked away with an embarrassed shrug. As Johnny and the Consoler locked stares again, Middenface exchanged a chagrined glance with Doubletalk. Like him, the Consoler's adviser was reduced to watching and waiting for the outcome of this contest of wills. Middenface was backing his partner to win, of course.

The Consoler was already on the ropes. He looked tired and far less sure of himself than normal. "I need to think about this," he pleaded. "The information you brought me last night has changed everything."

"So, you know who your enemy is now," said Johnny. "That should make your decision easier, not more difficult. It makes you even more responsible for what's happening on Miltonia, and you need to put a stop to it!"

It was clear from the Consoler's resentful glare that he knew what Johnny was trying to do. That made the ploy no less effective, however.

"I can't help thinking," the Consoler said, "that if I could only see my brother, speak to him..."

"Has talking to Kit ever helped in the past?" asked Johnny, mercilessly.

"Our psychic bond used to be so strong. When he was hurt, I felt his pain, and vice versa. We were inseparable. Then, Kit changed. No, that's not right. It was *I* who changed."

"Kit doesn't want to talk," said Johnny.

Middenface had expected him to take advantage of his foe's weakness and go in for the kill. Instead, Johnny had softened his voice as if in sympathy. He would never get the hang of this diplomacy business, Middenface thought.

"He sent Moosehead here to assassinate you, and then when he failed to do the job, he sent us," Johnny continued. "If you hadn't been so well-hidden and well-guarded, we'd have had you trussed up and halfway back to Clacton Fuzzville before we even smelled a rat."

"Still, I have to try."

To Middenface's surprise, Johnny nodded, seeming to accept the point. "Then I have a proposal to put to you."

"One that ends, no doubt, with my brother in your custody."

"It isn't just about that anymore," said Johnny with quiet anger. "Leonard Leadbetter was a Mutant War hero and a colleague of mine. It's bad enough that Kit took his dream of equality and perverted it. Think how he must feel, confined to that vat: his senses working but unable to communicate; watching as your brother runs this world as he pleases while claiming to speak for him. And I was there, with Middenface. We were standing beside him, taken in by that usurper's lies, and he couldn't reach us, couldn't warn us. He must have been screaming inside!"

"Very well," the Consoler said wearily. "Tell me your plan and I will give it my due consideration. That is, if I am to have a say in the matter."

"Nobody's turned against you," said Johnny. "You command a great deal of respect around here. Your people would follow you to hell and back if you asked them to. They're just waiting for the order."

The Consoler nodded and smiled sadly.

"Does this mean we've got whit we wanted, Johnny?" Middenface piped up. "Braw!"

* * *

Johnny slept soundly that night, but he was one of the

few who did. He woke up four hours before dawn to the same sounds to which he had dozed off: the whisper or hushed conversation and the clatter of activity, much of it to no end. It was as if the camp had been charged with electricity from the moment the Consoler had called all its occupants together to explain what was about to happen.

The Salvationists' leader had given a short speech, mostly emphasising the fact that he didn't expect anyone to do anything that made them feel uncomfortable. Then he handed over the reigns to Elephant Head who had given an expert mission briefing. It was concise and yet so thorough that Johnny hadn't felt the need to interrupt once.

It was as he was kitting himself out in the armoury hut that he felt the first pang of anxiety, and Moosehead was the inadvertent cause. Johnny had found his old friend testing the weight of a bow, his eyes a hundred light years away. He had suggested that maybe he should sit this one out in the volcano base. After all he had been through, no one would deny him some recovery time. Moosehead's reply was fierce, and Johnny smiled to see a trace of his old obdurate self, if only in the depths of his eyes.

"I've waited a long time for this, Johnny," he said stubbornly. "Now the wind's blowing my way again at last. Trust me. Even in this body I still got a nose for these things." Johnny smiled at that but the smile froze as Moosehead continued. "Anyway, who's gonna be fool enough to mess with us? You, me and Middenface: brave heroes of the Mutant War, and the meanest, toughest agents the Doghouse ever produced. This is gonna be like old times, eh?"

And in that moment, Johnny was transported back to his youth, to his home world, to a time when he had fought not for money, but for simple survival.

It was the atmosphere in the camp that reminded him

of those days, although the circumstances now were very different. Still, it was the same heady mixture of apprehension and excitement, of fear and camaraderie. Suddenly, he felt a strong kinship with each and every one of the Consoler's guerrillas. It was the bond that came from knowing they were about to fight together, and possibly die together, and that they would have to rely on each other implicitly. It occurred to him that, terrible though the Mutant War had been, he had never made better friends than on the blood-soaked fields of Earth.

Only, back then, *he* hadn't been the one sending those friends to their deaths.

He felt a new respect for the mutant generals who had had to make such decisions on a daily basis: brave leaders like Clacton Fuzz, the Ooze, the Torso from Newcastle and Middenface McNulty.

He found Middenface in his element surrounded by admiring Salvationists as they begged him to recount details of his exploits and impart a few last-minute pointers in the art of dishing out laldy. It hit Johnny once again that many of the eager audience were norms, but norms who knew what it was like to be persecuted.

"Ah still wish ah wa' comin' tae the camp wi' ye, Johnny," said the big guy when the pair had a moment to themselves at last. "I'da liked a few minutes alone wi' those guards who took pot shots at us."

"I know," said Johnny. "But your mission is just as important, if not more so."

"Whit, because it keeps the Consoler sweet? Ye don't really think he can git through tae that scunner brother o' his, dae ye?"

Johnny shook his head. "Not for a minute. But if he can draw Kit out into the open and distract him…"

Middenface grinned and smacked his right fist into his

left palm. He understood.

"Take Kit out and this war's over before it begins," said Johnny. "Not to mention the other seven hundred thousand reasons."

A heavy footstep alerted him to the presence of somebody behind him. He turned to face the Consoler and was briefly worried. How long had he been there? Had he heard what Johnny and Middenface had said? No, he reassured himself, the Consoler's many mutations had made his gait slow and laboured. There was no way he could have snuck up on them.

"Elephant Head informs me that everybody is ready," said the Salvationists' leader. "It is time."

Johnny nodded. "We are doing the right thing, you know," he said.

"I think that may be true," the Consoler conceded, "albeit for the wrong reasons. You are a cleverer man than I gave you credit for, Mr Alpha. I think you will get your man, whatever the cost. I just hope you are proud of yourself."

CHAPTER FOURTEEN
LIBERATION

The convoy was two and a half hours late already.

This didn't seriously affect Johnny's strategy, but it was making his soldiers anxious. War, in his experience, was all about waiting; long periods of boredom punctuated by brief bursts of frenetic activity. Seasoned fighting men and women knew how to deal with this, but Johnny's soldiers weren't seasoned. No more than twenty of them had any kind of military experience, and only half of those had seen action. They had trained the others as best they could, but for all the pressure he had put on the Consoler to act, in his heart Johnny wasn't sure they were ready.

The rush of adrenaline that they had all felt upon taking their positions in the mountain foothills had passed, and many of them were getting the jitters. Johnny had already disciplined three men for straying from their posts. He didn't like coming down hard on them, but it was crucial that they remained hidden until it was time to strike.

He gazed down at the route the convoy would take, and at the ravine where the ambush was to take place, checking one more time that everything was in place.

"Excuse me, Mr Alpha, sir." It was Fingers, one of the mutants from the hunting party he and Middenface had followed to the Salvationist base camp. "The signal's just come through."

He handed Johnny a telescope and he focused on a promontory about a kilometre away. Johnny saw small clouds of smoke rising from it. It was the signal that the convoy had been sighted. Moosehead might have been robbed of his good looks, thought Johnny, but he had lost none of his skills as a scout. He was only sorry that his old friend wouldn't be beside him in the first skirmish.

Johnny nodded to a norm who was standing by with a bow. The archer lit his arrow and fired it into the valley below. At this signal, a small group emerged from hiding, clutching bottles and jars. Almost simultaneously, the convoy of four trucks chugged and wheezed into view, blowing out foul-smelling smoke from their exhausts. The information the Salvationist network had picked up was correct: the government was stepping up the numbers they were sending to the camp.

The Salvationists ran towards the trucks and threw the bottles and jars at the ground in front of them. The first two trucks rolled onto the broken glass and the rubber coverings on their wheels burst. Caught by surprise, the drivers couldn't stop their vehicles from swerving and juddering to a halt. Armed guards jumped out of both trucks into a volley of arrows from a hidden group of Salvationist archers. Most of them fell without ever knowing what hit them.

Two more groups of Salvationist volunteers charged down on the trucks and swiftly overpowered the drivers and the few remaining guards. Johnny swore and cursed them for their incompetence. They had forgotten the plan and moved too soon.

The third truck had been stopped by the broken glass, but the driver of the fourth had had time to see what was happening. He pulled out to avoid the Salvationist volunteers and drove around them, accelerating as he approached the end of the ravine. Johnny broke from his position and ran down to intercept him.

"Aim for the wheels, shoot at the wheels!" he shouted at the hidden archers. They obeyed, but most of their arrows missed their targets by a long shot. Some thudded into the main body of the truck, and some even struck the prisoners inside.

Three arrows struck true, however, causing the rubber around one wheel to burst apart. The truck skidded badly, spinning around and around as the driver lost control.

Johnny raced towards it, commanding a group of volunteers to follow him. As the truck came to a halt, he tore one of the doors open and leapt inside. One guard sat beside the driver – a mutant with a long, thin nose – but he was shaken from the skid. Before he had a chance to reach for his weapon, Johnny brought the heel of his hand up hard against his nose, breaking it and forcing the shattered shards of bone up into his brain. The guard was killed instantly.

The Salvationists dragged the other stunned guards off the truck and overpowered them. Hyped up with the frenzy of the struggle, they made short work of their enemies, using their own weapons against them.

"Don't kill me, please don't kill me," pleaded the driver as Johnny grabbed him by the throat and dragged him out of the truck. "I've got three kids and this is the only job I could get. They were going to deport me."

"I'm not going to kill you just yet," said Johnny. "Do exactly as you're told and I might not have to kill you at all."

Meanwhile, the volunteers had opened the backs of the trucks and the prisoners emerged blinking into the bright sunlight. When they had all been freed from their shackles, Johnny gathered them together and addressed them.

"You are no longer prisoners of the Miltonian government," he said. "You will not be locked up in an internment camp. Soon, no one will be held in that camp again. We are on our way to liberate it. We have spare weapons; you are welcome to join the fight. If you do, you must obey all commands that are given to you. If you don't, we will not think any less of you. There are men and women standing by to lead you back to safety, a day's hike from here."

Twice as many of the freed prisoners stayed than Johnny had anticipated. There weren't enough weapons for all of them so they had to improvise. Not for the first or last time that day, he felt apprehensive about the level of casualties in the coming conflict.

The volunteers went to work patching up the rubber wheel coverings. They stripped the dead guards, fixed up the holes in their uniforms, and scrubbed off as much blood as they could. The most mutated volunteers donned the guards' uniforms, while the others piled into the backs of the trucks.

As Johnny climbed into the front of the lead truck, dressed as a guard, Youngblood bounded up to him. "Johnny," he said. "I would really consider it an honour to ride with you."

Johnny looked him over. He was wearing the uniform of a three-armed guard with its dead owner's extra arm still inside the jacket. Youngblood had cauterised the stump and strapped it to himself. It was gruesome, but effective, and they needed someone up front who looked heavily mutated. He nodded and Youngblood hopped in beside him eagerly.

Johnny turned to the driver and pressed the tip of a large hunting knife up against the mutant's chest. "Now, it's up to you to make this work," he said. "I want this to go as smoothly as any normal delivery. If you give the guards at the gate any hint that something is wrong, if you even smell like you're going to cross me, I will kill you where you sit. Do you understand me?" The driver swallowed hard and nodded, then turned the key in the ignition and started up the truck.

"I never thought I'd be glad to go back to that place," said Youngblood, "but I couldn't be prouder to be fighting alongside you. I owe you my life."

"Yeah, well, that life of yours cost me quite a bit to save," said Johnny. "You make sure you hang on to it, you hear?"

"Yes, sir," said Youngblood.

The first truck pulled up at the gates of the camp with the others behind it. The head guard sauntered over and banged on the window and the driver slowly wound it down.

"We expected you over four hours ago," said the guard.

"Yeah, well... We, er, ran into a bit of trouble."

"What kinda trouble? Terrorists?"

"No," said the driver quickly. The sharp point of Johnny's knife pressed harder between his ribs. "Hit some loose rocks on the way. Had a few blowouts. Took us a while to repair them. We didn't have enough spares. You know how it is."

The guard nodded, satisfied with the story. "I gotta ask," he said. "They've been on my ass about stepping up security ever since the escape."

He signalled for the gates to be opened and waved the trucks through. The first two carried on around to the second gate in the inner fence, which was on the far side of the compound. The remaining two turned in the opposite direction towards the guard's quarters. From their surveillance of the camp, the Salvationists knew the guards worked in strict shifts. At any one time, a third of them would be asleep inside the barracks. Johnny had figured that if they could take out these men before they woke, they could drastically reduce the camp's defences with hardly a struggle.

"Hey," one of the gate guards called out after the last two trucks. "Hey, where do you think you're going? That's the wrong way!"

Salvationists leaped out of the backs of both trucks and jumped the gate guards. Surprised by the attack, two of them went down without much trouble, but the other four put up a spirited defence. Two Salvationists were wounded, and one guard broke free, racing towards the barracks and screaming to raise the alarm. An arrow flew from one of the trucks and hit him in the throat. He fell to his knees in a geyser of blood but not before his cries for help had been heard.

Johnny cursed again. Fortune was not favouring them so far. They were losing the element of surprise. Leaning out of the window of his truck, he yelled, "Plan C. Go to Plan C!"

Trucks three and four slowed down just enough for the volunteers in their backs to leap out. Led by Elephant Head, they stormed the barracks, but the guards in the closest machine gun tower opened fire. Bullets sprayed the crowd, cutting several of them down. The trucks, in the meantime, had sped up again, driving at the towers themselves. The first struck its target dead centre and the whole structure crumpled with the force of the impact. The two guards fell from the top, but a stray bullet from the machine gun hit the truck's petrol tank.

Johnny winced as the vehicle went up in a raging ball of flame along with the three volunteers who had still been in its driver's cab. He turned swiftly to watch as truck four struck the second tower. As it smacked into its base, two volunteers were thrown through the shattered windscreen. This tower didn't fall, but it was damaged. It listed to one side and one guard fell, but the other kept his position and tried to fire the machine gun. It jammed.

A third volunteer – a giant of a man whose only mutation was his increased size – emerged from the truck and climbed the broken structure. He overcame the terrified guard easily by lifting him above his head and hurling him to the ground.

Shots rang out in the barracks and two guards came running out of its doors. They were dropped by rifle fire from behind them. Johnny took this as a good sign. Elephant Head's team must have found the barracks' small artillery before their enemies could.

A bullet flew by his ear and several more found his windscreen, shattering it. The mutant driver hit the floor and Johnny grabbed the wheel. The truck was accelerating towards the second gate. Six guards with rifles stood in its path, shooting wildly.

Johnny put his foot down hard and the guards scattered. He crashed into the gate. The bonnet of the truck crumpled and the front axle snapped, but the gate buckled and was torn off its hinges. Johnny pulled on the handbrake and the truck skidded to a halt. He jumped out as the second truck pulled up beside him.

The camp exploded into pandemonium. The guards had no means of communication so they couldn't receive orders. They reacted slowly to the attack, unused to acting on their own initiative. This played well into Johnny's hands, but the actions of the prisoners didn't. Many of them were panicked and ran for whatever cover they could find. A whole gang of them raced for the gate where two guards opened fire on them. With all this activity, it was difficult for Johnny and the Salvationists to get a clear shot at anyone.

Johnny drew his knife and shouted out orders. "We'll take the guards in close combat. Formation threes, just like we discussed." The tactic was simple and Johnny had been pleased to learn that the Salvationists were familiar with it. Three of them would attack one guard at a time; two drawing his attention while the third went in for a close-contact attack with a knife or other short-range weapon.

Flanked by Youngblood and Fingers, Johnny headed for a rifle-wielding guard. When he was in range he drew his knife and threw it, aiming for where he estimated the man's heart ought to be. Unfortunately, due to the guard's mutant physiology, he missed his mark. The guard's left arm dropped to his side and hung limp as he tried to raise his weapon to return fire. Youngblood kicked the rifle from his hand and Fingers sucker-punched him. With the guard's focus torn between the pair, Johnny went in hard, grabbed the handle of his knife, twisted it and tore it free, causing maximum damage in the process.

The guard grabbed Johnny's throat with his right hand, trying to crush his windpipe. Youngblood punched him in the kidneys and, while he was reacting to the pain, Johnny drove his knife into the guard's bicep. He relinquished his hold and Johnny sliced through his jugular vein.

He grabbed the dying guard's rifle and climbed up onto the corrugated iron roof of the ramshackle structure where the prisoners were fed slops. From here he would be able to pick off the other guards as a sniper. His first few shots, however, drew the attention of two more guards with rifles. His disguise had confused them for a while, but soon the game was up and he had made himself a target. The guards leapt out of his sight beneath the roof he was standing on and started firing up at him. Their bullets shot through the flimsy metal and one nicked his shoulder. Johnny winced at the sharp pain and rolled off the side of the roof, landing heavily on the ground.

As he climbed to his feet, a rifle butt smashed into the back of his head. The force of the blow sent bright lights ricocheting around the inside of his skull. His eyes lost their focus and he dropped to his knees, stunned.

He expected the next blow to kill him, but it never came. Instead, as his eyesight returned and his head cleared, he heard a piercing shriek of pain. He stood up slowly and turned to see one of his attackers lying face-down with a knife in his back. Youngblood had another guard on his back and was choking the life out of him with a rifle barrel.

And right behind Youngblood, a three-eyed guard was aiming a crossbow.

Johnny barely had time to yell a warning. Youngblood sprang to his feet, spun around, and took three bolts to the chest. Pure, blind rage exploded inside Johnny and he flew at the guard with his knife drawn. The guard had no chance to reload before he was knocked to the ground. Johnny sat astride him, pinning his arms with his knees, and drove his blade into the base of the guard's throat just above the collarbone. He struck again and again, blood welling between his fingers.

It was only when his battle frenzy subsided that he remembered Youngblood and rushed back over to him. The young mutant was still breathing, but he was awash with sticky, green blood that stung to the touch. Oblivious to the pitched battle around him, Johnny carried him beneath the shelter of the cast-iron roof and propped him up against a trough.

"It's not as bad as it looks," lied Youngblood. "I don't think he hit anything vital. It hurts when I breathe, though."

"Hang on in there," Johnny ordered. "Don't you dare die on me now. Just because you've repaid me for saving your foolish life doesn't mean I'm going to let you die on me. I'll be back with help as soon as I can."

"Okay," said Youngblood with a brave smile.

Johnny surveyed the progress of the battle so far.

The barracks had been taken. Those guards who had survived the attack had either joined their comrades in the inner compound or fled the camp altogether.

The guards in the compound had been in retreat, but now they regrouped, using the prisoners as human shields. The inmates were gathered around the guards in a circle of at least five deep. They were dead scared. Months of ill-treatment and torture meant that many of them were still in thrall to the guards, but as Johnny watched, a few at the outskirts of the group found their courage and made a break for it.

To his alarm, a pair of crackling blue bolts shot out from behind them, passing through the crowd without harming anyone but exploding as soon as they found the would-be escapees. Johnny swore.

"They're using controlled detonation blasters," he said to Fingers who had just appeared at his shoulder. "How in hell did they manage to get them to work out here?"

"Listen up!" called one of the guards from the centre of the human shield. "I want you all to drop your weapons and surrender. If you don't, we'll kill all these prisoners and you along with them."

"Hold your ground," Johnny ordered. "We've got them outmanned and outgunned."

A protracted volley of blaster bolts shot through the prisoners, hitting more than twenty Salvationists and tearing them apart.

"That's just for starters," the guard shouted. "I won't tell you again. Now lay down your weapons!"

"What are we going to do?" cried Fingers, an edge of panic to his voice. "They've got us over a barrel. We can't get to them through that crowd and we daren't fire on them for fear of hitting innocent people. In the meantime, they're just picking us off."

"Listen to me," said Johnny, addressing the hostage prisoners directly. "Your liberty is now in your own hands. By my guess you outnumber the guards behind you by at least six to one. It doesn't matter how well-armed they are, you can still bring them down by sheer weight of numbers."

A blaster bolt shot through the crowd directly at him and Johnny hit the ground as it exploded over his head in a burst of fierce heat.

"I don't die that easily," he boasted. "As you can see, their weapons aren't infallible. What do you think will happen if our attempts to liberate you fail? If you thought you had it bad before, think how bad it's going to get. Is that any kind of life to cling to? Would you rather live on your knees, or fight on your feet?"

Another volley of blaster bolts shot out, but most of them misfired or crackled off into the sky without hitting anything. A scuffle was obviously going on at the centre of the crowd. More and more of the inmates turned inwards to engulf the guards, months and years of resentment at their mistreatment ignited by Johnny's words. Their fear turned to righteous fury, but more than that, they were motivated by hope; hope that the Salvationists had suddenly brought them.

The battle was over.

The remaining guards dotted about the camp surrendered without firing another shot. The inmates could hardly believe they were free. Many of them wept openly, giving vent to the grief that they had kept locked up inside them for so long.

Johnny despatched several parties to hunt down and capture or kill the guards who had fled. He didn't want word of the camp's liberation getting back to General Rising and Kit until it had to. Then he went to check on Youngblood.

The barracks had been turned into a makeshift infirmary where the camp's one physician was attending the wounds of the injured Salvationists at gunpoint.

"Is this really necessary?" he asked Johnny, indicating the blaster that was levelled at his head. "I was practically a prisoner here myself and I'm just as glad to be freed." The man was nearly a norm. The only thing that distinguished him was the extra hand that sprouted from the end of each of his arms. Johnny nodded to the volunteer who was covering him and she stood down.

Johnny went to Youngblood's bedside with the physician. "How is he doing?" he asked the doctor.

"Not too good. I'm afraid some cadaveric tissue got into the wounds and poisoned his blood. He doesn't have long."

Youngblood motioned for Johnny to come closer and Johnny bent down to talk to him. "This wretched blood of mine, hey Johnny?" Youngblood whispered. "I knew it would be the death of me one day. I let you down, I'm afraid. I couldn't hang on to this life that you saved for me."

"No," said Johnny. "No, you didn't let me down at all."

"All the same," Youngblood continued, "the short life I have lived, since you rescued me, has been fuller and more fulfilling than anything I've ever known. Whatever it cost, it was worth twice the price we paid for it."

Youngblood even managed a faint smile before his eyes rolled up into his head and he was pronounced dead.

Johnny closed the young mutant's eyelids and walked outside. He looked at the corpses of all the mutants strewn about the camp: mutants he had helped norms to kill. He thought about how much this war had cost him so far. He knew it had hardly even begun.

CHAPTER FIFTEEN
DOUBLE BLUFF

"You are surrounded. Dismount from the animal and lie face down on the ground with your hands above your head!"

Middenface took a good look around him, careful to turn his head slowly and not to make any sudden moves. The soldier was telling the truth, but he had already known that. He counted a dozen more emerging from the rocks around him. A dozen blasters were trained upon him and he only had his knife and club. He had walked into a trap. He would be dead before he could take out more than four of them.

Everything was going according to plan.

After Johnny's group had left for the internment camp, Middenface had waited in the nearly deserted volcano base for an hour, staying out of the Consoler's way. He would have more than enough of his company to look forward to.

At the agreed time, the pair had climbed the ladder and squeezed down the passageway to the camp entrance. Middenface had walked a short way ahead, alert for any sign of threat. Since every other able-bodied Salvationist had gone off to fight, it was up to Middenface to make sure that the Consoler was protected. Their camp and their leader had never been so vulnerable.

He had also hoped that, by putting some distance between him and his companion, he could discourage conversation. No such luck. The Consoler had been in a contemplative mood and had insisted on grilling Middenface about his past on Earth of all things. Then, faced with a truculent silence, the Consoler had begun to guess the answers for himself, and came uncomfortably close to the truth.

"I know what it's like to be brought up in an atmosphere of violence," he said. "I know what it does to you. It programmes you to believe there is no other way. It erodes your ability to reason beyond the most immediate links of cause and effect."

At first, Middenface had thought he was being insulted, but it was worse than that. He was being pitied. And not for the endless struggle that had been his childhood on the rough streets of Glasgow, but for what that life had made of him. It was too much.

"Listen, pal," he growled, rounding on his tormentor, "ye can say whit ye like aboot me, but ye insult ma upbringing, and ye're insultin' ma dear auld granny. And anyone who insults ma granny gits tae pass his teeth through his bladder, dae ye see whit I'm saying?"

The Consoler saw.

Middenface had forgotten about the animals Elephant Head had mentioned. Certainly, he had seen none around the camp, but the Consoler had led him to a concealed cave a short distance away which had been kitted out as a makeshift stable. Straw was strewn about its floor, tethering posts hammered into the stone. The six beasts inside had seemed too frail to bear his weight, let alone the Consoler's too, but they were stronger than they looked – and faster.

They had been christened heffalopes, and were indigenous to Miltonia. They were lean and wiry with hungry looks on their doglike faces and two pairs of double-jointed legs. The heffalopes were easily domesticated,

but the Consoler had warned Middenface to hold tight to
him all the same. He soon found out why. One prod and
their mount had shot out of the cave opening like a bullet. It was incredibly agile and surefooted on the
treacherous rocks, bounding between plateaus with a
zigzag motion that made Middenface's stomach lurch. At
one point, to his horror, the heffalope had leapt over a
cliff edge. Somehow, it had found a safe way down, ricocheting between a series of footholds that were almost
invisible to Middenface.

The Consoler sat in front of him, holding the reins.
He'd been jabbering about something but with the wind
in his ears Middenface hadn't heard a word. For that reason as much as any, he'd decided he liked this method of
transport, and once he was used to predicting the heffalope's erratic motions and shifting his weight to counter
them, he had been able to relax and enjoy it.

An hour passed before he knew it. The Consoler
brought the heffalope to a sudden but graceful halt and
announced that it was time to switch places. Middenface
had been apprehensive at first, but the creature reacted
quite decently to his amateur tuggings.

Once he'd got used to controlling it, Middenface began
to concentrate on the next step of the plan: to knock out
his co-traveller.

They had used a preparation provided by Moosehead
from the same plant that had almost killed Middenface.
For a minute or more, Middenface had been certain that
it did not work. Then the Consoler's many eyelids had
drooped and he'd slipped into a deep sleep. Middenface
lashed him to the back of the heffalope with a rope. He
kept their speed down to a trot after that, but he hadn't
had too far to go in any case.

They had been following a course described to Middenface and Johnny in the air cruiser on their way into

the mountains. Rising's lieutenant had been circumspect about what lay at its end, but Johnny had guessed that there was a military base out here somewhere. Sure enough, Middenface's keen eyes soon found a concealed camera. He figured he was at the edge of the mountains now, and outside the magnetinium field. His every instinct had urged caution, but to make this work, he had to act as if he had no reason to distrust the government's mutant militia. He flashed a cheery grin at the lens and trotted on.

The soldiers had appeared less than three minutes later.

"Steady on, fellas," Middenface said as he struggled to climb off the heffalope's back while keeping his hands in sight. For his trouble, he caught his foot in a stirrup and almost fell flat on his face.

"Ah'm a frien'. Name's Middenface McNulty. Ye call the palace and ask General Rising aboot me." He nodded toward the unconscious and bound form of the Consoler. "Ah've fetched him a prisoner."

Middenface's return to the palace was in very different circumstances to his first visit. He arrived incognito in the back of an army transport, and was all but smuggled in through a side entrance while two mutant soldiers carried the Consoler between them. There was no talk of taking weapons from him, but then again, what use were his knife and club when everyone else had blasters?

He was met by Rising, who was flanked by two guards. The general led Middenface to a large service elevator which creaked and whined its way down to the second sublevel. Here, they were greeted by stale air, reinforced walls and sterile lighting panels that buzzed quietly. Middenface filled the silence with an account of his great victory over his prisoner. He concentrated on the fun parts, almost getting carried away as he explained how he had punched the Consoler repeatedly in the face. He sighed sadly at the fact that none of it was true. Fortunately, the target of his imaginary violence was so mutated that nobody could tell if he was bruised or not.

The Consoler began to come round as he was manhandled into a tiny, dark cell. Without waiting for him to struggle, his bearers dashed him to the ground and kicked him into submission before closing the heavy door on him.

"Was tha' necessary?" protested Middenface, realising his mistake as half of Rising's eyes narrowed in suspicion. "Ah mean," he added quickly, "ye said the poor guy'd been brainwashed by them Salvationist scunners, it's no' his fault he wa' helpin' them."

"Nevertheless," said Rising, "he is an enemy of the state. We can't afford to take chances with him. Now, if you would follow me, please."

Rising led Middenface to a small room a short distance away. It was furnished with a table and two chairs, and reminded him uncomfortably of the interrogation room at the spaceport. Johnny had warned him to expect something like this.

Rising dismissed the two soldiers, but his own guards took up positions inside the room, flanking the door. He motioned to Middenface to take one of the seats and lowered himself into the other.

"I do apologise for this," he said with a smile, still faking congeniality. "I know you must be tired and hungry, but there are one or two matters we must clear up." Warily, Middenface nodded his assent.

"May I ask what happened to your partner?" Rising asked first.

"Och, Johnny Alpha!" Middenface spat with feigned distaste. "Always too fond of the chatter, that one was. The Consoler here, he brainwashed him too. Kept tellin' him how his group were the injured party, can ye credit it? Ye ask me, it's a bit rich fer any norms tae be complainin' o' persecution after all they've done tae oor kind."

Rising was keeping his expression carefully blank, but Middenface detected a flicker of approval there.

"Ah said tae Johnny," he continued, "Ah said, 'This ain't oor business, let's just dae what we came here fer an' collect oor bounty,' but he wouldnae have it. So, I saw ma chance, an' I bagged the Consoler fer myself and scarpered."

As Rising mulled over his story, Middenface sat back, proud to have got the words out in the right order. Even as the eight-eyed soldier opened his mouth to speak, though, Middenface started and blurted out: "Och, ah fergot tae say, ah reckon it's 'cos Johnny ain't so mutated as us, 'cos he can pass for a norm sometimes, that he fits in better wi' that Salvationist lot."

Johnny had told him to say that. He said it would help. Middenface was glad he had remembered in time.

A look of bemusement crossed Rising's face but it passed as his eyes hardened. "There's something I'd like you to explain to me. Yesterday morning, two mutants attacked a resettlement camp in the mountains and broke out three illegals. We have no pictures, of course, but the descriptions given by the guards are uncomfortably familiar."

Middenface nodded. Johnny had prepped him for this question too. "That wa' Johnny's idea," he said, playing nervously with his hands. "We found yer camp while oot lookin' for the Salvationist base, an' Johnny pointed out that some o' the people in there, being treated so bad like, they were mutants."

"Lesser mutants," interjected Rising sharply.

"Aye, well, ah didnae twig that till later on. Johnny said that maybe this had somethin' tae dae with Identi Kit, an' we should break out a couple of these, um, lesser muties, fer questioning like."

"And you just went along with him?"

"Aye, that's right." Middenface nodded eagerly. If Rising was going to prompt him, then this would be easy.

"And what about Identi Kit? Did you find him?"

"Oh, we found him all right. He was with the Salvationists, like ye said he would be. Running aboot in his own body like he thought he were untouchable. He came oot wi' some cock-and-bull story aboot not being who we thought he was." Middenface stared into Rising's centremost eyes as if daring him to react to that, but the general revealed nothing. "Then he tried tae run so ah shot him," he concluded bluntly.

Rising raised all eight of his eyebrows. "Shot him?"

"Wi' an arrow," said Middenface, realising the flaw in his story. "Johnny took the head so we'd have proof to tak' back tae the Doghouse. Ah just hope he comes tae his senses soon. Ah wouldnae wanna have tae go after him tae git that head back, y'ken what I'm saying? An' speaking of collectin'..."

Rising nodded. "You've done us a great service by rescuing the Consoler. The whole of Miltonia is grateful to you."

"Aye, well, ye can git that Nose Job guy doon here tae show me *how* grateful," Middenface said eagerly. "Fifty thousand, we agreed."

"Mr Johnson is in conference with the president at the moment," said Rising. Middenface scowled his disappointment. "He knows you're here and he'll be with you as soon as possible. In the meantime, there are a few more things I need to know from you. The location of the Salvationists' base, for example."

"After ah get ma fifty thou," said Middenface firmly, "and ma hardware back, and ye'd better no' have been mistreatin' it or there'll be some laldy dished out."

"Patience, Mr McNulty. I'm sure you know the president well enough to trust that he will honour his debt." Middenface bit back a retort and forced a smile. "As for your equipment, it is safe in our stores and will be returned to you shortly."

Rising pushed back his chair and stood. "While you're waiting, I thought you might care to sit in on my interrogation of the Consoler. I'm sure you'll be interested to hear everything he has to say for himself."

Middenface groaned inwardly.

The next hour was one of the longest of his life. His one consolation was that the Consoler's unflappable loquaciousness was, if anything, even more exasperating to Rising than it had been to him. And the more exasperated the general became, the calmer the Salvationists' leader appeared to be in contrast.

"I have already explained," he said with infinite patience, "that I believe in non-violent protest. I have certainly not sanctioned any acts of terrorism, and if any such acts were carried out by my people, then I am deeply sorry."

"If?" roared Rising. "Is that what those criminals told you? That they were squeaky clean, that this is all a conspiracy?"

"I have also explained that I am not an unwitting dupe as you believe. It was I who formed our organisation."

"And you expect me to believe that you spend your time sitting around your campsite writing protest songs and painting up banners?"

For the first time, the Consoler looked uncomfortable. He squirmed in his seat, unable to hold his interrogator's stare. Sensing that he was onto something, Rising leaned closer to him, his nose wrinkling into a snarl.

"You're planning something, aren't you? What is it? Some contingency for if you were captured? What did those little fanatics say they'd do, storm the presidential palace?" The general laughed at the absurdity of his own suggestion, and then his face hardened again. "I think you should face it, Consoler, you're on your own. The Salvationists don't care about you. They were using you! It's just you and me now, and I can promise you things will go a lot easier for you if you tell me what I want to know."

He barked out the questions again; the questions he had asked a dozen times already. How many Salvationists were there? What weapons did they have? Where did they intend to strike next? Did they have friends in the government? And, over and over again, where were they hiding out?

Sandwiched between the general's guards, Middenface shifted from foot to foot. For now, Rising seemed determined to crack the Consoler almost for the sake of the victory. Ultimately, though, he would have to accept defeat, and then he would turn to his other source of information: his supposed ally.

It wasn't supposed to be like this. Kit, in his Nose Job guise, was meant to have been here by now, lured by his brother's presence. What was keeping him? Could he suspect a trap? The attack on the immigration camp would have begun long ago. Only the magnetinium field, with its ability to block radio communication, was keeping word of it from Rising. He wouldn't remain ignorant of events forever, though. How would he react when he found out? Would he put two and two together and throw Middenface into a cell with his other prisoner?

"Unfortunately for you, general," said the Consoler, "I am not concerned with making things easy for myself. My only wish is to live in a fair and equal society."

"Look at you," said Rising contemptuously. "Do you really think any norm could see you as an equal? You're

ugly, misshapen – a freak! They don't deserve your loy-
alty. They're laughing at you behind your back!"

"I don't believe that is true."

"They aren't like us. Norms stick together and that is
what we have to do if we are to resist them. Do you want
Miltonia to become like every other world? Is that what
you want, to sell your own kind back into slavery?"

"You speak of norms and mutants," said the Consoler.
"I believe the distinction is irrelevant."

"Irrelevant?" Rising howled. "Perhaps you've never
been to another world, Consoler. Perhaps you've never
applied for a job as a mutant, or asked for a meal in a
norm café, or tried to book a seat on a transport ship.
Perhaps you've never been spat at in the street. Your
mutancy may be 'irrelevant' to you, but believe me it is
very relevant to our enemies, the people who begrudge
us our contentment here!"

"I have seen my share of prejudice, I assure you. That
is why it matters to me that Miltonia should be different,
better."

Rising lowered his voice, his tone heavy with threat.
"I'm trying to reason with you here. I know no true
mutant would talk like this if he were thinking clearly. I
know the tactics those scum probably used on you.
They'll have starved you, beaten you, torn down your
self-esteem, turned you around until you don't know
which way is up. Well, believe me, Consoler, we have
men who know those tactics, too, only I'm trying to spare
you that. Give me something, some indication that
there's still a good man, a loyal mutant in there, and
things needn't get unpleasant. Tell me about the Salvationists!"

That was when Middenface realised something about
General Rising. He realised that whenever he spoke
about the norm threat, or about the Salvationists as terrorists, and about their supposed brainwashing of the

Consoler; when he spoke about all that, he actually believed it.

Another hour passed before Rising straightened, let out a tired sigh and rubbed three of his reddened eyes. He gestured to Middenface to follow him outside, but the S/D agent caught the look that passed between the general and his two guards as they left. He knew what that look meant.

The door closed, leaving him alone with Rising in the grey corridor. The sounds of muffled violence reached them a moment later. Rising shot Middenface a look as if daring him to protest. He said nothing. The Consoler had accepted this possibility when he had agreed to Johnny's plan. He had been so eager for a chance to meet his brother that he hadn't cared about the risk to himself. Middenface had enough to worry about himself now, with Kit nowhere to be seen and Rising's attention focused back upon him.

"His conditioning is stronger than I thought," said Rising. "It'll take us some time to break it. If we don't break him first." He smiled a humourless smile and continued. "Pity. His information would have been useful, but we can't afford to wait for it."

"Ye've got somethin' planned?" asked Middenface.

"Let's just say that in a few days from now, our men will have the weapons they need to end this war. And with all you must have learned about the enemy..."

Middenface swallowed. "Ah awready told yer," he stalled. "Cash first." A particularly nasty sounding thud from behind the door made him wince.

"May I remind you," snapped Rising, "that this is a matter of planetary security!"

Middenface folded his arms and squared up to him stubbornly. The general sighed again and marched up to a wall-mounted intercom. He asked to be patched through to Nose Job Johnson, and Middenface felt a small thrill of anticipation as the familiar voice of the president's advocate crackled from a tiny speaker.

"Yes, Rising?"

"I'm down by the detention rooms with our bounty hunter friend," said the general. "He's impatient for his money. Can you deal?"

There was a long pause on the other end of the line. Too long, thought Middenface.

"I'm tied up at the moment," Nose Job finally responded. "I'll send down somebody from admin." And he signed off with a harsh click.

So he *did* suspect. He was staying out of their way on purpose.

Middenface seethed with frustration. His first instinct was to fight his way up to Nose Job Johnson's office and wrap his hands around his scrawny neck, but he knew he'd never get there.

In the room behind him the beating continued. The Consoler, however, hadn't cried out once. Middenface could picture him enduring the punishment with his usual equanimity. He respected that, but he could also imagine how it would goad his torturers to greater efforts. He might be an aggravating son of a bitch, he thought, but he didn't deserve that. And Middenface needed somebody to punch. What the hell, he thought, and punched Rising.

The blow landed squarely in the middle of the general's face and its effect was startling. Rising's body went rigid, his eight eyes glassy, and he toppled backwards to land like a plank of wood. Middenface looked down at the unconscious soldier as he wrung his grazed knuckles, feeling a little satisfied that he'd been right about him all along. He was nothing but a desk monkey.

A brief search revealed that, to Middenface's chagrin, Rising was carrying no weapons. Still, the odds were only one against two and he had the element of surprise.

He shouldered open the door to the interrogation room and charged in with fists flying.

Middenface helped the Consoler up off the floor and back into his seat. The Salvationists' leader slumped over the table. "Thank you, my friend," he said hoarsely. "I'm not sure I could have taken much more of that treatment."

"Sorry I couldnae have been less violent aboot it," he said wryly, glancing at the bodies of the two guards.

The Consoler winced and then nodded, accepting his point. "Unfortunately, I'm afraid you have rather blown your cover here."

"Aye, I'd say I have at that. Can ye walk? If we're quick, we can git upstairs and oot that back door and awae in one of their own trucks before anyone knows whit's happened."

The Consoler shook his head. "You're right. You should go. But I'm staying here." In response to Middenface's questioning look, he explained. "My brother is in this building. I sensed it as soon as we arrived. I thought our psychic link had dissipated, but I was wrong. It feels stronger than ever." He seemed happy about that. "I can sense Kit's feelings, almost read his thoughts and, I'm afraid, he mine. Kit suspected that I didn't come here as a prisoner, that's why he stayed away. He's worried."

"He's got good reason tae be."

"I know you had your own motives for coming here with me," said the Consoler, "but I only ever wanted to talk to Kit and I believe that is still possible. Once you are out of the way, he will feel safe to come down here and see me."

"And ye're really sure ye want that? 'Cos twin brother or no, we're talkin' aboot a nasty piece of work, here. If you and Kit have got this cyclical link, then how come he didnae lift a finger tae help when his own people were laying into ye?"

"I know my words are unlikely to make a difference," said the Consoler with a sad sigh, "but I could not live with myself if I didn't try every method to win peace without bloodshed. Go, Mr McNulty. Return to your partner and the others, tell them what's happened, and do what you must. I will continue to do all I can for our cause, but in my own way."

Middenface felt he should argue, but he didn't have the Consoler's mastery of words. He was trying to think of something to say, opening and closing his mouth like a goldfish, when his companion suddenly flashed him a kind smile and said: "I wish I had known your grandmother. I'd have liked the chance to congratulate her on raising such a fine young man."

Middenface returned his smile awkwardly and realised that there was nothing more to be said. He turned instead and did as the Consoler had requested.

He ran.

CHAPTER SIXTEEN
ARMS RACE

A cheer went up in the camp.

Johnny was in one of the main buildings when he heard the noise. The building was usually used as a meeting hall, but it had been converted into headquarters for the War Council. He looked up from the schematic of the presidential palace that he had been studying.

"Any big celebrations planned?" he asked Elephant Head.

"None that I know of," she replied with a shrug.

One of their Salvationist guards burst into the room. "Middenface is back!" he announced with great excitement. Elephant Head fixed him with a stern look. The man looked apologetic, took a deep breath and said: "Sorry, Middenface is back, ma'am and, er... sir. Permission to join the others, ma'am?" Elephant Head exchanged looks with Johnny and then dismissed the guard. They followed him outside to investigate the commotion.

The whole camp was elated. Everyone was crowding into the centre, and there, right in the thick of things was Middenface, being carried on the shoulders of two norms and brandishing a bottle of Scotch in both hands.

"Johnny," he called out as he saw his partner, "have a drink on me!" He tossed him one of the bottles. "I liberated a crate o' them on my way back here."

Johnny handed the bottle to Elephant Head. "And now we're going to put every one of them under lock and key.

Most of these soldiers have training and manoeuvres for the rest of the day. This is not the time for recreation or celebration. We've just started a war and now we need to win it."

"Right enough," said Middenface. His mood quickly became sombre and he climbed down from the norms' shoulders. He picked up the pilfered crate of bottles and handed them to Elephant Head. "Here's a few more prisoners fer ye." Then he grinned and slapped Johnny on the shoulder. "So it's good tae have me back, aye?"

Johnny's mood softened and his usually austere expression cracked into a smile. "You don't know how good," he said.

"That's it, party's over!" Elephant Head told the assembled crowd. "You heard the man, it's time to get back to work."

The Salvationists began to disperse, but not without a number of groans and mutters of discontent. The rush of enthusiasm that had come with the decision to take action had now dissipated in the face of the hardships of a military campaign. In spite of their success so far, many of the volunteers were beginning to have misgivings about its cost. Most of them had lost friends or family members. Some were starting to suggest that they should have stayed on the Consoler's path of non-violent revolt, and others dared voice the opinion that terrorist tactics would have been more effective. Johnny knew he would have to maintain a firm hand if he was to keep everyone in line and on board with the programme.

Back inside headquarters, Johnny was keen to hear Middenface's story. Also in attendance were Elephant Head, Doubletalk, Walrus and Moosehead. Unfortunately, Middenface wasn't a great one for detail except for when it came to recounting his fights, and Johnny had to keep going over points again, pressing him for precise answers.

"Aye, but it felt good tae lay that scunner oot," Middenface was boasting. "Ye shouldae seen 'im go doon. One punch an' he was oot."

"Okay," said Johnny patiently, "but I need you to go over everything Rising said *before* you punched him. In detail."

"Och, my blood was boilin' an' ah was distracted by the beatin' the Consoler was takin'. Ah'm not sure ah can recall."

"Try!" Johnny said in a tone that left no room for protest.

"They were workin' 'im over pretty bad, though." Johnny could see that the others were distressed by this news. Walrus in particular had advised very strongly against the Consoler's return to the palace.

"But he said they couldn't wait for any intel the Consoler might have because..." Johnny prompted, steering his partner away from the violent part of the story.

"That's right, they had somethin' planned. Rising didnae say what, but he said his men would soon have the weapons they needed tae end this war. He kept pumpin' me fer the exact whereabouts of this place but I gave nothin' away."

"He must mean those special blasters we recovered from the camp," said Elephant Head. "You don't think they've found a way to mass-produce them, do you?"

"I don't know," said Johnny. "What's the name of that norm we have working on the blasters again? The one who's trying to backward engineer them?"

"That'll be Valerie," said Doubletalk, "and she isn't a norm. I understand she's made some progress and she wants to talk to you."

"Bring her in," said Johnny.

He recalled that Valerie was one of the prisoners they had liberated on their way to the internment camp. She had chosen to join the Salvationists and fought alongside

Elephant Head in the attack on the barracks. Elephant Head spoke very highly of her. It came to light later that she had been an engineer for Miltonia's top mining organisation until the political climate had changed and she been fired and ultimately interned for not being mutated enough.

Valerie was escorted into the room by two guards. She was carrying two of the blasters recovered from the internment camp, both semi-dismantled.

"So what have you discovered?" asked Johnny as she placed the blasters on the table in front of him.

"Quite a lot, actually," said Valerie. "I'm afraid it cost me two blasters to discover everything, but I think it's worth it."

"I'm not keen on losing any weapons at the moment, so convince me the information is more valuable," Johnny said sternly.

"I will," said Valerie. Johnny liked her attitude.

She opened up one blaster and pulled out a small metal case. "This is what protects the circuitry from the EMPs generated by the magnetinium field. It's a rare alloy that is both non-ferrous and electrically non-conductive."

"But surely it's far too small to hold all the necessary circuitry?" said Doubletalk.

"And what about the power pack?" barked Walrus.

Valerie continued, unfazed by the barrage of questions. She took an identical case from the second blaster which had its end sawn off. She extracted a thin tube with a green crystal pulsing in its centre. "This is specially designed liquid circuitry powered by an insulated dilithium crystal. It's extremely specialist stuff. It certainly wasn't made here on Miltonia, I can tell you that."

"How can you be so sure?" asked Johnny.

"Liquid circuitry is a specialised field," said Valerie. "It's as much an art form as it is a science. There aren't many organisations undertaking this work and each of them has its own special signature. This one comes from Earth. Plus this alloy isn't produced anywhere in this quadrant. I've worked at what passes for the cutting edge of technology here on Miltonia, and it's too new a planet to have the talent, the infrastructure, or the raw materials to construct this sort of thing. It had to be made offworld, and a custom job like this wouldn't have come cheap. No one has the money or the expertise to mass-produce these yet."

"Then the government must have commissioned a limited number of them," said Doubletalk, alarmed, "just for the purpose of crushing us."

"I would suggest that the weapons we seized from the camp were a prototype, to road test the design before they committed to having a whole batch made," said Valerie.

"Did Rising give you any idea of when his attack might take place?" Johnny asked Middenface.

"Aye, he said somethin' aboot 'a few days from now'. And it took me three days tae find ma way back through these sneckin' mountains tae ye!"

"Moosehead, your scouts have been watching the army base in the foothills. Have they seen any trucks or carrier ships come in?"

"No," said Moosehead, "but they've just been joined by a new battalion. At first we thought they were there to relieve the current soldiers, but no one has left and our agents inform us there's another battalion marching to join them from the south."

"That gives us some idea of the numbers we'll be facing and how many weapons they're bringing in," said Johnny. "How are they likely to deliver them?"

"For a cargo that size, it would have to be an air carrier," said Elephant Head. "It's the only thing the armed forces have that could handle the job. That means that if it's to avoid the magnetinium field, there's only one feasible route it could take from Clacton Fuzzville."

"But two *possible* ones," Moosehead corrected her. "My guess is they'll use the less obvious of the two. They'll assume Middenface has told us everything he knows, and that we'll have the direct route staked out. The alternative route is longer and more dangerous, but also more secluded. They've used it before when they needed to move troops and equipment in secret."

"How did you find out about it?" asked Walrus.

Moosehead grinned. "I just happen to stumble across these things now and again."

"We have to stop it," said Doubletalk. "But how?"

His words cast a pall of gloom over the room. No one dared say it, but they all knew there was no way they could hold off such a sizeable attack. Johnny knew he had to be decisive to keep spirits high.

"We'll attack them in the one place they're vulnerable!" he announced.

"Where's that, Johnny?" asked Middenface.

"Where they least expect it," he replied. "In the air!" He turned to Valerie who was waiting to be dismissed. "Do you think you could adapt the liquid circuitry from these blasters to rewire some fried jetpacks?"

"It could be done," she said, "but we'd have to be out of the range of the magnetinium field."

"That's all I need to know. Moosehead, you must have entered the mountains the same way we did, using a jetpack. Do you remember where you left yours?"

"In one of the hideaways I had in the mountains," said Moosehead. "I can take you there, it's not far."

"Good," said Johnny. "We'll need to take a detour to where we stashed ours as well. Elephant Head, you need to organise manpower and transport to meet us after we've done the job. Time is of the essence. We leave in two hours."

* * *

"I haven't had the time or the tools to finish this job properly," said Valerie. Surrounded by dismantled blasters, she was sitting on the floor of a cave in the foothills to the west of the mountains, fixing the last of the jetpack casings.

"I haven't the time to listen to excuses," said Johnny. Time was short since the trek to the hidden jetpacks took longer than anticipated. "Will they work?"

"More or less. I've rewired the controls so you can navigate, but I haven't totally recalibrated them so you won't be able to turn as sharply or as quickly as before. Please bear that in mind. I've also increased the flow of fuel to give you the extra power you need to reach higher altitudes. This also means that you'll burn fuel twice as quickly and, as none of these jetpacks has a full tank, you won't have much time in the air."

"We'll have enough for what I need to do," said Johnny.

He left her to make the final adjustments and walked outside the cave. Middenface and Moosehead were scoping the terrain. "Any sign of the air carrier?" he asked.

"It'll be along in twenty minutes or so," said Moosehead.

"How the sneck can ye tell that?" asked Middenface.

Moosehead pointed to the sky. "Shape of the clouds, quality of the air, movements and flight patterns of the birds. It all adds up."

The carrier pulled into view about twenty minutes later. Johnny nodded when he saw it, and then buckled on one of the rebuilt jetpacks and checked his detonation blaster. Moosehead had lost none of his touch.

The carrier was a large, flat ship built for transporting cargo and troops. It was flying at a low altitude just above the tops of the mountains. Johnny, Middenface and Moosehead fired up their jetpacks and flew towards it. Moosehead shot forward over the top of the carrier and headed towards its rear. Middenface pulled around to the side, and Johnny made for the pilot's deck at the front.

As the carrier approached him, Johnny could make out six guards and three pilots behind a sheet of plexiglass. He levelled his blaster, adjusted the range, and let off eight shots in rapid succession. The shots sailed through the glass and then detonated on deck. Five guards and one pilot fell before they'd even seen their attacker.

Through the portholes in the carrier's side, Middenface counted twelve guards inside the cargo hold. They were sitting around, supposedly guarding the precious crates that were stacked high around them, but in reality expecting no threat. Middenface targeted six, his first volley catching four of them completely off guard. He swore violently at having missed the other two who by sheer luck had happened to move just before the blaster fire detonated.

Before they could see him, he flew beneath the metallic underbelly of the carrier and came up on the other side. He readjusted his blaster and loosed off seven more shots, taking out five more guards. The remaining three took cover so Middenface couldn't get a bead on them. Still, he had done what he had planned to do: he had severely depleted the carrier's defences.

Moosehead hovered above the carrier's onboard engines. He counted six. He let off a shot at the furthest right engine. As he did so, the carrier hit an air pocket and jumped, causing his shot to go wide and explode out of range. Moosehead tried again, sending off three shots in frustration. The engine blew apart in a fierce burst of flames and thick black smoke.

The carrier started to bank steeply to the left. To level it out, Moosehead sent two shots into the furthest left engine. It exploded so violently that it came away from its fixtures and shot off into the sky, hurtling straight towards him.

Moosehead opened the throttle on his jetpack and sped off to the side. He was just in time to dodge the flaming engine but he had to use another thrust to catch up with the moving carrier again. He took out two more engines, causing the carrier to shake and veer to the right and lose height. As it did so, his jetpack began to make an extremely unhealthy spluttering sound. Moosehead checked the fuel gauge to find that it was practically empty.

He had only one option. He opened the throttle one last time and flew straight at the roof of the carrier. His jet-pack cut out and he rolled just in time to land on his back and let the spent pack take the force of the fall. The impact knocked the breath out of him and also caused an injury. With his left shoulder dislocated, he slid along the carrier's roof, forced backwards by the velocity at which it was travelling. He would be thrown off within seconds.

Moosehead unbuckled the jetpack and rolled to the right, managing to catch hold of the twisted fuselage of a wrecked engine mount. Fighting the forward motion of the carrier, he crawled into a crevice formed by the mount's support. He flattened himself against the blackened, hot metal – safe for the time being, but out of the fight. He only hoped that Johnny and Middenface could land this thing gently.

Middenface joined Johnny at the cargo hold door. The big lug gave him a thumbs-up sign to show that all was going according to plan.

There was no sign of Moosehead, but Johnny had seen the explosions from the engines so he knew that he had succeeded in undertaking his part of the job. There was no time to worry about anything else. They would just have to pray that their partner was all right and press on without him.

Johnny shot the lock off the door and he and Middenface tugged it open and flew inside. The decompression of the air inside the cargo hold yanked one guard right out. The other two guards could not be seen as Johnny and Middenface wedged the door shut and their jetpacks finally gave out.

"No way offa here now, hey Johnny?" said Middenface cheerfully.

"Only one," said Johnny, "and that's down."

They were checking the hold for the surviving guards when the door to the pilot's deck burst open and a giant of a man jumped Middenface. He must have been at least seven feet tall and was covered with hair. He looked for all the world like a gorilla in an ill-fitting uniform. The guard had Middenface in an armlock and he was clearly struggling.

"A little help here, Johnny," he cried out.

Johnny couldn't get a clear shot for fear of hitting his partner. He charged instead and brought the butt of his blaster down hard at the base of the guard's skull. The blow, which would have floored a normal man, hardly even fazed him. The guard swatted Johnny aside with the back of his left hand, sending him sprawling. But Johnny had provided enough of a distraction for Middenface to wriggle free.

Middenface hit the ground and kicked the guard's feet out from under him. The guard fell backwards and came down hard. Johnny took the opportunity to release three shots into the guard's chest, which erupted in a fountain of gore and charred ribs.

Middenface picked himself up and they entered the pilot's deck. The two surviving pilots were having serious problems with the controls.

"Now listen carefully," said Johnny, pointing his gun at the chief pilot's head. "There's a plateau coming up on your left. You've got less than two minutes to land this carrier there."

"I don't make deals with terrorists," the pilot said with contempt in his voice.

"You don't have any other choice," said Johnny. "You're rapidly losing altitude anyway. Do exactly as I tell you and you might just live."

"What makes you think I won't crash this bird for the hell of it?" asked the pilot.

"Because you're no hero," Johnny said menacingly, leaning in close to him.

The pilot swallowed hard and brought the carrier slowly down towards the plateau. "I'll do my best but you've not left the old bird in much of a shape," he complained.

They came in fast and low. Up until the last minute, Johnny didn't really fancy his chances of walking away from this one, and indeed, it was not a smooth landing. As they bumped along the floor of the plateau, he and Middenface were knocked off their feet. They could hear the high-pitched shriek of metal rending and tearing as the undercarriage was torn off. Then, finally, they ground to a halt.

Elephant Head was waiting for them with a contingent of Salvationists and a host of recently assembled wooden carts to take the weapons away. Johnny and Moosehead's earlier calculations of where the carrier would end up was spot on. The Salvationists swarmed onto the grounded carrier, rounded up the two surviving guards and began to unload crates. A shaken Moosehead called out from on top of the carrier and ropes were found to help him climb down.

Johnny was surveying the operation when one of the captured guards broke free of his escort and ran up to him. "Johnny. Hey, Johnny! Remember me? It's Scaly! We fought together at the Siege of Upminster. I had no idea you were in the militia, or even on Miltonia for that matter. You must have been on the pilot's deck when they hit. Stinking terrorists, they won't get away with this! They don't know who they're dealing with! They won't break you, will they, Johnny? Not you, you're..."

The scaly-skinned mutant's voice suddenly trailed away, and he looked as if the bottom had dropped out of his world.

"Oh sneck, Johnny, no. Tell me it ain't true. You're not *working* with these terrorist scum, are you? I heard a rumour that you'd become a stinking Strontie, but this is worse, much worse!" Scaly's captors had caught up to him by now, and he didn't resist as they took hold of him again. "How much are they paying you, Johnny?" he shouted as he was dragged away. "How much did they give you to turn on your own kind? Those men you killed today, they had homes and families, you know. Whatever you're getting out of this, I hope it's worth the lives of all the innocent mutants you've killed!"

Johnny turned away, unable to listen to any more. He felt the hand of a norm Salvationist on his shoulder and a comforting voice said: "Don't listen to him, Johnny. What you're doing now is for a far better cause than taking blood money for bounties."

"Take your stinking hands off me, norm!" he demanded, his voice thick with venom. The norm fell back, shaken by the force of the verbal attack.

Johnny strode off and threw himself into the task of getting the weapons loaded onto the carts. Anything to stop himself from having to think about Scaly said. Was all of this really worth it?

Suddenly, seven hundred thousand credits didn't seem so much after all.

CHAPTER SEVENTEEN
THE WHOLE KIT AND KABOODLE

He was coming.

The Consoler had known it for some time, long before he heard the *hum* of the lift, the squealing of its doors and the footsteps that now halted outside his cell. He had sensed his brother's conflict: his fear of confronting his past, a touch of shame at the anticipation of its judgement, and the stubbornness with which he had fought those emotions. Kit insisted to himself that he was in control. He tried to make himself feel powerful.

It had taken him two days to make up his mind, but when he'd done so at last, the Consoler had felt a wave of bliss wash over him. Kit, in turn, had sensed this and became paranoid again. But the Consoler had not doubted his eventual decision. He had known it even before Kit had been able to acknowledge it to himself.

He climbed to his feet as the door was cracked open, spilling a little cold light into his tiny, dark cube. There was a sickness in his stomach, a thrill up his spine, and he didn't know which sensations were his own and which his brother's. He could feel their lungs drawing breath in unison, their heartbeats syncopating, and he felt as if he had regained a part of himself.

Then he was there: a menacing silhouette with the light behind him and flanked by muscular guards. The brothers faced each other for the first time in over ten years. It was the moment that the Consoler had dreamed of and rehearsed over and over again, only this time he had forgotten all his carefully chosen words. For one of the few times in his life, he didn't know what to say. And he knew that Kit felt the same so they just stared at each other, adjusting to each other's new physical forms.

Kit's current shape meant little to the Consoler, of course. Nose Job Johnson was just a man he had seen a few times on the holo-news, with a sprawling, mutated nose and a smart suit. But that body was no more than a shell and the Consoler could see through it. He saw a pale, frightened child huddled in the corner of a one-room shack in a Thulium ghetto, with tears in his eyes and a bruise on his cheek.

And he reached out to him.

"Who did this to you, Kit? Was it the Rockets again?"

Kit shrugged away the proffered hand and buried his face. He didn't want to talk but as usual his brother wouldn't shut up. He could feel Kaboodle's presence inside him, in his head and heart, comforting and cajoling him. He tried to resist it but it was like denying a part of himself.

He raised his head to face his own mirror image. "I tried to do what mom said," he blurted out. "I tried to stay away from them, honest I did."

Kaboodle nodded and squatted beside him. "I know. It isn't always that easy. Once they've singled you out, they'll find you. It's not your fault."

"Then why do they keep on picking on me?" he wailed.

"They're norms," said Kaboodle. "It's their problem, not yours. They're afraid of anything different."

He always knew what to say. Kaboodle was only eleven, like Kit himself, but he was older than Kit by an hour and he seemed wiser than any grown-up. Kit didn't know what he would have done without him.

"I tried to be like them," he said. "That older kid, Spike, they call him. He was calling me names and everyone was laughing, like they always do. They all dress like him and talk like him and laugh when he laughs, so he leaves them alone. And I thought, why can't I do that? So I started to laugh, too."

Kaboodle looked at him with a kind smile. "You did more than that." He brushed a lock of chestnut hair away from Kit's forehead – hair that Kit hadn't had that morning. No wonder Spike had looked so surprised, afraid and angry in quick succession. No wonder he'd lashed out.

"I was only trying to fit in," Kit said sullenly.

"That's where you made your mistake," said Kaboodle with a sigh. "We can never 'fit in' with people like that. They won't let us."

"But they don't give you a hard time. Not like they do me."

"That's because they know I'll stand up for myself. I've told you before, Kit, you have to fight back and meet violence with violence."

"There's too many of them."

"Then you have to find their weaknesses; find a way to beat them. It's the only language they understand."

"Mom says–"

"Mom doesn't understand. She's a norm, too, and drokk knows she has the patience of a saint to have raised mutant twins, but she doesn't know what it's like to be us. She won't accept that we can't fit in here."

Kit gaped at his brother, alarmed. "You snuck out to the township again!"

"I've been going there every night. I want to take you there, too."

He shook his head stubbornly. "Mom says the people who live there are crooks."

"They're mutants, Kit, like you and me. And yes, the norms would call them criminals, but that's because the only way for a mutant to better himself on this world is through taking what they won't let us have."

"You'll get into trouble."

"You're the one with the black eye." The remark wasn't meant to be nasty, but to be an observation. Kaboodle was examining Kit's face. "You know, you're getting better at that. Anyone who didn't know you like I do, I'd swear they'd think you were Spike's younger brother. Funny, though."

"What is?"

"Our power never worked on a norm before."

Kaboodle looked searchingly into Kit's eyes and Kit knew he could hide nothing from him. He squirmed and his cheeks burned hot. Bad enough that he had changed again since it would be hours before his face returned to normal and he could show it in public, but this time, there was something else. Something unspeakable. Something that had twisted and corrupted his body, making him outwardly the freak he had always been on the inside. And he was afraid that it wouldn't go away.

His brother felt his fear and calmed him with a smile and a telepathic hug. "Interesting," he said. "Very interesting indeed." He stood and extended his hand again. This time, Kit accepted it and let himself be hauled to his feet.

"I think we've found our friend Spike's weakness," said Kaboodle, and his smile held no trace of warmth now. "Come with me tonight, Kit. To the township. Just once, that's all I ask. Come with me and I'll show you how to deal with his kind. I'll show you how to make sure they don't hurt you again."

It was only later that Kit learned everything his brother had done for him that day. Later, when Kaboodle's actions had become the stuff of urban legend.

He had walked right up to Spike in front of his followers in the Rocket gang and challenged him to a fight.

Spike had laughed in his face and accepted, seeing an opportunity to enhance his reputation at the expense of a younger, weaker opponent. It wasn't the first time Kaboodle had taken a beating for his brother, nor would it be the last.

The turning point came as Spike was driving a booted foot into the prone Kaboodle's ribs and the underdog saw his chance. He reached up, took hold of Spike's waistband and yanked his trousers down. The humiliation alone would have ensured that his opponent lost more face than he could gain from the encounter, but in this case, that was the least of his problems.

For nineteen years, Spike and his family had concealed his disgrace. There was no hiding it now. The other Rockets gaped in horror at the sight of a short, reptilian tail, glistening and twitching behind him.

It took less than six hours for Spike to be disowned by his parents, sacked by his employer, and assaulted by his old gang. He arrived in the mutant township shortly before midnight to find that Kaboodle had organised a reception for him.

Kit was one of the vengeful mutants who had gathered around the newcomer as he kneeled in the dirt and whimpered. Tomorrow, Spike would be one of them. For now, he was still a norm in their eyes; someone who had hated and mistreated them, and they would take a grim pleasure in seeing him suffer.

He watched in silence as the older mutants had their fun. They left Spike a bloody, blubbering mess and dispersed into the shadows. And then Kaboodle was at Kit's side, beckoning him forward and urging him to take a good look at his one-time tormentor. Kit was reluctant at first, his legs feeling heavy, each step seeming to cross a mile. A part of him expected to see that old sneer on Spike's face, but he drew on Kaboodle's courage and made himself confront it.

And when Spike looked up at him through teary eyes half closed from injury, Kit saw no trace of the monster he had feared so much. Just a crushed and frightened mutant, his eyes pleading for mercy as Kit's eyes must have pleaded on many occasions.

Kit kicked him in the face. Then he kicked him again. And again and again.

"I was proud of you that day."

The Consoler didn't have to explain what he meant. He'd been thinking back to that time so he knew that Kit had been thinking about it, too.

"I was proud of myself," said Kit. "All my life, I'd been so weak and frightened. That day, I learned to take charge of my own fate, thanks to you."

"Don't say that!"

"Why not?" Kit sneered. "It was you who taught me to take what you want from life." He suddenly remembered that they weren't alone. He sneaked a self-conscious glance at each of his guards, but they were facing dead ahead as if deaf to anything they shouldn't hear. He dismissed them abruptly and closed the cell door behind them. He knew as well as the Consoler did that he had nothing to fear in here.

"Everything I am," said Kit, "I owe it to you, my brother." And he really meant what he said; the Consoler could feel that he did, even though he knew how much pain it would cause him.

"I was wrong, Kit," he said. "It was never about getting justice, only about revenge. We made ourselves as bad as the norms who persecuted us."

"Is that what they drummed into you in that prison? Know your station; conform to their rules; accept your lot?"

"They gave me time to reflect on my actions."

"They broke you!" said Kit contemptuously. "No norm gangbanger would have pulled down five years, but you were a mutie. No one cared what they did to you. They could keep you clapped in irons until you were prepared to lick their boots!"

"My sole regret about my time in jail," the Consoler sighed, "is what it did to you, Kit. It made you bitter and more vicious. The things you've done..."

Kit snarled. "I'm not the one who changed."

"Violence only breeds violence, Kit. The cycle has to end somewhere."

"And you've found a better way, have you? By running away?"

"It's true, I came to Miltonia because I was afraid," the Consoler confessed. "I was afraid of what I had been, of what I might become again. And I begged you to come with me because I thought you could be happy here, too. But not like this, Kit, not like this. Miltonia *is* our better way. Things are different here."

Kit shrugged dismissively. "More to take, that's all."

When Kit looked back on his early life, he always saw it through a haze of tears. That changed, however, on the day that Kaboodle introduced him to the township.

He was happy there, and even accepted by the older kids. They made him an honorary member of one of their street gangs – the Blades – and gave him his first alcoholic drink and taught him how to scrape a living on the black market. They understood all he had been through and they hated the norms as much as he did. Sometimes, there would be clashes between the Blades and the Rockets on the edge of Bogweed, and despite his youth Kit was allowed to join in if he pleased. As a rule, he would go along if his brother was going and stay behind if he was staying.

By the time they were fourteen, Kit and Kaboodle had ceased even their infrequent visits back to their mother's home. It wasn't just that the streets of what they called

Normtown were dangerous, but it was that they n
longer felt they belonged there.

At the age of fifteen, then considered adults, they spl
from the Blades after a heated argument over somethin
trivial. Kaboodle formed a new gang which he named th
Chameleons in honour of the brothers' shared abilitie
Within three years they became one of the most feare
organisations on the planet, and the most wanted. Bu
the posters that hung in every sheriff's office feature
only blurred photographs and inaccurate artists' impres
sions.

The next time Kit cried was on his nineteenth birthday
the day it all went wrong.

He remembered the lights of the saloons streakin
around him, diffracted by the water in his eyes as he ran
He remembered also his heart pounding in his chest an
shouts ringing in his ears. The marshals rarely entere
the township and he had counted on them to give up a
he crossed the border. But this time they were deter
mined to get their man.

He didn't know what to do. He wasn't physicall
strong and he didn't know how to fight. They outnum
bered him, anyway. He had always relied on his stealth
and his cunning, but he couldn't shake them off lon
enough to hide or to change shape. Only one though
formed clearly through his panic: Kaboodle. He had t
find Kaboodle. And in that moment, Kit became th
bullied child again, looking for protection from hi
brother.

They talked for a long time in the bar they had mad
their home, sequestered in their private room while th
rest of the Chameleons waited outside knowing that th
building was surrounded, knowing that this was bad.

Kaboodle took the news calmly but Kit could feel hi
disappointment. "I told you she was off-limits. She's th
sheriff's daughter, Kit."

"I know," he snivelled, "but she's been seeing that Blade, Tusk. I just thought..."

"You thought you could kill her and frame him, bring the whole affair out into the open, and set the norms and the Blades against each other. I told you it wouldn't work, but you're cocky, Kit. That's always been your problem."

"It *should* have worked," insisted Kit. "I was watching the Blades' hideout, disguised as a street sweeper, and when I saw Tusk, when I realised I could get right up to him without him suspecting... It was a good disguise, too. I'm getting better at it, Kaboodle, like you always said I could. I can read their DNA now like a map. I mean, the eyes weren't quite right because they're the hardest part, but so long as I wore my hat jammed down..."

"What happened?" Kaboodle prompted.

"Stun pellet," said Kit, miserably. "It wasn't my fault. I mean, I had to let them see me, didn't I? I had to let them see the tusks. Only they came quicker than I thought. I still had my hands around her throat and she was still kicking. They got lucky, that's all. The pellet grazed my shoulder, and I just... lost control. It was like my body just shot back to normal and they could see my face. My real face!" He was shaking. "You have to help me, Kaboodle. I can't go to jail, I can't! I'd be at their mercy again!"

Kaboodle thought for a long time. Then, in a quiet, resigned voice he said: "Go back into the bar, Kit."

"What... what are we gonna do? Fight our way out?"

"We can't win against them, Kit. Even if we could, the cost would be too high. Those people out there trust me. I won't sacrifice them."

"Then what?"

"Borrow a face from Spike or one of the others. Find a dark corner and do nothing to draw attention to yourself."

"Hide from them? B-but they know I can change shape now. They won't let anyone out of here until–"

"I'll deal with it," Kaboodle said firmly.

Sometimes, when he looked back at that moment, when he saw again the quiet resolution in Kaboodle's face, Kit wondered what he would have done if he had known what his brother had planned. There were times when he almost admitted to himself that on some level he *had* known. After all, neither of them could have made a decision of such import without the other being aware of it. Back then, though, it hadn't mattered.

A moment earlier, Kit had been unable to see a way out. Now, he was saved because his brother was here.

He would make everything all right again.

"I knew you couldn't face doing hard time," said the Consoler. "I knew it would destroy you. But sometimes, Kit, when I look at you now... Drokk help me, I wonder if I did the right thing."

"Of course you did," said Kit. "Your going to jail was the best thing that ever happened to me. It taught me to stand on my own feet. My abilities developed and so did my confidence. I became as good a leader of the Chameleons as you'd ever been; everybody said so. They respected me. And not because I was your brother, but because I'd earned it. Don't you see? I always wanted to be like you, and then I was!"

"I wouldn't have attacked the sheriff's daughter," said the Consoler darkly. "And I wouldn't have dreamed of doing some of the things you've done since then."

"You think I'd have been happy stuck on Thulium 9 all my life? There were opportunities out there, Kaboodle, and I wanted to take them."

"You preyed on our own kind."

"And the ironic thing is that, again, I have *you* to thank for it. The only limitation of my power was that I couldn't copy norm DNA. If I was to make myself rich, I had to find some wealthy mutants, and we both know how few of them there are. It was you who first mentioned Miltonia to me, Kaboodle. It was you who gave me the idea of finding rich mutants here and ripping them off. You did that on the day you left; the day I realised there was nothing to keep me on Thulium 9 any more."

Kit prided himself on being hard-hearted and pragmatic. Even so, it had taken him many years to stop feeling guilty about his brother's sacrifice. He had managed it, eventually, through an unexpected turn of events. Kit's guilt had left him in the moment that Moosehead McGuffin zapped him with a paralysis ray.

His captor had paraded him in front of the very mutants from whom he had been stealing for years, his duplicity exposed by the most solid evidence possible: Kit himself, frozen in mid-transformation. His game was over. He had experienced a lot of emotions that day: shame, humiliation, denial, impotence, anger, and even a touch of despair. But not fear. Not this time. Not even when he thought about what the norms would do to him. And this, he realised, was how Kaboodle must have felt, all those years ago. For someone in their profession, jail was just an occupational hazard – an inconvenience, to be sure, but no more than that. He could handle it.

As for what had happened to Kaboodle, well, that had been his own fault. Kit had no intention of being broken like his brother. He had developed new abilities that nobody knew about. He was still in control.

He wouldn't be like his brother. He wouldn't stay caged for long.

"I didn't plan to keep McGuffin's body at first," said Kit. "Why would I want to be a Strontium Dog anyway? But I soon realised that the longer I was walking around as him, the longer he'd be left to rot in Shawshank. Also, Moosehead was something of a war hero and had a bit of respect in certain quarters despite his trade. I used that to my advantage."

"Moosehead McGuffin is a good man," said the Consoler. "A man whose reputation and life you destroyed."

"I did no worse than what he tried to do to me," said Kit. "Anyway, first chance I got, I contacted some of the wealthy Miltonian mine owners and reminded them of what good ol' Moosehead had done for them. They fell over themselves to return the favour and got me a Miltonian passport in double-quick time. I handed in my notice at the Doghouse and got outta there before anyone could smell a rat."

"You must be very proud of yourself," the Consoler said dryly, "conning the same people twice."

"They didn't suspect a thing," said Kit with a broad grin of satisfaction. "And why would they? After all, the heinous Identi Kit was locked up out of harm's way."

"And now you've found the perfect career for somebody so obviously skilled at lying, cheating, and betrayal. You've gone into politics."

"My new friends in business were more than happy to sponsor my campaign. It wasn't just that they were grateful to poor old Moosehead. As soon as I scratched the surface of our utopia, here, I found what lay beneath it: fear."

The Consoler nodded. "I discovered that for myself."

"The norm population was growing faster than ours, and they were taking mutant homes and jobs, demanding rights and representation. The mutants could see a day when they would become a minority again, when Miltonia would become like every other world."

"And you appealed to that fear."

"I gave the people what they wanted. I promised a hard line against immigration and was returned to office by a landslide. I looked for you, by the way. Once I had access to government records, I searched for your name. I didn't find it. It was only when you formed your ridiculous resistance movement that I knew you were here. Mr George Smith... Were you really so ashamed of where you came from?"

"Some of it, yes." The Consoler shook his head sadly. "All that skill, Kit, all that guile and courage, and you had real power, too. You could have done so much good. If only I could have made you see."

"See what? That I should be like you? Devote my life to helping others? Why should I, Kaboodle? Nobody ever put themselves out for me."

The Consoler raised an eyebrow. "Nobody, Kit?"

Kit hung his head but the Consoler could feel that he was more angry than ashamed; angry at having his past thrown back in his face again.

"You have to fight back," muttered Kit, parroting his brother's words of so long ago back to him, "meet violence with violence." Then he looked up and met the Consoler's eyes defiantly. "I did what you told me, Kaboodle. I stood up for myself. And now I have everything we ever wanted. I'm rich, I'm comfortable. Hell, I'm even respected!" A snarl pulled at his lips. "And every day, I get to make life miserable for the norm scum who thought they could grind me down!"

"Then I'm sorry," said the Consoler, "for what must happen next."

They looked into each other's eyes for a long time but no more words were spoken. They were not needed. Each knew exactly how the other felt. The Consoler could see now that he would never talk Kit round to his way of thinking. The knowledge was a profound disappointment to him, and it surprised him only a little to feel that same disappointment reflected in Kit's heart. He felt responsible for having made Kit the person he was, and somewhere, buried deep within Kit's psyche and denied for many years, that same guilt resided, too.

The Consoler had never felt closer to his brother, nor so far apart.

"I will find out what your Salvationists are planning," said Kit quietly as he turned to leave the room. "For the sake of all we used to share, please answer General Rising's questions sooner rather than later."

Kaboodle Jones was left alone again with his misery, with the remnants of a desperate hope, and the bitter knowledge of what his failure would mean for his friends, his followers, his world. There was nothing more he could do. Events would play themselves out, as perhaps he had always known they would.

"The only language they understand," he muttered to himself sadly as he awaited the outbreak of war.

CHAPTER EIGHTEEN
RISING FALLS

General Rising was not having a good day.

His borscht had been scalding hot and when he'd dropped the straw from his lips, it had splashed all over his uniform jacket. The thick beetroot stains would not come out. It was his only clean tailor-made uniform, too. The other was covered in blood, thanks to that contemptible traitor McNulty. He hated the way he looked in standard issue uniforms. And to top it all, his tailor had just been sent to an internment camp.

He swore violently and then realised how stupid he sounded with his jaw wired up. This only angered him more and he swept the bowl of soup off his desk, splashing borscht all over his trousers as he did so.

Jenkins, his aide, popped his head around the office door at the sound of the bowl shattering on the floor. "Is everything all right, sir?"

"Yef, id'f fine, dank you. Diffmiffed," said the general.

"Is that blood on you, sir?" Jenkins asked with a concerned look.

"No id'f borffd."

"I'm sorry, sir?"

"Beedrood foup, you idiot. Now ged oud!"

Jenkins left with discreet haste and Rising slumped behind his desk. He knew he shouldn't take his anger out on his second-in-command. He was about the only person left in the palace that he could trust.

Having to abort his pre-emptive strike against the Sal
vationists had greatly embarrassed him. It would not do
his career any good, either. If he even had a career to
worry about after the fiasco of the crashed air carrier...
He had launched a full-scale investigation into what had
brought the carrier down and where its extremely expensive cargo had gone, but it was likely to be days before
any conclusive leads turned up.

He knew in his bones that Alpha and McNulty were
behind it, and he swore to make them pay. What he
couldn't understand was how two mutants who had
fought for the freedom of other mutants could suddenly
turn on their own. Perhaps it was simply money. They
were bounty hunters, after all. Perhaps it was money that
had caused members of the mutant militia itself to turn
traitor, too.

This was the issue that had been troubling him most of
late. Acting on an anonymous lead, his men had appre-
hended three Salvationists planting a bomb in a
schoolroom. The men had been quite heavily mutated,
and further investigations had shown them all to be
members of the elite presidential guard. Before Rising
had a chance to properly interrogate the men, they had
all committed suicide in their cells. His attempts to get
some answers from their unit about the corruption in
their ranks had been stonewalled. They'd simply insisted
that they weren't answerable to his authority and refused
to cooperate in any way with his investigation. Even the
president had denied him an audience when he
requested it.

Rising could feel his influence slipping by the minute.
He had few powerful friends left and his enemies, sensing his growing weakness, were circling. There was
obviously Salvationist infiltration at work in the highest
levels of government and he meant to get to the bottom
of it.

There was a knock at his office door. "Come," Rising said.

Jenkins's head appeared around the door again. "I think you ought to join me on the balcony outside, sir," he said.

"Nod now, I'm doo bufy."

"There's something going on outside that you really should see, sir," said Jenkins, politely but firmly. "I assure you it demands your immediate attention."

Rising exhaled sharply in annoyance, but he trusted his aide enough not to question him further. He joined Jenkins and walked to the balcony at the front of the palace. From their lofty position they could see that an enormous crowd was gathering in the large plaza at the front of the palace.

"Whad if de meaning of dif?" the general demanded. The sight of such a disorderly rabble disrupting a public place without permission brought bile to his throat. He was nearly blind with fury.

"I'm afraid I don't know anything about it, sir," said Jenkins, apologetically. "There were no public meetings scheduled to take place here, and our agents have told us nothing about a demonstration."

"Id'f dofe confounded Falvadionifd!" Rising said, the veins up the side of his head throbbing with rage.

"Who, sir?"

"The Salvajsionifz, you idiot. De terrorifz we've been fighding."

"Of course, sir. I'm sorry."

"Fummon de guard," ordered Rising. "I want dif rabble crusfhed. Crusfhed, do you hear?"

"Right away, sir," said Jenkins, and he left to carry out the general's order.

Rising turned his attention to the gathering crowd below. Their numbers seemed to be growing all the time as more and more norms and quite a few mutants joined them. Some of them were quite obviously drilled and were standing in formation. The others who were milling around without any apparent aim were probably just bystanders who had come along either out of curiosity or because they were caught up in the mood of defiance. He intended to put a stop to this right away. To make certain they were all cowed into submission. He was not going to stand for this sort of insubordination right on his doorstep.

As he watched, he saw that at three strategic places in the crowd the protesters were assembling odd constructs from planks of wood. As the constructs took shape, Rising realised that they were catapults; the type of catapult that would have been used in some ancient siege in humanity's early days on Earth. They didn't seriously intend to attack the palace with those, did they? Were they out of their minds?

As this was going on, two troops of the civilian guard in full riot gear formed a human shield between the protesters and the palace. At the same time, a small contingent of the palace guard, armed with blaster weapons, poured from the gates to take up formation behind them.

"CLEAR THIS AREA IMMEDIATELY!" the captain of the palace troops shouted through a voice amplifier. "THIS IS YOUR ONLY WARNING! CLEAR THIS AREA OR MY MEN WILL BE FORCED TO TAKE ACTION! YOU HAVE FIVE MINUTES TO BEGIN TO DISPERSE!"

A few people on the outskirts of the crowd made themselves scarce at this, but the majority of the protesters stayed where they were.

When the five minute period had elapsed, the captain ordered his men to ready their blasters for a warning shot. Before he could give the order, however, a voice from the crowd shouted out: "Slingshots, engage!"

At this signal, the nearest Salvationists took out makeshift slingshots and fired small rocks over the heads of the civilian guardsmen to bombard the palace guard. Fortunately, most of the missiles missed their targets, landing at the guardsmen's feet or behind them. In response to this attack, the civilian guard pushed forward with their shields and batons, and the rock throwers retreated as fast as they could.

For the first time in weeks, General Rising actually laughed out loud. He was beginning to enjoy this. The Salvationists' attempts at an uprising were laughable. They were trying to take on a well-drilled and well-equipped army with slingshots and catapults. Their leaders were idiots. To think he had been prepared to launch a major offensive against them, equipping himself with state of the art weaponry and combing the mountain terrain to find their hideout. Instead, they had come to him like brainless lambs to the slaughter.

This was the insidious threat that was eating away at the heart of Miltonian society; that was infiltrating the government and threatening his position. They were nothing more than a bunch of undisciplined amateurs. Rising would crush them mercilessly, once and for all. Let his political opponents try to manoeuvre him out of the palace, then!

The palace guard raised their weapons again. The captain gave the order to fire.

Nothing happened.

The captain shouted the order again. Still nothing. He began to berate his men who were looking puzzled and checking their weapons. Something wasn't right. Rising had never seen so many guns malfunction at once. Not one of them seemed to be in working order. He would have someone's head for this.

With the palace guard in a confused state, a second contingent of Salvationists stepped up to replace the

stone-throwers. Seemingly out of nowhere they produced
blasters of their own, and Rising was astounded to see
that these were the very same weapons he had ordered
from offworld. The weapons that were missing from the
downed air carrier!

The Salvationists fired an opening salvo. Their shots
sailed through the civilian guardsmen without harming
them, but mowed down at least half of the defenceless
palace guard. The remainder of these men beat a hasty
retreat, but the Salvationists unleashed another torrent of
blaster fire and many more guards fell at the palace gates.

The civilian guard, armed with nothing more dangerous than their batons, were left in a vulnerable position.
Rising heard Johnny Alpha call out to them: "Drop your
weapons and leave this area! We don't wish to kill any
more people than is necessary."

The soldiers didn't know how to respond to that. Miltonia had enjoyed years of peace and none of them had
faced a situation like this before. They were outnumbered
by more than twenty to one, and Rising could see now
that fully two-thirds of the Salvationists were carrying
controlled detonation blasters. He was angry, but not surprised, when most of the civilian guard threw down their
shields and ran.

Jenkins appeared on the balcony again. "Permission to
call a general alert, sir," he requested.

"Granted," growled Rising between clenched teeth.
Jenkins gave the order over the intercom and an alarm
sounded all over the palace. Rising knew that every
guard would be taking to his or her posts. He cursed the
fact that he had sent so many of them out into the mountains.

At that moment, the whole building shook and the
alarm stopped dead. Rising whirled around in alarm and
saw what had happened. The Salvationists were using
their catapults. As he stared open-mouthed, two more

boulders crashed into the wall below him, and all the lights suddenly went out. Rising tried the intercom, to order that long-distance guns be trained on the catapults, but this was dead, too.

"Sir," wailed Jenkins. "I don't understand. What is happening?"

"Magnedinium," the general hissed. "Dey're hidding us wid magnedinium!"

It was suddenly obvious. The Salvationists had been sitting on a secret weapon for years. They had shipped it down from the mountains and they were putting it to use. Every bit of technology in the building was at risk. They could disable all of it and disarm his men with nothing more than a handful of thrown pebbles. And, thanks to Rising himself, their own weapons would not be affected.

A moment earlier, General Rising had been in good spirits believing he had nothing to fear. He was gripped by the sudden terror of inevitable defeat.

Johnny led the troops up the final set of stairs and directed them to spread out.

The tactic had been the same on every floor: attack the command posts, take out the guards, then move to the floor above, leaving behind a contingent on each floor to maintain their territory.

Most of the firefights had been quick and one-sided. After an opening exchange of blaster fire, the Salvationists had pelted their foes with magnetinium ore and disarmed them. Then they moved in to mop up the opposition. The casualties on the Salvationists' side had been minimal.

Conversely, the palace guard had suffered huge losses. With their comms down, they weren't receiving any orders and had no idea what was going on. They were unprepared for the attack and did not know how to react. Almost every floor had fallen to the Salvationists, but two more remained, including the one that housed the president's quarters.

Johnny had spent a long time studying the palace's schematics and had directed the catapult fire quite specifically. He needed to take out most of the palace's electronics without putting President Ooze's life-support machines at risk. Johnny had also given strict instructions to his volunteers that the president's sanctum was off-limits to them. He intended to secure that area for himself. He also wanted to retrieve the weapons he and Middenface had left at the palace.

To do that he needed General Rising, and his office was on the floor they had just reached. Leaving Elephant Head to take over the general offensive, Johnny and Middenface made for the office and found it at the end of a long corridor. Johnny kicked open the door and a plasma bolt shot past his ear.

The general's aide was standing in front of the desk, holding a pistol. Before he could fire again, Middenface heaved a large chunk of magnetinium at him. The ore hit the man right in the face, flattening his nose and nullifying his weapon. He dropped the gun and put one hand in the air. The other went to his nose which was streaming with blood.

Rising was cowering underneath the desk. "I furrender, I furrender," he said as Middenface hauled him out.

"Whit is yon scunner sayin'?" Middenface asked the aide.

The man looked blank and turned to Johnny. "I'm sorry," he said. "I'm afraid I can't understand your friend's accent."

"He wants to know what the general just said," Johnny told him.

"Oh, right. The general wants to know your terms of surrender."

"Jenkinf," cried the general. "Ged him off me, dadf an order."

"Sir, you just surrendered," replied Jenkins. "We're at their mercy."

"Tell 'im tae gi' us back oor weapons," demanded Middenface.

Jenkins turned to Johnny again.

"You're holding some specialist weaponry that belongs to my partner and me," said Johnny. "We'd like it returned."

Jenkins turned back to the general. "Sir, they–"

"I heard dem!" snapped Rising. "Dey're in de fafe in de nexd room."

Jenkins took a handkerchief from his pocket and dabbed at the blood on his face before opening the door to the adjoining room. "They're through here," he said.

Johnny kicked the chunk of magnetinium out into the hallway so it was safely out of range and then followed Jenkins into the room.

"Och, but it's braw tae have the auld Westinghouse back," said Middenface. He was strapping on his much-missed weaponry as they climbed up a back staircase to the presidential floor.

At first, Rising had blanched at Johnny's order to take the bounty hunters to the Ooze's sanctum. He had plainly not believed their hurried assurances that they meant their former comrade no harm. Still, what choice did he have?

Fortunately, no Salvationists had been this way, so their newly recovered weapons were safe from any stray chunks of magnetinium. Johnny knew, however, that that was the least of their problems.

Jenkins punched a code into a keypad on the wall at the top of the stairs and a security door swung open. Johnny stopped him before he could step through.

"The general goes first," he said. The barrel of his Westinghouse was stuck in Rising's back. The general harrumphed in protest but Johnny pushed him forward.

Twelve heavily armed members of the presidential guard blocked their way to the president's inner sanctum. "Tell these men to lay down their weapons and step aside," Johnny told Rising.

"You heard de man," said Rising. "Drop your weaponf!"

The men didn't move. "I'm afraid we only take orders from the president," the head guard said stiffly, "and our orders are to let no one pass."

"Are you mad?" spluttered Rising. "Dey've captured de whole palafe and he hazh a gun on me!"

"Are you orders straight from the president," queried Johnny, "or from Nose Job Johnson?"

For a second, he could see the guards wavering as they weighed up the situation. Their stand was ultimately hopeless – even suicidal. Then a look passed, almost imperceptibly, across their eyes that betrayed their true mettle. Johnny knew exactly what that look meant.

"Move!" he shouted. He dived for cover and pushed Rising down with him. Middenface dived too, but Jenkins reacted too slowly. A volley of plasma bolts tore through him, lifting him off his feet. His smoking corpse was thrown backwards into the wall.

"They've got us pinned doon," cried Middenface.

Johnny unclipped a time bomb from his belt, activated it, and tossed the small metallic disc at the guards. There was a blinding flash of light followed by total silence. When he and Middenface looked up, there was just a large hole in the floor where the guards had been standing.

The bomb had blown them two days into the future. In two days, they would reappear in the selfsame spot, still standing on the missing part of the palace floor. By then,

Miltonia would have moved on in its orbit. The guards would continue to fire plasma bolts into the cold, empty wastes of space until they realised what had happened. Then, the vacuum would kill them.

Johnny stepped around the hole and moved cautiously into the president's sanctum. Middenface followed, his gun raised ready to provide covering fire. There was no need, however. Johnny swept the room and found nothing – nothing but the upturned bowl of the Ooze's nutrient tank and his life-support equipment.

He walked up to the tank and was relieved to see that its occupant was unharmed. "President Leadbetter," he announced formally. "We have deposed the impostor Kit Jones. This palace is now under the temporary control of the Salvationist Army." The Ooze's two large eyes gazed up from the tank with what Johnny could have sworn was gratitude.

"It's over!" sighed Middenface.

"Not while Kit is still at large," said Johnny with a grim set to his jaw.

CHAPTER NINETEEN
FACE OFF

Johnny took the steps down three at a time with Middenface's heavy footsteps clattering behind him.

"Whit's the hurry, Johnny? We won the war, didn't we? We've taken the palace and got the exits covered. There's no way Identi Kit's gettin' oot o' here."

"Not past you or me, maybe," said Johnny grimly, "but we got a lot of inexperienced volunteers out there. Can we really trust every one of them not to fall for Kit's tricks even after we warned them about him?"

"Ah guess not, but whit can we dae aboot it doon here?"

Johnny said nothing. He trusted that the answer to his partner's question would become clear soon enough.

They burst through a door onto the second sublevel where Johnny asked Middenface to lead him to the Consoler's cell. He watched as comprehension dawned in the big guy's eyes.

The cell door had been electronically locked, but magnetinium emissions had fried the mechanism so that it swung open to Johnny's tentative touch. The Consoler, however, was still inside, slumped in a corner. He raised his head to greet the S/D agents, blinking in the dim light.

"Is it over?" he asked. There was no hint of triumph in his voice, just a deep weariness.

"Not quite," said Johnny. "We need your help."

The Consoler looked a mess. Several of his eyes were blackened, and several of his noses bloodied. Even in the insane jumble of body parts that made up his body, Johnny thought he could see limbs that were bent out of shape or pulled out of their sockets. He had to have been in great pain but he made no complaint. Instead, he nodded in resignation and struggled to his feet. To Johnny's mild surprise, Middenface hurried to help him.

"You want me to find my brother, I assume."

"I hoped this psychic connection of yours might lead us to him."

"It doesn't quite work that way," said the Consoler, "but combined with my ability to sense other mutants in the vicinity..."

"And is he?" asked Johnny. "In the vicinity, I mean?"

"Oh yes," said the Consoler. "He's above us, in this building. He's worried but not afraid. He's lost his protection but trusts his own abilities. If he can get out of the palace, he knows he can disappear. He's disguised himself as a volunteer who died in battle; Kit stole his form and hid the corpse. He's watching, waiting for his chance. It will be difficult to pinpoint his exact position."

"Get us close," said Johnny. "I'll do the rest. He can't hide from me!"

They rode up to the ground floor in the service lift and found a crowd of Salvationists guarding the nearby side entrance. They reacted jubilantly to the sight of their leader, but their whoops of delight were muted as they took in the extent of his injuries. The Consoler smiled bravely and congratulated them on their great victory, raising their spirits again.

Down in the basement, his gait had been laborious and pained, and Johnny had half-expected him to collapse. He walked taller and more assuredly, buoyed by what? Pride at seeing what he had achieved? Or grim resolution at the thought of what he still had to do?

They heard gunfire. Johnny and Middenface sprinted to the main antechamber, which was filled with Salvationists, but the fighting was over by the time they got there. Elephant Head came running up to them, her grey face flushed. She explained that two palace guards had got the drop on a volunteer and stolen his blaster. Their surprise attack had taken down four men before they were overpowered. Elephant Head was all for killing them, but Johnny reminded her that their enemies thought they were fighting for their government.

"They were happy enough to support Kit's fascist policies," she grumbled. "That makes them as bad as he is." But she did as she was told.

The Consoler came huffing up to them, practically having to fight his way through his overjoyed followers. "He's in here," he reported urgently. "My brother is in this room somewhere."

Dismayed, Johnny surveyed the crowd. Of course this was where Kit would be. He could be easily lost amongst the horde of people who were gathered there. And there were too many exits. Any of the faces here could be his, and he'd be able to slip away or change his identity again before Johnny could even begin to interrogate even one of them.

Turning back to Elephant Head, Johnny nodded in the direction of the palace's main entrance doors. "You've got people down there? People you can trust?"

"With my life," she said. "They know not to let anyone pass."

"Not even you?" Johnny asked.

"Not even the Consoler. Not until we know where Identi Kit is."

"Then it disnae matter where he hides," said Middenface. "We'll find him sooner or later." He smacked a fist into his open palm in anticipation.

"Unfortunately," said Johnny, "it's not that simple."

Elephant Head knew what he meant. "We've beaten the palace guards," she said gravely. "But right now there'll be army units headed back here from all over Miltonia. As far as they're concerned, terrorist fanatics have just attacked the heart of their government. They won't stop to ask questions."

"Even if they did," said Johnny, "they wouldn't believe the answers. Not without proof. We need Kit."

"Whit aboot the Ooze?" interjected Middenface. "He must know whit's been goin' oan. Couldn't he tell them?"

"The president can't speak," Elephant Head reminded him. "He needs a mouthpiece."

"But if it was the *right* mouthpiece…" Johnny thought for a moment, stroking his chin furiously. "Rising. Where is he?" he asked Elephant Head. Catching a flicker of evasion in the Salvationist's eyes, he asked suspiciously: "What did you do to him?"

"Nothing he didn't deserve," she said mutinously. "You should have heard him talking. Rising wasn't one of Kit's dupes. He believed in everything he was doing. He'd have exterminated every norm on the planet if he'd had his way."

"Where is he?" asked Johnny, angrily.

Elephant Head indicated the glass-sided lift. "We've been finding rooms for our prisoners on the deepest sublevel. But you're not listening to me, Johnny. He won't help us."

"I think he will," said Johnny. "I think he'll follow orders whether he agrees with them or not. At least, I hope so, because he's just about the only person in this building who anyone will listen to." Johnny turned to his partner. "Middenface, find Rising and take him up to the Ooze's sanctum. You know what to do next, yeah?"

"Aye, he drinks doon some o' the Ooze, and the Ooze can speak tae him, tell him the truth. But whit aboot Kit, Johnny?"

"I'll keep searching with the Consoler. Elephant Head, see if you can find a working comms unit. If we can get

Rising on side, he can talk to some of his fellow generals and convince them not to slaughter us just yet. And keep clearing the magnetinium out of here. Throw it back out the windows; it might buy us a bit more time when the soldiers arrive, and we need all the time we can get, guys. This war isn't over until we've exposed the *real* culprit."

Middenface felt a chill as the lift doors opened. It wasn't just that the air was cooler down here, it was also the memory of the last time he had walked these corridors to view the body of a murdered friend.

Of course, a lot had changed since then.

He could hear footsteps, the banging of heavy doors, and occasionally, a yelp of pain. The sounds were all muted by concrete walls so it sounded like they were coming from a distance. The Salvationists were having fun with their prisoners, and who was he to stop them?

Rounding a corner, he came up short at the sight of the very man everyone was looking for: Identi Kit. Middenface gaped for a second until his brain caught up with him and reminded him that another man now resided in this body.

Moosehead McGuffin was slumped against a wall, trembling; his borrowed face even whiter than normal. "It was worse than I remembered," he wailed. "The blaster wound was bad enough, but now it's starting to…" And suddenly, Middenface knew what Moosehead was doing down here and what he had just seen.

"I wouldnae worry aboot it," he said with forced cheer. "Johnny says it's no' really *yer* body that's had its chest blown open, it just looks that way. He says we can make Kit swap yer DNA back wi' Nose Job's in there, and ye'll be ye're auld antler-headed self again." He thought Moosehead was about to say something more so he jumped in quickly and asked: "Ye seen any sign o' Rising?"

Moosehead shrugged and indicated in one direction. ". think Fingers and a few of the others took him dowr there. Middenface, what if-"

"Middenface!"

Two Salvationists had appeared in the corridor ahead of him. He knew the two norms' faces but not their names. He was grateful for the interruption; he didn't know what else he could say to Moosehead that would help him.

Then he saw the familiar figure between the two new-comers, an arm looped around each of their shoulders for support. The Strontie drew his blaster and yelled out to all three to freeze where they stood.

"Middenface?" said the Consoler, and the various folds of his forehead creased into an enquiring frown.

"Ye don't fool me, ye scunner," he said. "Now, put yer hands up and move away from the others or ah'll shoot ye doon where ye stand."

"I'm afraid I cannot comply. You see, if I put my hands up, I will lose the support of my friends, here, and then I will surely fall over."

The two Salvationists looked at each other, and at the Consoler, in confusion.

Moosehead sensed trouble. He pushed himself away from the wall and sniffed the air reflexively. "Where did you find him?" he asked.

"I-in a cell back there," said the first volunteer, indicating the direction with his thumb. "He was chained up and just coming around. Wh-what's..."

"I think I see the problem." Despite his earlier words, the Consoler let go of his escorts and lurched forward on shaky legs. "My brother brought me down here at knife-point and rendered me unconscious. It doesn't require a great deal of brainpower to deduce what he did next. Would I be right in assuming, Mr McNulty, that you have encountered another Consoler today?"

"Ah'm warning ye," growled Middenface. "Stay back!"

"If only I still had my sense of smell," Moosehead grumbled beside him. "Kit's abilities were never a match for that."

"I understand your caution," said the Consoler. "I'm sure your grandmother impressed upon you how dangerous it can be to trust too readily." He fixed Middenface with a meaningful look.

Middenface could almost feel cogs turning in his brain as he looked at the Consoler's face and slowly came to only one conclusion.

"Oh, sneck!" he groaned, lowering his blaster. "Johnny!"

"Mr Alpha, something's happening!"

Johnny turned to his companion with a sense of fatalism. The Consoler passed a hand over his eyes, looking as if he were concentrating to the point of pain. "Something…" he grunted. "I'm not sure what. Kit's trying to block me. I can't sense exactly… but… but, oh, he's excited. He thinks he's beaten us. He's… free! I don't know how, but… but he's outside the palace! He's getting away!"

Johnny felt his stomach sink. He turned and sprinted for the main entrance. As soon as he was within range of the guards at the doors, he shouted at them.

"You let somebody through. Who did you let through?"

The volunteers looked baffled, murmuring assurances to Johnny that nobody had passed them. He had no time for their excuses. "Somebody did just a minute ago," he snapped. "Think! Even the most unlikely pers–"

"Surely it would be better to ask these questions later," a voice interrupted. Johnny hadn't realised that the Consoler was still at his shoulder. He wondered how he had managed to keep up with his injuries. "For now, the important thing is to find Kit. If we're quick, we can catch him before he reaches the gates."

Johnny nodded and made for the doors. When he put his hand on one, the Salvationist volunteers brought up their weapons, obeying the orders they had been given. He opened his mouth to snap impatiently at them but the words caught in his throat. They were *obeying orders*. They'd been telling him the truth. Kit *couldn't* have got out of the palace this way.

Unless, in his blind haste to find his enemy, Johnny himself escorted somebody past the guards... Somebody whose apparently miraculous recovery from days of torture had already given him cause for suspicion, only he hadn't stopped to think about it clearly before.

Johnny snatched his gun from its holster and whirled around but it was too late. The disguised Identi Kit had seen his hesitation and had drawn a blaster of his own. Johnny threw himself to the ground as blue fire crackled over his head. Kit was already running. Scrambling to his feet, Johnny let off two shots which went wild. Kit was out of sight before his pursuer could fire again, and before the Salvationist guards could even work out friend from foe.

Cursing himself for his gullibility, Johnny gave chase.

"He's on the move," reported the Consoler as Middenface and Moosehead bundled him into the glass-sided lift. It had been slow-going dragging him all the way here, but his psychic link with his brother made him indispensable. Middenface just hoped that Johnny would last an extra few seconds. He was shrewd and could take care of himself, but if anyone could strike him down, it would be a foe in the guise of a friend. Johnny could be too trusting sometimes.

"I can feel his heart pounding, the air burning in his throat, his muscles aching," the Consoler continued. "And he's afraid. He wasn't afraid before, but now he knows he can't get out of the palace. He's running. Upstairs."

"Which floor?" asked Middenface. His fingers hovered impatiently over the buttons.

"I don't know. He isn't thinking clearly. Kit isn't used to losing control like this. He's desperate. I haven't sensed him like this since... Well, for a long time."

Middenface thought furiously. What would he do in Kit's situation? Only one answer occurred to him. That might have been because he knew so little about the lay-out of the palace, and Kit would surely have options open to him that Middenface couldn't even guess at. Still, his instincts told him he was onto something, and Midden-face rarely ignored his instincts.

He closed his eyes and tried to remember the clearance codes he and Johnny had been given the first time they had stepped into this lift. He had made a special effort that time to memorise them, feeling that they might come in useful. Concentrating hard, he punched the numbers into the keypad, and was gratified to hear the chirruping electronic signal that told him he had remembered right.

The lift lurched into motion and carried them up towards the president's sanctum.

Johnny, too, had realised where Kit was headed, but he was too late to take the lift and cut him off.

The few seconds in which he had lost sight of the iden-tity thief had cost him. He returned to the antechamber to find a scene of chaos. Kit had morphed himself into the image of the first mutant he'd been able to lay his hands on: an outwardly normal-looking woman. He had then dived into the crowd and spread that template from person to person, so that Johnny was confronted by dozens of clones. He had, however, picked out the real Kit in an instant, since there was only one person run-ning with a purpose. Unfortunately, he'd lost time pushing his way through the confusion of clones and could not catch up to Kit.

Johnny had gained some ground on the stairs as he was in better condition than Kit in his current form. Not enough, however, to keep the security door at the top from shutting in his face. It took him precious seconds to shoot out the lock and his heart leapt into his throat as he emerged into the corridor to hear blaster fire.

He burst into the inner sanctum of President Leadbetter, his own gun raised, and stopped short at the sight that awaited him.

Four figures faced each other around the Ooze's nutrient tank, their eyes and their gun sights flickering distrustfully between each other.

Four perfect replicas of Middenface McNulty.

"Johnny, thank goodness ye're here!" cried one of the Middenfaces.

"It's Kit, Johnny," said another in exactly the same voice with the same accent, "but ah cannae work oot which one of us he is."

"Ye have tae use yer alpha eyes," said a third.

"No, ye can't!" the fourth protested. "Remember what we wer' told, ye'll disrupt the life-support machines!"

Johnny realised that his mouth was hanging open and closed it. He didn't have time to be surprised. He had to think.

One of these Middenfaces was the genuine article because Kit would have needed him here to replicate his DNA. Or would he? His powers had evolved again. How else had he been able to copy his victims' clothing as well as their bodies? All four of the Middenfaces were dressed alike in the bounty hunter's customary tartan.

"Ye have to do something, Johnny." The first Middenface again. "Else Kit'll kill the Ooze."

"That's whit he was tryin' tae do," said Middenface number four. "If Moosehead hadnae jumped him..."

"No," argued Middenface two. "Ah think he only wanted a hostage."

"And I think everyone should put down their guns," said Johnny, "before somebody gets hurt."

"Are ye crackers?" protested the fourth Middenface. "No way do I put ma gun doon while that scunner's still got his trained on ma friends and me."

"Ah hate to suggest this," said Middenface three, "but ah think the only way tae end this standoff withou' bloodshed is tae let Kit go."

"Dinnae listen to him, Johnny!" cried Middenface one. "Ah'll lay odds he *is* Kit, tryin' tae talk his wae outtae here."

"No," said Middenface two. "He's right. Trust me, ah know Kit. If it even looks like he's about tae be exposed, he'll fire intae yon nutrient tank. The president would be dead before any o' us could blink."

Johnny's head was spinning. Middenface two claimed to know Kit. Who did that make him? The Consoler? Was he here? Or was it Moosehead, who was certainly present and had once tracked the identity thief across half a galaxy? Middenface three was another candidate for the Consoler with his talk of non-violence. Or had that been Kit, playing the part of his brother as a double-bluff?

Then there was Middenface four, who had used the word 'scunners' and warned Johnny against unleashing his alpha rays. Would the big guy really have remembered that detail from so many days ago? Or had Kit just ensured that Johnny didn't try to expose him that way?

He could pinpoint the impostor in seconds, of course, with a few well-chosen questions, but that would likely panic Kit into carrying out his implied threat. Was it worth sacrificing the president's life to get his man? How would they hold off the approaching armies without him?

"Okay, Kit, you win," he said, still watching the four Middenfaces and waiting for one to betray himself.

"Ye cannae mean that, Johnny!" protested the first Middenface, just as the real one might have done.

Johnny spied an intercom that appeared operational. "I'm gonna try to raise the Salvationists," he said, "and get them to clear a way to the exit. Then you can all walk out of here, one by one."

"Ye're just lettin' him go?" exploded Middenface four. "After all we went through tae find him? Listen tae me, Johnny, ah'm the real Middenface, and anyone who says otherwise is a lyin' scunner!"

The tension in the room shot up to breaking point. Johnny had little doubt now which of the Middenfaces was his partner, but he could only imagine how Kit would react to the revelation.

Then, Middenface three blurted out: "No, ye're the liar. *Ah'm* Middenface!"

Then suddenly, Johnny was confused again.

All guns were trained on each other, and so no one could shoot without being shot down in turn. Johnny shifted his aim from one of them to the other, fearing that at any moment the impostor would shoot into the Ooze's tank.

"Ah'm the real me, Johnny," cried Middenface four. "I swear it on ma granny's grave!"

"Dinnae bring ma granny intae this!" snarled Middenface three. "She may o' been a daft auld bat, but–"

He never got to finish the sentence. Johnny turned his blaster decisively upon him and pulled the trigger. At the same moment, Middenface one fired, too.

To Johnny's horror, not one but two Middenfaces crumpled to the floor.

CHAPTER TWENTY
KIT BAGGED

"Middenface!" Johnny cried out in confusion and fear.

"Ah'm awright," said one of the Middenfaces who was still standing.

"Ah'm okay, too," said Middenface number one. "I'm Moosehead."

Johnny looked down at the two figures on the floor. "The Consoler?" he guessed.

"I'm afraid... I don't have much longer to live. That was good shooting, by the way. It's only thanks to my mutant anatomy... that I didn't die instantly."

"Hang oan a minute," cried Middenface. "It was ye that Johnny and Moosehead shot?"

"As I... hoped they would."

"But why?" asked Johnny, kneeling beside the Consoler and cradling his head.

"It was the only way to stop my brother," said the Consoler. He was breathing with some difficulty and he let out a soft moan. It was echoed from the other side of the president's tank. Kit was dying, too.

"We were... apart for so long," the Consoler continued, his face twisted with pain. "During that time, our powers grew so much. My time here at the palace confirmed my suspicions... that the bond between us had also grown. We were feeling the same emotions... even seeing and hearing the same things, as if we were one person. I knew that if one of us died, so... so would the other."

"But why did ye no tell us?"

"Kit was threatening the president. He was going to get away. He would go to some other world where he would cause more pain and misery for countless more people. I couldn't have that on my conscience again. I had to make certain... he couldn't hurt anyone else."

"You made me what I am," spat Kit, writhing with pain. "You got me into this life."

"I know," said the Consoler. "That's why I had to put an end to it once and for all. For the good of Miltonia... so it could live up to the promise you tried so hard to stifle."

"What about the Salvationists?" asked Johnny. "How will they get along without you?"

"From what I've seen today, I should think they'll get along rather well. I've done all I can for the cause. Now it's up to them. I would only have gotten in the way had I lived. They were growing away from me even before you joined us... I can be much more of an inspiration... like this."

Violent coughs wracked the Consoler's body. He was bleeding profusely from his twin wounds and blood frothed up in his mouth, spilling over his chin. Middenface pulled out a handkerchief and bent to wipe it away, showing uncharacteristic gentleness. Kit was not bearing his pain anywhere near as stoically. He moaned and cursed everyone in the room.

"Wait!" cried Moosehead, kneeling beside the Consoler. "What about me? Can't you do anything about me? I can't spend the rest of my life looking like this!"

"An' whit'd so bad aboot that?" demanded Middenface, bristling.

"No offence intended," said Moosehead. "Consoler, I know you don't have much strength left, but if there's any way you can undo what Kit has done to me..."

"I understand," said the Consoler. "And though I haven't used my powers in quite this way before, I can try."

He summoned the last of his strength and placed his hands on Moosehead's face. Nothing happened at first and Johnny wondered if the Consoler was too weak after all. Then Moosehead's skin began to ripple. The ripples became larger and then his whole physique began to distort. This obviously caused Moosehead some discomfort but he didn't complain. Slowly, Middenface's rugged exterior disappeared as Moosehead's body started to rebuild itself. His features blurred and shifted their shape, and finally he looked like...

He looked like Kit, again.

"I'm sorry," said the Consoler. "You've spent too long in this form. I can't find any trace of your original DNA. It seems there is still much of my brother's handiwork I cannot undo, and I will take that regret with me... to the... next... world..."

With that, the Consoler slumped against Johnny and his eyes closed. Kit let out one last defiant scream of pain and rage at what he obviously perceived to be the injustice of it all, and the two brothers died together.

"Ye know," said Middenface, "fer someone who talked so much, he wisnae such a bad feller."

"There are few brave enough to give their lives so that a whole planet can prosper," said Johnny. Moosehead just nodded sadly.

The three of them bowed their heads and stood in silence.

"There has been mistrust and there has been recrimination," said the figure of Moosehead in the hologram. He was standing on a podium in the plaza in front of the palace. Beside him, President Leadbetter floated in a portable nutrient tank, his words relayed by his new mouthpiece to an audience of thousands. "But now is the time for reconciliation. We need to put our fears and our hatred behind us. To forgive, in order that we ourselves can be forgiven."

The speech had been recorded three hours earlier and now it was being broadcast all over the planet. Johnny and Middenface had the honour of watching the holo-cast from the president's sanctum, alongside Moosehead, the president himself, and General Rising.

"We have learned that bigotry and intolerance are not the sole auspice of any one race, creed or kind of human being," the holographic Moosehead continued. "They are mistakes to which we are all prone. History is rife with examples of oppressed peoples who became oppressors themselves when they finally achieved power. It is a pattern to which we, too, have fallen prey. A pattern we must break. We have lived through some dark times, but they are over now and the people responsible are no longer in a position to harm us."

"Miltonia has never had a better chance to live up to its promise as a world in which mutants can live free from prejudice – including our own. I come before you today to ask for your help in building that world, to ask you to dream that dream along with me."

Float-a-cams swooped over the audience as they went wild. Johnny detected more than just approval on the faces of the cheering mutants; there was also relief. The fear had gone: fear of getting a knock on the door in the middle of the night, fear of the constant threat of a terrorist attack. Maybe they *did* have a chance of a better life, he thought.

"Well, it's too early to tell how that went over with the voters," said Rising, reading from a column of statistics that had just popped up alongside the holo-cast, "but you just had the highest ratings of any presidential speech, so the early indications are good."

The eyes in the presidential vat rotated a fraction of a degree towards the general, who beamed proudly and said: "Why, thank you, Mr President." He was revelling in the status that his new psychic link with the president gave him. A far cry from his reaction, Johnny recalled, when they had first pushed a straw into his wired-up mouth and forced him to drink a small portion of the Ooze.

To Rising's credit, he had acted in an honourable fashion once he knew the truth. He had immediately ordered that no retributive action be taken against the Salvationists, and he'd dealt fairly with all sides during the negotiated disarmament of the rebel troops and the return of the palace to the government.

One of the terms of the treaty had been that several seats in the president's new cabinet should be given to Salvationist leaders. Elephant Head had landed Kit's old job as minister for immigration – apparently, ministers with animal heads were very popular with the public – while Moosehead was delighted to be offered one of the most important of government roles, and to settle permanently on Miltonia as he had long dreamed of doing.

Johnny was still a little concerned about Rising's newfound influence. He could see the sense, though, of having two political opponents in communion with the president. After the ease with which Kit had duped the whole of Miltonia, it was good that Moosehead and Rising would act as checks against each other. He remembered the hatred with which Rising had spoken about norms, however, and wondered how much of it was ingrained and how much was an understandable reaction to the lies he had been told. Certainly, his attitude had changed enormously; he even appeared to hold Johnny and Middenface in some esteem since their defeat of Kit.

"The president has just asked General Rising about the progress of the investigation into the school bombing," said Moosehead for the benefit of Johnny and Middenface.

"Ah yes," said Rising. "I still have a few loose ends to tie up, but thankfully the corruption appears to have been confined to a small cell of fanatical operatives in the presidential guard. They believed themselves to be acting under your orders, Mr President, when in fact those orders came from Identi Kit. How they could have thought you would sanction the bombing of your own people, though, is beyond me."

"Fear is a great political motivator," said Moosehead. Johnny was fascinated by the way his voice changed when he spoke on the president's behalf. His pitch became lower and his speech patterns were completely different. "It can be stronger than hope, determination, or even morals. The threat that Kit created through manipulation and exaggeration scared people into accepting his policies without question."

"Och, come oan," said Middenface. "Ye cannae mean tae tell me yer own soldiers did all that just tae get a bunch of policies passed."

"They thought they were saving Miltonia from itself. A few innocent lives were a sacrifice they were willing to make. If you think about it, your own actions weren't entirely dissimilar. To stop Kit and capture him, you were prepared to kill fellow mutants and even former comrades."

"But ye cannae compare oor actions tae theirs. We did ye a favour gettin' rid o' the scunner."

"And Miltonia is grateful for that service," said the president. "In a way, that was the flaw in Kit's strategy. By stigmatising a whole section of the populace, he empowered its militant tendencies."

Johnny completed the thought. "Kit gave us the army we needed to defeat him. His own twisted tactics proved to be his undoing."

"I don't suppose we'll ever know how many of the atrocities we've seen in recent weeks were committed by one side and how many by the other," sighed Rising.

"The important thing is that it's over," said the president. Moosehead turned to Johnny and Middenface. "I'm only sorry that you won't consider a role in the rebuilding of Miltonia. There are still powerful factions within our society that oppose our new integrationist policies. I could use your help in dealing with them."

"Aye well, thanks and aw," said Middenface hurriedly, "but there's far tae much talkin' and no' enough daein' in politics fer my likin'. In fact, ye'd have got along well with the Consoler on that score."

"I'm sorry I never got a chance to meet him," said the president. "It's a shame that circumstances pitted us against each another. I am considering a proposal to erect a monument in his honour."

"I'm sure he would have appreciated that," said Johnny. "Now, I hope you won't think us rude, but we've got a shuttle to catch and we still need to retrieve Kit's body."

"Of course. Moosehead here will escort you to the mausoleum."

Realising that the president had just mentioned him, Moosehead looked surprised, as though he had just come out of a trance. "Oh, yes of course," he said, his voice becoming his own again. "We'll take the lift down."

Moosehead swiped his key card and the concrete door creaked open.

"I still get the creeps coming down here," he said. "So much for the glamorous life of a politician, eh?"

"Ye dinnae have tae tell me," said Middenface, his breath condensing in the cold air. "Now I know how ye felt seein' yerself laid oot like this."

Kit's body lay in a coffin-shaped anti-gravity container. It had not reverted back to its original form like Middenface had hoped.

"It's gonnae be mighty strange goin' back tae the Dog-house wi' ma own dead body in tow," the bounty hunter muttered.

"Sort of gives you premonitions, doesn't it?" said Moosehead. "Makes you realise how close to death we all are at any time, especially in our line of work. At least you didn't have to bury your body and say goodbye to it forever."

"Look on the bright side," said Johnny. "Now you get to help undo everything in Kit's body that he did in yours. That's some kind of payback, I guess."

Moosehead smiled bravely but Johnny knew his words were not that helpful. For the rest of his life, when he looked in the mirror, he would see the face of the man who had taken everything from him.

They closed the lid on Kit's casket and guided it out of the morgue towards the service lift. As they walked, Moosehead handed Johnny a holo-disc. "This contains all the relevant documentation plus the core DNA signature scan you'll need to prove this is Kit's body. The Miltonian government also contacted the Search/Destroy Agency to confirm your part in Kit's capture and update them about the extent of his criminal career here on Miltonia. We've sponsored another one hundred thousand credits to be added to your bounty."

"Crivvens," whistled Middenface. "That's over two hundred an' fifty thousan' each, split three ways."

"Three ways?" said Moosehead, looking baffled.

"You didn't think we'd cut you out of your share, did you?" grinned Johnny. "You were looking for a nice score to retire on, and it looks like you've found it."

"Fellers, I don't know what to say," said Moosehead. "I'm speechless!"

"Aye," said Middenface. "That's why ah prefer yer company tae that of the president. There's still one question ah gottae ask before we leave."

"What's that?" asked Moosehead.

"What did the auld Ooze taste like?"

Moosehead smiled and thought for a moment. "I don't remember exactly. I do remember I gagged and nearly threw up, just like Rising did."

"Aye, that's right," recalled Middenface happily. "We had tae mak' him drink the Ooze twice."

"I do remember what it felt like when he trickled into my brain. One drop of consciousness at a time, until he was right there sharing my mind with me. I'm still getting used to him being there all the time, to hearing everything he thinks. It's kind of comforting in a way. He knows exactly what Kit put me through. He went through something similar, only his prison was his nutrient tank. Kit stole his life and his dreams from him too. I think we can support each other through the days ahead."

Upstairs, a hover limousine waited for them at the palace's side entrance. "I thought you'd want to avoid any excess publicity this time around," said Moosehead. "Before you leave, I just want to thank you again for everything you've done... Not just for Miltonia, but for me as well. For believing a story most people would have dismissed as impossible."

"Nothing was impossible where Kit was concerned," said Johnny.

"I could tell something wisnae right frae the word go," said Middenface with a wink. "I've got a nose fer these things."

"So, back tae normality, then," said Middenface as the limousine headed off to the spaceport. "Would ye ever want tae settle on a planet like Miltonia, Johnny? Maybe try for a normal life?"

"I gave up any chance of that the minute I put on this S/D badge," said Johnny. "Moosehead was one of the lucky ones; he found a way out. The rest of us have got only one end to look forward to."

"Aye," said Middenface, lounging back in his seat and putting his feet up. "But ah'm gonnae drink a lot o' whiskey and hand out a lot o' laldy before then."

"Middenface," said Johnny, clapping his friend on the shoulder. "The minute we get to a bar, I'll drink to that!"

ABOUT THE AUTHORS

Jaspre Bark writes fiction and comics for adults and children. Prior to this he toured extensively and made numerous radio and TV appearances as a stand-up poet. He has also worked as a national film and music journalist, and written scripts for short films, radio and stage plays. He has written for the BBC, The Theatre Royal Stratford East, The Short Film Bureau, *Empire*, *Mixmag*, *SFX*, *The Independent* and countless others. He has published two books of poetry and was awarded a Fringe First at the Edinburgh Festival in 1999.

Steve Lyons has written over a dozen novels, several full-cast audio dramas and many short stories, featuring characters such as *Doctor Who*, the *X-Men*, *Spider-Man* and *Sapphire & Steel*. He has co-written a number of books about television shows, including *Cunning: The Blackadder Programme Guide* and the bestselling *Red Dwarf Programme Guide*. He lives in Salford, near Manchester.